THE NIGHTMARE

The Mist - Book 2

REGINE ABEL

Cover by
Regine Abel

Copyright © 2020

CONTENTS

THE NIGHTMARE

She was his obsession.

For years, Zain has stalked Naima until she slipped through his fingers. He longs for the delectable taste of her terror and the divine sound of her screams. She occupies his every thought, and he aches for her. Eager to reclaim the only female that can ever complete him, Zain carefully plans his passage into the Mortal Plane. However, when next the Mist rises, instead of hiding from her Nightmare, Naima makes him the most improbable proposition. Is his woman truly surrendering herself to him, or is this a trap to eliminate him for good?

He was her darkest desire.

For a long time, Naima feared the Mist that engulfs the world for three days every month, and especially the monsters that dwell within it. After facing her own demons, she becomes a psychotherapist to help others deal with trauma. When given the opportunity to join the governmental agency that deals with the Mist, she jumps at the chance. Except, she never expected it would mean facing her greatest Nightmare. He's a bloodthirsty psychopath, with no sense of compassion or empathy. So, why can't she resist him? Why does he make her crave things she shouldn't?

DEDICATION

To those with a big enough heart to love even the most unlovable. To those able to see and nurture good even within those who seem to have none. To those who strive to bring light to darkness with love and kindness rather than with violence and cruelty.

To anyone who had the courage to face their demons and conquer them.

To my wonderful cousin Gena Abel, LMHC, CCTP, for helping me validate my assumptions about the psychology and behavior of a psychopath.

CHAPTER 1

NAIMA

I gave my invitation card to the agent screening the candidates, proud that my hand didn't shake despite my nervousness. Plastic and completely dark, you'd never guess its purpose if you'd stumbled on it by accident. The agent waved the card in front of a scanner, then stared at his screen for a second before examining my features. He didn't smile but kept the same neutral, professional expression his other colleagues also had plastered on their faces. Seemingly satisfied, he handed the black card back to me.

"A non-disclosure agreement was given to you along with your invitation to participate in the program, another copy of which has been handed to you upon arrival. Have you read and understood it?" the agent asked.

"Yes, Sir. I have read and understood it," I answered.

"If you consent, please look straight into the camera. When the red light turns on, state your full name and that you agree to abide by the terms of the NDA as spelled out in the document."

I turned towards the round camera hooked to some kind of

rod. The camera moved up by a few centimeters to align with the center of my face before a red light turned on, indicating it was recording.

"My name is Naima Connors, and I agree to abide by the terms of the Fourth Division's Mist Project non-disclosure agreement."

The red light turned off.

"Thank you. Please proceed to the next station," the agent said, gesturing at the counter near the two full-body scanners blocking the access to whatever awaited us beyond.

I gave him a stiff smile and nodded before complying. Another man welcomed me at the counter.

"Please give me your invitation card and all personal electronic devices you are carrying, including smart watches, phones, cameras, tablets, and anything else with the ability to record videos, audios, or images," the man said without preamble.

We had already been warned against bringing any such items as we wouldn't be able to keep them with us. I had only brought my phone, which I handed over to him. An exhaustive list of all other things that weren't permitted were outlined on a display panel sitting on top of the counter. The agent placed the phone in a brown envelope, asked me if that was all, then sealed the envelope once I confirmed there was nothing else. The seal looked like a small chip. The agent waved my card over it, causing it to beep.

"Your phone will be returned to you upon your departure at the end of the Mist," the man said. "Any metal items on you, such as keys, should be placed in this container along with your bag," he added.

He placed my card inside a large, rectangular tray, similar to those found at airports, then pushed it my way for me to put my overnight bag in and other items. While its contents were being scanned, a female agent had me step through the full-body scanner. As I waited to recover my bag, I glanced at the other candidates going through the same process I just had.

A million questions ran through my mind as I wondered who they were and what had brought them here. I still didn't quite understand how I personally had qualified. But these questions would soon be answered.

Or would they?

Another agent ushered me down a long hallway. So long in fact that it turned into a moving walkway. I hated that there were no windows allowing us to look outside. In a few minutes, the city defense sirens would blare throughout every town, in every country, and at the same exact moment. Then the Mist would rise, swallowing up the world in a thick fog filled with nightmarish creatures for the next three days.

This year marked the fifteenth anniversary of the dreadful day that changed the world. No one knew exactly what had caused the tearing of the Veil, which opened portals between our world and the mysterious one of the Mist. Then again, we all believed our governments were somehow involved. It had likely been some experiment gone wrong. Naturally, no one confessed. However, considering every single country on the planet had been hit, conspiracy theories implied it had been a concerted effort by our worldwide leaders. The alternative, that a single country was the culprit would give it an even greater incentive to keep quiet. If it was ever exposed, that country would never recover from the reparations the rest of the world would demand.

The moving walkway ended at the entrance of a small underground transport system. A shuttle, reminiscent of the car of a subway train, stretched the entire length of the short platform. However, its interior couldn't have been more different. All the seats faced each other and were equipped with seatbelts that crossed over the chest. Just like the hall and corridor I'd come in through, the shuttle was entirely white, except for the dark-grey floor and leather cushion of the seats. The dozen or so passengers onboard were scattered in the space, each one having left at least an empty seat between them and their closest neighbor. I hesitated for a second before heading towards one of the only two males in the shuttle.

He looked friendly with a handsome, boyish look to him, even though he had to be in his late twenties or early thirties like me. Fit, a little on the androgynous side, his light-brown eyes sparkled with intelligence and undisguised curiosity. We exchanged a timid smile as I placed my bag in the overhead compartment before sitting one spot over from him. I buckled my seatbelt and began the waiting game.

Thankfully, the wait turned out not to be all that long with only a handful more candidates joining us onboard. The doors closed, but seconds ticked by as we remained stationary.

"Please, fasten your seatbelts so that we may depart," said a soft and polished female voice over the intercom, startling me.

All eyes zeroed in on a petite, dark-haired, gothic-looking woman in her mid-twenties as she scrambled to rectify her omission. She appeared so mortified as she buckled up, I almost felt sorry for her. As soon as she did, a green light appeared above the four doors of the shuttle. Seconds later, it began to move, gaining speed at a mind-boggling rate. In a blink, the need for the seat belt became obvious. We were moving so fast, it felt like the beginning of the centrifuge effect one experienced on a roller-coaster.

Still, after about five minutes of this underground high-speed ride, the shuttle came to a smooth stop. Nothing happened for a few moments while everyone exchanged wondering glances. Then the shuttle shook slightly with a loud, clinking sound, as if something had grappled the car from above. The same blossoming panic I felt was reflected on everyone else's face.

"Docking complete. Initiating takeoff," said that same feminine voice over the intercom just as everyone seemed on the verge of freaking out.

"That's not creepy or unnerving at all," said the man sitting next to me.

I snorted and gave him a sideways glance. "Agreed," I said with a nervous smile.

"The name is Riley," he said, smiling back.

"Naima," I replied.

"Pleasure to meet you. Might as well make friends since we're headed into the Twilight Zone," he added with a mischievous glimmer in his light-brown eyes.

I chuckled, agreeing with that statement as well. "I mean, I understand they don't want us to know where the selection will be taking place, but this feels like a bit of an overkill."

Riley shrugged. "This stuff doesn't impress me anymore. I'm an engineer with NASA, but I've been studying the rifts in the Veil for a while now with other governmental agencies. This type of excessive security is becoming commonplace for me. Although, it's never been this crazy for a mere job interview."

"Wow," I said. "A bona fide rocket scientist!"

He snorted and shrugged in that way of meaning 'what can you do?'

"I'm nothing that fancy," I continued. "I'm a psychologist.

5

I work mostly with psychopaths and sociopaths, as well as their victims with PTSD."

"Wow!" Riley said, echoing my own reaction to his profession. "It must be crazy trying to get into the mind of these types of patients, no pun intended. However, it now makes me wonder what makes you want to work for the Men in Black. That seems like quite a stretch."

"I mostly work with convicted criminals of Mist homicides and their surviving victims," I answered, knowing I would likely face the same question once the interview process began. "A better understanding of what lurks in the Mist will not only help me in my career, but frankly, it will also help me face my own demons."

And God knew I had plenty of those. As a surviving victim myself, I still had the occasional nightmare about the incident.

"I'm really dying to know what this interview entails," I mused out loud. "Why did it have to take place during the Mist? And where are they taking us? Even the requirements to sign up were super vague. Frankly, I still cannot believe I was selected. And now, hearing your profession makes me even more confused as to what the role will be."

"That makes two of us," Riley said pensively. "I know they're looking for people with something specific. And it has nothing to do with our jobs. That's all I could get out of my contacts in high places."

Before I could reply, the intercom came to life again.

"Dear passengers, we are preparing for landing. Please remain seated with your seatbelts fastened until the doors have opened," the female voice said. "Careful opening the overhead compartments to retrieve your belongings as the bags may have shifted during the flight. Once you disembark, please go up the escalator into the Observatory. Spread out and walk around the bay windows. Do not be afraid by what you see. Your safety is guaranteed. Continue until an agent approaches you to let you know whether you will proceed to the next stage of the recruitment process."

Riley and I exchanged a baffled look. That did nothing to reassure me, not to mention increase my confusion level a thousand-fold. While their selection process was making even less sense to me, the female's comment about walking around the windows was what truly freaked me out.

Heart pounding, I followed the other candidates as we filed out of the shuttle. I had speculated about a million different things that this recruitment process could involve. A part of me had known that it would be what I was certain awaited me upstairs. But I'd convinced myself otherwise. My skin heated, and an invisible weight suddenly crushed my lungs, keeping me from drawing enough air. I focused on my breathing, more grateful than ever for the escalator that spared me from also having to pay attention to where I stepped. As the landing came into view and, with it, the massive circular room ahead, cold shivers ran down my spine.

I stepped off the escalator, moving out of the way in a nearly panicked daze. Floor-to-ceiling windows surrounded the aptly named Observatory. In the time it had taken to complete our registration, security check, and travel here, the Mist had risen outside. Many of the Mist Beings lurking within had already reached our location, drawn by the lights and so many visible prey to feast on—us.

When the Mist first appeared, taking the world by surprise, countless lives were lost, devoured by the creatures dwelling within the otherworldly fog. Livestock and indigenous tribes weren't spared. Since then, once a month, the world shut down while the Mist took over. Every house was now equipped with metal shutters and reinforced doors to keep it secured from the moment the city's defense siren heralded the beginning of the Mist until it resounded again to announce its end three days later. No one looked directly at the Mist or allowed its dwellers to look back at them. Why tempt the devil?

But I had seen it once before. Walked within it even... against my will.

I shuddered, casting away the traumatic memory that I had foolishly believed myself far more recovered from. The overwhelming urge to turn tail and run back to the shuttle tugged at me. Pressing myself against the white wall next to the escalator, I closed my eyes and practiced the visualization and breathing exercises I often used with my patients.

This is why I'm doing this. To face my demons and put them to rest, once and for all.

It shamed me to admit it. But while being a better psychotherapist for my clients remained part of my motivation for my presence here, more selfish reasons were also driving me. Moments later, my eyes flicked open as the strong sense of being observed took hold of me.

The first thing I noticed were two of the candidates that had already been in the Observatory upon our arrival being escorted back towards the escalator. Their dejected expression led me to think they'd been cut. My gaze flicked around the room to settle on a tall agent, with blond hair and penetrating blue eyes staring at me. My heart skipped a beat, and my stomach sank at the realization he was likely about to come escort me out as well.

Just like that, the burning desire to flee faded to be replaced by the urgent need to make it to the next stage, whatever that involved. I averted my eyes from the agent for fear he might signal for me to come towards him. Pushing myself away from the wall, I walked with what I hoped would pass for confident steps closer to the window on the far-left side of the room. Keeping a two-meter distance from the other candidate in front of me, I adjusted my steps to her pace as she walked the perimeter of the room.

Up-close, I could now see the incredible thickness of the windows, likely bullet-proof. It went a long way into alleviating part of my fears, unfounded though they were. After fifteen years of the Mist, it had been demonstrated beyond any doubt that the Mist Beings never attacked buildings. They would seek an opening, as they were now, circling around the Observatory, but wouldn't force their way in if they found none.

I willed myself to gaze upon the creatures. They were divided into two groups. The biggest one seemed to be the Beasts who could go from cute to horrifying, and from the size of a medium dog to a towering behemoth as tall as a building. The second group was the Walkers, commonly referred to as Mistwalkers. They didn't actually walk as they had no legs and resembled shadow wraiths with glowing, yellow eyes.

I shuddered, seeing a few of the Walkers close in around the windows. They almost appeared to be looking for something or someone inside the Observatory. My one and only encounter with one, more than a decade ago, had nearly cost me my life. Instead, my abusive boyfriend had perished at his hand.

As I reached the midway point of the Observatory, I forced my gaze away from a strange creature. It looked like a twisted mish-mash of the xenomorph alien queen's head attached to some kind of giant bug body with a massive stinger. It settled instead on a mammoth Beast that could have been the ungodly love child of Cthulhu, a tyrannosaur, and a praying mantis. As if it had sensed me observing him, the Beast turned to look at me.

Unlike the Walkers, the Beasts' eyes didn't glow yellow, but white. As our gazes locked in the oddest staring contest, I felt nearly hypnotized, like a moth drawn to a flame. Time appeared to stand still as the white light grew, swallowing me whole.

It took a few moments for the sound of the alarmed voices around me to penetrate my mind. I snapped out of my trance to find myself leaning against the window, my palms pressed against it as if I'd wanted to get outside. I'd previously kept at least a two-meter distance from it. Startled, I took a step back only to see the dark form of a Mistwalker charging towards us.

A frightened gasp escaped me, joining the voices of the other candidates. The Mistwalker appeared to be on a collision course with the window. At the very last moment, he tilted down and crashed into the Cthulhu Beast. It roared in pain, the sound so powerful the building shook. I shuddered at the sight of its gaping maw, filled with dagger teeth, partially obscured by the tentacles from its upper lip. It reared, flailing its praying mantis arms this way and that in a vain attempt to knock off its assailant.

Suddenly tilting forward—giving us a perfect view of the Mistwalker clawing savagely at its nape—the Cthulhu Beast swiped at its own back with its long tail. Seconds before it would have struck him, the Mistwalker flew up above the creature's head to come hover in front of its face. Four tentacle-like, shadowy tendrils shot out of the Walker's ethereal form. They wrapped around the length of his prey's praying mantis arms before the Beast could strike. The tendrils tightened, crushing the monster's limbs. Simultaneously, the Mistwalker's razor-sharp claws lacerated the Cthulhu's face, chopping off its facial tentacles, which turned to ash as they fell. No blood gushed out of the terrible wound.

The Beast bellowed. As soon as it opened its maw, the Mistwalker leaned forward, and a stream of energy appeared to transfer from the creature's mouth into him. The Cthulhu Beast, clearly in distress but not yet defeated, reared on its hind legs before brutally bringing down its bound arms towards the ground. Once more avoiding getting crushed, the Mistwalker released his prey and flew around it at dizzying speed, savagely whipping it with his tendrils. Long, dark gashes appeared on the Beast's back wherever the shadowy tendrils made contact.

Using both its tail and broken mantis arms, the behemoth attempted to knock down its aggressor, but the Walker was much too fast for it. Worse still, each blow appeared to slow the Beast further. The Mistwalker resumed siphoning his prey's lifeforce through the open gashes on its back, while inflicting more wounds with his tendrils. When the Cthulhu Beast all but ceased fighting back, the Walker flew back to its face and used his tendrils to open wide the creature's maw. Hovering before it, he greedily sucked the very life out of the monster, whose massive body began to shrink and wither before our very eyes.

My heart all but stopped at this dreadful déjà vu. That fateful night in the Mist, eleven years ago, this was what Jared had intended for me. I could almost feel again the bruising hold of his big hand around my wrist. It all but crushed my bones as he opened the shutters before throwing me out of my own house and into the Mist. A different Beast had been roaming the street. It immediately converged towards me the minute I stumbled down the five steps of the front porch's stairs. I tried to run back inside, but Jared slapped me then dragged me a few meters down the path before shoving me towards the sidewalk. I fell so hard on my knees it was a miracle I hadn't broken something.

That was when a wraith-like, dark shadow swooped down. I covered my head with my arms, thinking my final hour had come, but it continued past me to tackle Jared. I could still hear his horrified screams as the Walker pinned him down. I scrambled back to my feet, terrified at the thought I had to walk past them to get back inside the house. Yet, I didn't hesitate.

Immobilizing Jared's arms and legs with his shadowy tendrils, the wraith held my ex's head by the hair while he drained the life out of him. My hair stood on end from the energy swirling around them as I rushed past their location. A choked sob of relief escaped me when the tendril I'd expected to wrap around my ankle never did. I jumped up the stairs in two steps and slammed the door shut behind me. I ignored the sickly-sweet scent of the white clouds of the Mist that had made it inside the house and were slithering on the floor. Wasting no time, I locked the front door and slapped my hand on the button activating its metal shutters.

They lowered before the front door, increasingly blocking the nightmarish view outside. I stared in horror at other Mist Beasts gathering near my house, while staying at a safe distance from the Mistwalker. He was the last thing I saw, dropping the desiccated corpse that had once been Jared, while staring at me with glowing eyes.

Shaking away the dreadful memory, I refocused on the

Mistwalker outside. In the seconds that followed, the energy flow between him and his prey ended. The husk that remained of the Cthulhu Beast collapsed like a sandcastle of ashes. The Mistwalker turned towards the window, his yellow eyes glowing with the intensity of the sun at its zenith. He glided gracefully to the window, his gaze locked with mine. He placed both his shadowy palms against the reinforced glass, his featureless face a hair's breadth from it.

"Hello, Naima... Missed me?"

I gasped, and my hand flew to my throat at the sound of the otherworldly voice that resonated inside my mind. Although he didn't have any visible mouth, I could have sworn a malicious smile had appeared on his face.

The long and lethal claws of his right hand started tapping on the surface of the glass. My brain froze, and cold shivers ran down my spine as I recognized the rhythmic pattern. My ethereal stalker had played it on my shutters every day of the Mist for years following that fateful day, attempting to lure me out to finish what my escape had cheated him out of.

My Nightmare had found me again.

CHAPTER 2

NAIMA

I wanted to run away screaming, to find a dark place to hide in. How had he found me, so far away from my house? Why return now when he'd been quiet for so long?

He can't get me in here. If he could, he already would have.

Those words only partially reassured me. He'd never spoken to me before. In fact, I didn't know of anyone ever being spoken to by one the way this Walker just had. It then struck me that the other Beasts and Walkers in the Mist were giving him a wide berth, like they had done at my house all those years ago. How could they not in light of such a display of power? Inside the Observatory, too, people were giving *me* a wide berth.

Frazzled, I started moving again, more out of need to distance myself from the Walker than out of any real desire to proceed with the 'interview' process. At this point, I was entirely fine with not being selected. I wasn't as strong as I had presumed, and I had not as thoroughly recovered from that traumatic experience as I'd thought. But the wretched creature immediately followed suit, his shadowy claws raking the surface of the window with an aggravating sound, only to resume his tapping whenever I stopped walking.

A movement at the edge of my vision drew my attention. I jerked my head right to see the same blond agent who had stared at me earlier approaching me. I stopped walking with a sinking feeling in the pit of my stomach. My jumbled thoughts no longer made any sense. A part of me was hoping he would tell me this thing was over, so that I could go back to whatever room had been temporarily assigned to me, curl up into a ball, and wallow in self-pity. Another part of me, that stupid pride I'd inherited from my father, and stubborn streak passed down by my mother, refused to be sent packing. I hadn't bailed, despite my fear. I deserved to go through.

Heart pounding, I waited with bated breath for the agent to pronounce my sentence.

"Ms. Connors, please follow me to the next stage," the agent said with an oddly soft, almost youthful voice for such an imposing and stern-looking man.

My heart leapt in my chest, and I gaped at him in disbelief. Without a word, he turned and started heading towards a door at the opposite end of the Observatory. But before he did, I could have sworn the ghost of an amused smile had stretched his lips.

Two dozen pairs of eyes burned holes in my back as I silently followed the agent. I couldn't recall anyone else going through this specific door—at least, not since my arrival. Those who had not been retained had been escorted back down the escalator. The others—only a couple as far as I had noticed—had been taken through another door, closer to the center of the room. Like me, a Mistwalker had followed them, but at a respectful distance, displaying none of the antagonistic behavior my stalker did.

That same stalker was now banging on the window, not to break it, but apparently to draw my attention back to him. We hadn't followed the window on our way to that far exit, but cut through the large, circular room. The Mistwalker seemed angered to have thus been cast aside. He took the long way around, batting away the few Mist Beasts and Walkers who hadn't moved quickly enough out of his path. There was something beyond creepy about the way his eyes never strayed from me, and the obsessive urgency with which he followed me.

He reached the door at the same time we did, his palms once more pressed against the window. The agent waved his hand in front of some kind of bio scanner on the wall, and the large door swished open. To my surprise, a very long hallway —at least two hundred meters in length—stretched before me. The reinforced windows lining its left side, while a solid white wall lined the right side. Whatever doubt I'd had before vanished in that instant: they wanted candidates stalked by a Walker.

"Please, follow this corridor all the way to the end," the agent said. "Further instructions will be given to you at the appropriate time."

I wanted to ask what appropriate time that would be other than when I reached what seemed to be an elevator door with no button to call it. Biting my tongue, I gave him a stiff nod and proceeded as told, shadowed by my creepy companion. When the door closed behind me, a sudden impression of being trapped washed over me. I didn't suffer from claustrophobia, but right this instant, the walls felt as if they would soon start closing in on me. Worse still, I began wondering what could possibly lie beyond those doors. What if I was being offered as some sort of sacrificial lamb to the Mistwalker?

Refusing to give in to paranoia, I forced myself to put one foot in front of the other. My wretched stalker had resumed dragging his claws on the glass, clearly trying to irritate the hell out of me, and likely to frighten me. He was some sort of bully, and I wasn't one to allow myself to be pushed around.

Maybe a third of the way in, I stopped advancing to glare at him. "Cut it out!" I said, although he probably didn't hear me through the thick windows. "You're not scaring me with this, just annoying the fuck out of me. If you're going to stalk, do so in silence."

Although I'd known it would be as effective as throwing stones at the rain to tell it to go away, it had felt good to take an assertive stance. I'd let my fears overwhelm me from the moment that woman had mentioned not to be afraid before we disembarked from the shuttle. That wasn't... Or rather, that was *no longer* me.

To my surprise, the Mistwalker stopped and pressed his palm to the glass, turning to fully face me. He seemed to wait expectantly for me to do something. On instinct, I took a couple of steps towards the window to have a better look at him. Despite the absence of features on his face where only his yellow eyes glowed, he clearly perked up at this response. Aside from the way his ethereal body moved closer to the window, I couldn't say how I seemed to know what expression flittered over his shadowy face.

He placed his other palm against the window, his eyes glowing with accrued intensity. With a will of its own, my right hand pressed against his left. He stared at my hand with an air of disbelief and rubbed his over mine, as if he could feel it through the thick glass. My palm tingled. I couldn't say if it was real or just my imagination messing with me.

"Naima..." the Mistwalker whispered in my head with something akin to reverence.

The ghostly, ethereal sound of his voice sent a shiver down my spine. But it wasn't fear that had provoked it. It was beautifully haunting, deep, and gravelly, and yet breathy.

I opened my mouth to ask him his name when the sudden appearance of a bright light on his side of the window, at the other end of the corridor startled the both of us. My head jerked right to look at it, stunned to see some sort of luminous globe moving towards us. I then noticed the most stunning creature following it. A giant seahorse, the size of a five-year-old child, with a white unicorn horn and huge fairy wings, was flying towards the light. It was mesmerized, like I had been by the Cthulhu Beast. The creature looked diaphanous, its body shimmering with soft, pastel colors, and translucent scales that shone like so many diamonds. With the trail of what I could only call pixie dust behind it, you could have sworn the creature had come right out of a fairy tale.

I yelped at a loud bang on the window. My head snapped back towards the Mistwalker who, had he possessed features, would have likely been snarling. Could he actually be jealous? I no sooner cast a sideways glance at the seahorse, unable to resist its lure, than the Mistwalker viciously clawed the glass before darting towards the stunning creature. I immediately started running forward towards its location.

"NOOOOO!" I shouted when the Mistwalker grabbed the seahorse by long and slender neck and aligned its face with his.

To my surprise, the fairy didn't struggle or attempt to flee. It remained passive and didn't even try to continue pursuing the light sphere as its line of sight with it had been severed by the Mistwalker. Even when his assailant began siphoning its lifeforce, the seahorse fairy stayed stoic.

I frantically tapped on the window. "Stop! Stop! Please!"

He abruptly stopped. That last word appeared to have gotten through to him—although I still couldn't be certain he could hear me through the glass. He turned his yellow eyes towards me, and our gazes locked in a silent contest.

"Please, Mistwalker. PLEASE!" I pleaded again when he appeared intent on resuming draining the seahorse.

His entire body seemed to relax, and he looked at me with what I could only interpret as a satisfied expression.

He enjoys this! He enjoys being begged. He enjoys this power...

He slowly glided towards me, his fingers still firmly wrapped around the creature's neck.

"Zain," he said in my mind.

"Zain?" I repeated, forcing myself to focus on him despite my burning desire to seize the opportunity of an up-close view of the fantastic creature. "Is that your name?"

He didn't respond, but again, I knew beyond any doubt that he was smiling. He once more pressed the palm of his free hand against the window while the other one held the seahorse next to him, at eye level. The sudden certainty that he was daring me, tempting me even, to look at the fairy—and face the consequences—blossomed with perfect clarity in my mind.

He's testing me. But why?

"Well, Zain, I don't need to tell you my name as you already know it," I said, keeping my eyes locked on his face. "Now that the introductions have been made, I would like you to please let that creature go."

"Why should I? It's just a Spark. It's not even sentient. I can feed from it."

I gaped at him in disbelief. "There's no way you can still be hungry after that massive Beast you siphoned," I argued.

Zain puffed out his chest, and his smug, throaty laughter echoed in my head. It was surprisingly pleasant.

"I was magnificent, wasn't I?" he asked.

Narcissist...

Although I was starting to think he was rather a psychopath. His gratuitous violence towards the Cthulhu Beast, his cold indifference at taking the life of the 'Spark' simply because it had taken my attention away from him, his need for praise were ticking a number of the right boxes.

"Yes, you were," I said, playing along, but also with sincerity. "With your much smaller size in comparison, I didn't think you stood a chance, but it was the other way around."

"Naturally," he said with the same unrepentant ego.

"Please, let it go," I repeated.

Zain immediately stiffened, and his hand tightened around the seahorse's neck. That my mind had wandered back to the fairy mid-praise apparently stung him.

"You don't need it," I added quickly. "Clearly, you are the strongest Mist Being here. All the others, Walkers and Beasts alike, cowered before you. What would feeding on this wispy fairy do for you? Please."

"I like when you beg me, Naima," Zain said, mollified by my words.

"So I'm starting to see," I said with a bit more sarcasm than I intended.

To my surprise, he didn't take offense. Chuckling in that sexy fashion of his, he tossed away the seahorse. I almost turned to look at it, but thankfully caught myself at the last minute. However, from the corner of my eye, I saw the light sphere lure it back from whence it came. I instantly knew then that the Fourth Division—the official designation of the Men in Black's organization—had sent the fairy out as part of my interview process.

"Why are you following me?" I asked.

"Because you're mine," Zain replied, slightly stunned, as if the answer was self-evident. *"Because you want me to, even though you convince yourself otherwise."*

"That's insane. You sound like a stalker," I replied, feeling a little creeped out.

Zain recoiled, as if I was the one talking crazy.

"Of course, I do. Because I am," he replied, sounding baffled. *"That's what you made me."*

"WHAT?!" I exclaimed, taking a step back away from him.

Before he could answer, the chime of the elevator at the end of the corridor echoed through the empty space. My head jerked towards it only to see the door slide open, beckoning me. I cast a sideways glance at Zain, feeling somewhat reluctant to end the conversation there.

"Don't go," the Mistwalker ordered in a commanding voice.

For some reason, that prompted me into challenging him instead.

"I must," I replied in a gentle but firm tone.

He followed me as I made my way towards the lift. To both our surprise, as we approached the end of the corridor, a door opened on his side of the window. Mist already swirled within, indicating it would be safe for him to enter. We stopped and exchanged another glance. I didn't know what kind of fucked up mind game the Fourth Division was playing with us, but I wanted to get to the bottom of this.

"Don't go!" Zain repeated.

I gave him an apologetic smile then entered the lift. There appeared to only be three levels, with this one being the middle one. However, I didn't have to interact with the panel. Seconds after I stepped inside, the door closed on the sight of Zain staring at me with glowing eyes.

CHAPTER 3

NAIMA

It was a short ride up to the top floor. It opened on a disturbingly normal office space. The central area had an open floor layout with a dozen desks in two columns of three pairs facing each other. Along the left and right sides of the room, a few offices with frosted glass walls lay empty except for one. I couldn't see who the two people inside were, only their silhouettes. A small coffee station occupied a nook between two of the offices on the right. At the back, a large boardroom with its door closed led me to think the rest of the agents had gathered there. But it was the man in his early fifties standing in front of the open door of a big office on the right corner of the back wall who held my attention.

I immediately started moving towards him. He was tall, at least 6'3, with lovely blue eyes wrinkled by a welcoming smile, and brown hair sprinkled with grey. As expected, he, too, was dressed in a black suit, black shoes, and black tie over a white dress shirt. Instantly at ease, and grateful for the first agent to show any warmth, I returned his contagious smile as I closed the distance with him.

"Good evening, Ms. Connors," he said, extending his hand towards me. "My name is Alfred Thomson, Director of the Mist Squad Program. Congratulations on making it this far."

"The Mist *Squad* Program?" I repeated while shaking his hand, emphasizing the word 'Squad' that had never featured in any of the very cryptic literature about the program.

He smiled and gestured for me to come in. "I will explain everything."

I stepped inside the imposing space and took a seat in one of the two comfortable black leather chairs in front of his massive desk. The bookshelf behind him contained a few personal decorations, many official looking books and manuals. A worktable occupied the right side of the room, next to a window with drawn metal shutters, preventing me from getting an idea of where exactly they'd taken us. A family portrait of him, his wife, and a pretty young woman I assumed to be his daughter, sat on his desk. That further put me at ease. There was something reassuring about dealing with a family man.

"So, I'm guessing I'm here talking with you because Zain followed me?" I asked without preamble, stunned by my boldness. It was common courtesy to always let the interviewer initiate the conversation.

His brow shot up, impressed. "Zain is your Walker's name?" he asked.

I nodded. "Yes."

"He told you?" Director Thomson insisted.

"Yes. But I heard his voice in my head," I said, immediately feeling self-conscious, and wondering if he'd think me wacko.

His eyes flicked to my chest—which was completely

covered by the burgundy, sleeveless, leather top that I was wearing with black leggings—before locking back with mine. A slight frown creased his forehead.

"Did he touch you?" he asked. "Do you bear his brand on your chest?"

I blinked, utterly confused, then looked down at my chest. My top's frontal zipper was raised all the way up to my neck, showing no cleavage. Normally, I wore it open fairly low, but this wasn't the place to be sexy.

"I don't have any markings on my chest," I said, baffled. "But what are you talking about? I mean, there was a thick glass all around the Observatory—"

"I don't mean tonight, but during that tragic incident at your house over a decade ago," he specified with a sliver of impatience or annoyance, I couldn't tell which.

I gaped at him in shock. "How—?"

"We investigate every candidate that applies before sending out the invitation," Director Thomson said, interrupting me again.

I wrapped my arms around my waist, feeling suddenly unnerved. "No," I replied, shaking my head. "I never came in direct contact with him anymore than I have here."

"Ms. Connors, do you realize that Zain acts as your champion?" he asked cautiously.

I recoiled. "What? No," I said, disbelievingly. "What would make you think that?"

"Back then, he saved you from your boyfriend's attempt to murder you by killing him instead, just like he freed you tonight from the Beast's hypnotic gaze by killing it as well," Thomson explained. "Had you been outside, you would have stood there, immobile, while it devoured you."

I shuddered and rubbed my upper arms in a comforting

gesture. I still wasn't sure the word champion applied to Zain. However, thinking back, I could now see the pattern in his behavior, charging the threat to me, no questions asked, and siphoning the life out of them until nothing remained but ashes and a desiccated corpse.

"Do you know how the Mist Beings come to life, Ms. Connors?" Thomson asked, slightly tilting his head to the side.

Something in the way he asked the question poked my curiosity.

"Mist creatures have Mist sex and make Mist babies?" I said, having no real clue. So much mystery was kept around those beings, despite the Mist having been around for nearly fifteen years now.

He chuckled and shook his head with an amused expression on his ruggedly handsome face.

"Have you noticed how familiar they look?" he asked, not providing the answer to his original question.

I took a moment before answering, reviewing in my mind the appearance of the monsters I had seen. However, the Walkers all looked similar, aside from their size.

"Well, they aren't creatures found on Earth," I said carefully. "But they do remind me of chimeras created by matching parts of Earth creatures with parts of fantasy creatures, like that Cthulhu praying mantis that hypnotized me."

He nodded, visibly pleased with my answer.

"Even in that strange mishmash, what are the odds that creatures evolving in a completely different parallel universe would develop in such identical, easily recognizable parts?" he further asked with an unnerving intensity.

I hesitated and nervously licked my lips. "Honestly, I have no idea. One of the conspiracy theories lurking around claims that the portals between our world and theirs had opened in the past and that DNA cross-contamination occurred, which would explain those similarities. I mean, you guys have been fairly quick at removing the ash statues of the Beasts that fail to get back to their world through the portals when the Mist recedes. But there are tons of pictures of Beasts circulating on the net. So…"

I shrugged as my voice trailed off, feeling like a freak conspiracy theorist.

Thomson nodded slowly, a neutral expression on his face. His blue gaze boring into mine made me squirm on my chair.

"And what other theories have you heard?" he asked.

"Oh, the other one is completely cuckoo," I said with a derisive snort. "Apparently, the Mist is the dream world, and the Mist Beasts are our dreams and nightmares."

I'd expected him to chuckle with me. Instead, he held my gaze unwaveringly and without the tiniest sliver of humor on his face.

"That *is* insane. Right?" I asked, refusing to believe what his body language was telling me.

"It is not," Thomson said in a very serious tone. "The first theory you mentioned is partially true in that the human mind is a doorway into the Mist. The Mist itself is the realm where dreams are born and normally die when we stop dreaming about them. But sometimes, those dreams thrive and become self-aware."

I shook my head in denial. That was just too crazy, even though it echoed the wildest claims from those conspiracy theory websites.

"I know how it sounds, but it's the truth. That's why we never bothered cracking down on those conspiracy websites," Thomson said as if he'd just read my mind. "Their telling the truth only convinces the majority of the population that they've got a few screws loose. But in reality, they often help us figure out what is actually going on since the people who actually interacted with Mistwalkers are usually too afraid to speak to the government, but not to those guys."

Yeah, I could see that. When my ex had tried to kill me, I had not wanted to contact the official number for incidents related to the Mist. I'd been afraid they'd make me disappear to avoid terrifying the population. But with Jared's shriveled up remains lying on my front lawn, I'd had no choice but to contact the authorities.

"But... How?" I asked, confused and still struggling to believe any of this.

"Every time you fall asleep and dream, it creates a Spark —an ethereal version of whatever being or creature you've imagined," Thomson explained. "Like that seahorse fairy you saw earlier. It likely stems from the dream of a child, but is already forgotten. We know this by how translucent and mostly apathetic it behaves. In a few hours, maybe even up to a few days, that seahorse will fade away unless it is eaten by another Mist creature. And then, you have others like Zain that are the result of recurring dreams—in your case, of recurring nightmares."

I shuddered, my eyes widening at the undeniable truth of his last words. I hadn't known the name of the dark figure that used to lurk in my darkest dreams before I began therapy, but it had undeniably been a Mistwalker.

"You see, the Walkers are divided in two groups: the Wishes and the Nightmares," Thomson continued. "If you desire something strongly enough and dream of it with suffi-cient intensity and frequency, your Wish may become aware and then deliberately seek to communicate with you. But the same applies to your greatest fears if they haunt you often enough at night. The majority of the creatures you saw outside the Observatory were frequent dreams, but only a handful of the Mistwalkers become sentient. Those were the ones following their creators around the room, the same way your Zain was shadowing you."

"And you're assuming he's a Nightmare because of his violent attack on that Cthulhu Beast?" I asked.

"Yes," Director Thomson said with a nod.

"But what do they want?" I asked, still struggling to accept this as reality.

"It all depends on what you wished or feared," Thomson said with a shrug. "Wishes will always seek to do something beneficial to you. Children, especially bullied ones, wish for a true friend and protector so that they're not so alone or mistreated. Adults will often hope for someone that can get them out of whatever their greatest hardship is about. However, most of them are pushing for the perfect life part-ner," he added with an amused glimmer in his eyes.

"Like a spouse?" I asked, my eyes bulging with disbelief. "How is that even supposed to work? Ghost sex?" I froze as a thought straight out of crazy town crossed my mind. "Don't tell me that the lore on Succubi and Incubi comes from Mist-walkers?!"

Thomson burst out laughing. "Actually, I wasn't going to say that, although it does partially apply. Mistwalkers feed on emotions and the lifeforce of others. When they mate with a human, sex is the best non-lethal way for them to acquire the energy needed to fuel their power."

"But they're made of smoke!" I argued.

"Smoke that taunted you by tapping on the window and clawing at the glass," Thomson deadpanned.

That shut me up.

"Have you heard about the Thornhill Killer?" he suddenly asked.

I recoiled, taken aback by this abrupt change of topic. "Who hasn't?" I asked. "But what does that have to do with anything?"

"The images I'm about to show you are very disturbing," Thomson said, ignoring my question. "After that, what I'm about to tell you is the main reason for the existence of the Fourth Division and of the program you're currently being interviewed for. If any of this became public, there would be complete panic and chaos in every major city in the world. We are currently in a race against the clock that could determine the place of humanity in the food chain."

Those ominous words were my only warning before he handed me a folder with a huge, red 'confidential' slapped on top. Heart pounding, I hesitated, knowing that once I opened it, a line would be crossed, and my life would change in a way that could never be undone.

Fingers slightly shaking, I flipped the cover open and was relieved to see the normal portrait of a pretty young woman named Emily Gates. She had been the first alleged victim of the serial killer of the Thornhill borough. Below, a standard form provided general details about her: date of birth, address, education, employment, contacts and relatives, and a summary of the date and place her body was found. When I flipped to the next page, a horrified gasp rose for my throat. I closed my eyes and jerked my face left, wishing to unsee the desiccated remains of the lovely young female she had once been.

If not for her dress and the handful of long strands of hair still attached to her skull, she could have been the twin of

Jared's dried up remains. Taking a few deep breaths to regain my composure, I forced myself to turn back to the folder. As I flipped through the pages, the same pattern repeated itself. Each and every one of the victims found sucked dry of their lifeforce.

And yet, none of this matched up.

"That's not possible," I argued, shaking my head in denial. "A couple of these cases were filed a day or two after the end of the Mist. So, I'll buy that. But the others occurred well over a week after it. This last one took place less than four days before the following Mist. The Beasts and Walkers turn to ashes as soon as the Mist recedes if they are still in our dimension. How would that be possible?"

A glimmer of approval showed in his blue eyes. Under different circumstances, I would have been pleased to score points. Right now, however, I just needed to know what the fuck was going on, and if he was just messing with my head.

"Normally, you would be correct," Thomson answered before running nervous fingers through his greying hair. "However, and in response to your earlier question, mating between a Mistwalker and a human is possible because the sentient ones, if they want it badly enough, can crossover into our world and take a human appearance."

"All right," I said, fed up and shaking my head. "This is where I draw the line. What kind of stupid mind game is this? Why go through all this expensive process just to pull this stunt? Do I have 'gullible' written on my forehead? I'm done with this nonsense."

I rose to my feet, ready to leave. He imitated me and lifted his palms in front of him in an appeasing gesture.

"Please, Ms. Connors, hear me out," Director Thomson said in a pleading tone.

"I don't want to hear anymore. This is bullshit!" I snapped angrily. "First, you make me almost believe the monster that killed my sadistic ex is the figment of my imagination. And now, you're trying to make me believe someone dreamed up some psychotic serial killer that somehow figured out how to become human, and is now roaming the streets murdering people? Do I look *that* stupid to you?"

"I assure you, Ms. Connors, this isn't a game," Thomson said in a less friendly tone. "Please, sit down so that we—"

"I don't want to sit down," I interrupted. "I want to leave."

"SIT DOWN!" Director Thomson shouted, startling me.

A sliver of fear blossomed in the pit of my stomach at the sight of his anger. Gone was the gentle family man who had first welcomed me. I swallowed hard then quietly settled back down in my chair, not daring to provoke him further. He glared at me for a moment longer as if he wanted to smack some sense into me. As I stared at him, a sense of dread washed over me.

He's not bullshitting.

His entire demeanor and body language confirmed it. But how could that be?

"Oh my God! You're serious?" I whispered.

He closed his eyes and sighed heavily before settling back in his chair. His anger faded away, and he leveled me with a sad, almost discouraged expression. He picked up a small, flat, black remote control that turned on the large, wall-mounted TV on the left wall. Seconds later, the camera footage outside an office building showed a tall and handsome man running up to one of the victims in the folder and attacking him. The man was clearly terrifying the victim for a few moments before shadowy tendrils started protruding from his back. The same way Zain had done with the Beast, the killer immobilized his victim with the tendrils then siphoned his life away, leaving a shriveled corpse on the floor.

I realized tears were rolling down my face only after Director Thomson ended the playback and extended me his box of Kleenex.

"I'm sorry that I'm forcing you to relive a traumatic experience," Thomson said. "However, this is not a joke or a stunt. That monster is out there on the street killing people. The news has stated that there have been thirty-two victims so far. But the reality is that more than three times that number has been recorded."

I lifted my hand to my throat and gaped at him in complete shock.

"Nightmares used to be few and far between in the first decade of the Mist. But now, they're taking over our world. Every time the Mist ends, at least two or three new ones are born in our city," Thomson said in a grim tone. "Your Zain is the most powerful Walker I've seen in my entire career. There is no question in my mind that he was planning on crossing over at the end of the current Mist. Creating a human body requires a tremendous amount of energy. If the Walkers don't have high enough reserves before they initiate the shift, they die within hours."

I recoiled, a horrified expression on my face. "Are you saying that Zain intends to cross over to become the next serial killer?"

He hesitated, which frightened me even more.

"There is no question that Zain is a Nightmare," Thomson said carefully. "He has the potential to become a serial killer. However, after watching his interactions with you, I believe him to be exactly the solution we seek. But that can only work if we have your full collaboration. Zain is clearly coming for you."

"He's coming here to kill me?!" I exclaimed, straightening in my chair.

"No, no!" Thomson responded quickly, lifting his hands in an appeasing gesture. "Mistwalkers never want to kill their creator, especially when they cross over. You would be his anchor in this world. If you die, there is a chance he would fade away with time, unless you had bound him to our world, and he'd become human enough to survive on his own. Zain is a psychopath. He wants—"

"Rewards," I interrupted, seeing where his mind was going, as relief flooded me.

"Yes!" Thomson said with a smile. "And both *you* and your emotions are his rewards."

"But he wants my fear," I argued, not too crazy about that thought.

"And both your attention and admiration," he countered. "Your gratitude and focused attention on him rewarded him far more than demonstrating his dominance by killing that fairy."

"So, you want me to manipulate his impulses into getting him to…?" I asked, my voice trailing off.

"I want you to convince him to join his forces to ours to fight the Nightmares," Director Thomson said forcefully. "We're losing this battle. The entire middle drawer of this cabinet is filled with the files of my agents who died at the hands of a Nightmare in the past fifteen years. Half of them occurred in the past six months since the Thornhill Killer entered our world. And the deaths are accelerating."

I stared at him, lips parted in both shock and understanding. "But… But why my Nightmare?" I asked, confused.

"Zain is still unpredictable. I agree that he might be controllable with the right rewards, but wouldn't a Wish be safer and more appropriate? You don't recruit psychopaths or sociopaths in law enforcement."

He nodded with a friendly smile. "That was our initial thought as well. But Wishes are... too nice. They have the same simple desires and needs as your everyday person on the street. It takes a different type of person and a different type of dedication to want to become a police officer, join the military, or become a firefighter. And even then, we don't need a good cop or soldier, we need a ruthless predator to combat fire with fire."

"So... The Mist Squad Project... You want to form an army of them," I said, matter-of-factly.

"Yes," Director Thomson said with a sharp nod. "We want them to hunt down existing Nightmares already on the loose, eliminate new ones as they are born during and after the Mist, and help police the streets when we can't during the Mist to protect potential victims like you almost were."

Before he was even done speaking, I already knew I couldn't walk away from this. Of all the things I had imagined this project would be, this would never have been it.

"Where do we start?" I asked.

Director Thomson grinned, a triumphant expression descending on his features. "First, we go say hello to your Nightmare who has decided to play along."

CHAPTER 4

ZAIN

I hovered in front of the open door, taunting me, beckoning me. My Naima had gone within, and I wanted to be near her again. The wretched window was cheating me out of her emotions, which were rightfully mine to revel in. She was even more beautiful than I remembered when I'd first seen her all those years ago. She had been so close, almost within my grasp. I should have gone after her first instead of yielding to my rage at the sight of that vermin brutalizing what was mine.

I once more glanced at the endless corridor ahead of me. I had seen others go in before like that little Spark and never return. I had no doubt this was a trap. The others have been too stupid, but I was not. Granted, I had sufficiently gorged both on Beasts and weak Wishes. Worst case scenario, if I was locked within, I had enough energy to pierce through the Veil and return to the safety of my world. But that would delay my plans to crossover into the Mortal Plane.

My prey had never been so close than in those few moments with her hands pressed against the glass. I wanted to touch her flesh, taste her fear, drink the flow of her emotions. If I could brand her, then this slight delay will have been beyond worth it.

That last thought convinced me to proceed.

I entered the dark corridor, unfazed by the absence of light. We didn't need it to see clearly. The door closing behind me didn't frighten me. I didn't scare easily, if ever. And I *always* had a backup plan whenever I embarked on one of my reckless adventures. The tunnel began to descend at a slight incline. Thick panels blocked the access to connecting corridors along the way. I hated feeling that they were leading me like a sheep to the slaughterhouse. But, surely, they weren't foolish enough to think they could control me?

Still, the thrill of the unknown and excitement of potentially seeing my Naima again overtook my emotions. The corridor curved twice before I reached my destination. It was a reasonably large rectangular room, empty but for the Mist. The same thick glass windows as those outside delimited the space. A single, perfectly sealed door gave access to the antechamber on the other side. I made a beeline for it and tried to push it open. Naturally, it didn't budge. The lack of handle on this side of the room made it all the more obvious they didn't want me to escape.

However, testing the hunch that had been bubbling at the back of my mind, I raked my claws against the surface of the glass wall. I barely managed to repress the triumphant shout rising in my throat.

The sliver of pain—although rather pleasant—I had felt earlier when I'd raked my claws against the windows of the large room didn't manifest itself now. I intensified the pressure, still nothing. As creatures of the Mist, we couldn't enter a room or a house within the Mortal Plane without the owner giving their express consent. Attempting to damage anything in the human world in a place where we weren't welcomed would cause considerable pain. However, if the Mist could penetrate that location, we, too, were free to enter.

By opening the outside door to let me in, they had in fact granted me access to the entire facility. And this glass wall, in spite of its thickness, would be no match for my incredible power—free of pain.

And then, you will truly be mine, my little Naima.

The thought of my ethereal essence swirling inside Naima had me burning with excitement. I glanced around the room beyond what I believe to be a holding cell. A working desk was propped against the wall at the opposite end from where I stood. An oddly out of place chair sat a couple of meters in front of the cell. I could only presume it was to make a human comfortable while discussing with me from a safe distance. Cameras both inside and outside of my cell told me they could see everything happening within from any angle. It was good to know as I didn't want to give away my intentions too soon.

Once more, the thought of Naima's fear made me hot and cold all at once. I glided around the space, knowing the agents —and hopefully my female—would shortly come to converse with me.

I couldn't tell how long it took, maybe ten minutes. But I was growing increasingly angry to have been made to wait this long. Patience didn't sit particularly high in my list of personal traits. Just as I was considering bashing in the glass wall to go hunt for my female, the door opened at last. My disappointment at the sight of a tall, slender male quickly vanished when my Naima walked in after him.

She stopped in front of the door, and he placed his hand on the small of her back to urge her in. Although it had been brief, an instant, all-consuming jealousy flared within me that he would dare touch my mate. I advanced menacingly, glaring at him. Naima stopped again a few steps in, a frown marring her forehead, no doubt in response to my threatening demeanor. The male seemed amused and discreetly lifted his hands in a surrendering gesture. Naima didn't notice, but his surrender mollified me.

Dismissing him from my thoughts, I moved up to the glass wall and pressed my right palm against its cool surface. My female glanced at my hand, knowing what I wanted. Although she tried to maintain a neutral expression on her beautiful features, I could see her wheels turning as she tried to decide what kind of power dynamic she wanted between us.

As if that was even open for debate...

"Come to me, Naima," I mind-spoke to her, impatient to taste her emotions again.

The wretched wall blocked too much of them and, from this distance, I perceived nothing at all except for what her body language conveyed. She wasn't scared right now, but worried. Her blossoming fear was such a turn on. I would make her tremble, plead, and beg for the mercy that only I could grant her. While I drowned her in the sea of torment and despair she craved, I would feast on the whirlwind of her emotions—a perfect blend of fear, pain, and pleasure. And then, I would comfort and gently love her, as she deserved and also hungered for. She was my prey and my bride.

My beautiful Naima... I had missed her so much. Since her troubled youth, she had often dreamed of me, asking me to punish her for ruining her parents' marriage. Whenever I complied—and I always did—she would flee. How I had loved the chase. I almost always caught my mate and punished her before consoling her. As Naima grew older, our encounters became darker and more intense. She no longer wished me to comfort her after the fact. It coincided with the increasingly bad relationships my woman got involved in, with wretches that physically marked her, bruising the perfect skin that was mine and mine alone. You didn't damage such perfection.

"Come to me, Naima," I telepathically reiterated, this time more forcefully. She should have answered my first call.

Naima flicked her long, natural black curls over her shoulder and pinched her lips. It was subtle, but I knew her too well for such things to escape me. Her hazel eyes shone with a rebellious glimmer as she sustained my gaze somewhat defiantly. However sexy it made her, I was greatly going to enjoy curing her of this sass and attitude with a proper spanking.

Still, the impertinent female strutted towards me with pretend confidence that could have almost fooled me if not for the waves of her inner turmoil oozing through the glass to me. It was still much too faint to my liking. I felt like a parched man who was only given water with a dropper. The clicking sound of the medium heels of her short boots quieted as—to my utter annoyance—she stopped at least a meter away from the glass and crossed her arms over her chest.

"Hello again, Zain," Naima said in a casual tone. "I hear you're my Nightmare."

I scoffed, offended to be associated with such inferior creatures.

"I am no Nightmare," I snarled with disdain. *"They are stupid creatures, controlled by their impulses and primal needs. They relentlessly pursue their goal in a single-minded fashion. They may appear clever at times in the methods used to sate their addiction. But in the end, it always ends up being*

their downfall. I am far more refined," I said, puffing out my chest.

She gave me a dubious look. "Of your own admission, you are my stalker. You seem to take great pleasure in frightening me by clawing the glass and tapping on it with that little riff that reminds me of too many terrifying dreams to count. While I don't fully remember them, I know you chased me, chained me in dark places, made me beg, and who knows what else! I just remember waking up screaming. That rather sounds like nightmares to me," she concluded in a clipped voice filled with sarcasm.

I would have to spank her out of that, too. But Naima's words were such a turn on as I visualized various scenarios where each of these instances played out in her prior dreams we shared.

"You're such a tease! How can you speak such naughty words to me and yet stand so far out of reach?" I said in a purring tone.

She gasped and shook her head.

"Oh my God! You are disturbed!" Naima exclaimed, staring at me in disbelief.

"No, my beauty. I am your Darkest Desire," I countered. *"And I will prove it to you. Open the door, my love."*

"No fucking way!" she said, taking a step back. "Why would I wish for someone who wants to hurt and terrify me?"

"Pain has always been one of your fetishes," I retorted matter-of-factly. *"Why do you think you've only dated abusive men? You love being a victim."*

She recoiled. For some reason, the hurt and betrayed look on her face stung instead of giving me the malicious gratification emotionally distressing her normally gave me in the Mist.

"Fuck you! This conversation is over," Naima hissed, her

eyes suddenly too bright with what I assumed to be repressed tears.

The sour scent of her emotions knotted my insides. The sight of her distress should have been sweet, should have given me a hard on even. Was the Mortal Plane twisting my perception of her feelings, or was the glass wall distorting them instead?

Naima turned around and headed towards the exit with determined steps. That both angered and excited me.

"Naima, get back here!" I ordered in an imperious tone, knowing she wouldn't comply. *"Come back and open this door, or you will regret it!"*

She ignored me. Once again, my bride had provoked me before fleeing. She wanted to be hunted down, and I would gladly oblige. My threat would only raise the stakes and intensify the emotional rush we'd both get out of it. It was the way we played this game; an enjoyment she'd deprived me of for far too long when she began therapy after Jared's death.

The male, who had watched our entire interaction with increasing worry, had only heard Naima's words, mine having been spoken telepathically to my mate. His frown as he questioningly watched my mate stomp her feet towards the exit suddenly shifted to panic. Alerted by his expression, Naima stopped and looked at me over her shoulder. Her horrified expression at seeing my fist drawn back with massive amounts of ethereal energy swirling around it, gave me a pleasant tingle. Too bad she was too far for me to taste her fear as well.

Putting my back into it, I swung as hard as possible. The booming sound of the impact resonated like thunder. The glass cracked, forming a compact web at the point of contact, before spreading veiny tendrils in every direction.

"That's impossible!" the male whispered, his pale skin draining from blood.

"You are not welcomed in this place!" Naima shouted, thinking quickly on her feet, while taking a couple of steps backwards.

I chuckled when the ominous vibrations from buildings we were forbidden access to failed to manifest themselves.

"Nice effort, my love," I taunted, while raising my fist again to bring down the barrier keeping me from my prize. *"But one with greater authority over this dwelling than you gave me access."*

"RUN!" the male shouted to Naima as the glass wall came down under the force of my blow. "I banish you from this building!" he then added for me.

I immediately felt the shift. The walls glowed with a light, neon green hue, reminiscent of a radioactive pool. While touching their surface would be safe although unpleasant, any attempt to damage or break them would feel like acid had been poured on the attacking limb. By rights, now that I'd been banished, just gliding into the antechamber should have subjected me to excruciating pain. But the Mist from my glass cell spilled into it, allowing me to advance further unscathed.

Summoning four of my shadow whips, I projected one forward to slam the door shut before my mate could escape. I swallowed back the mind-numbing hiss of pain from the tip of my tendril touching the door. Two more of my tentacles wrapped around Naima's midsection and thighs, yanking her back to me. And the fourth one smacked out of his hand the unusual gun the male had just pulled out of the holster hanging on his hip.

As soon as my bride's back hit my chest, I possessively closed my arms around her and receded back into the glass cell where the remaining Mist was thickest. The orgasmic feel of her warm flesh against my ethereal form was nearly driving me insane. But I needed to focus as time was ticking. The Mist in the cell was thinning as it also tried to occupy the antechamber.

"Open the way back to the outside world," I ordered the man.

"NO!" Naima shouted, struggling in vain to free herself of my embrace.

The acrid scent of her terror, multiplied a thousand-fold now that no barrier between us dampened it, was making me nauseous. I had expected it to energize me, to be the sweetest—the most divine even—aroma I had ever inhaled. Not this... What was wrong with our connection? The male's horror and fear for my mate was delicious. I could gorge on it for days. Hers should have been even more delectable.

"You cannot take her out there!" the male exclaimed. "She will get killed!"

"If that had been my intention, no harm would have come to her," I replied with disdain before turning to my mate to telepathically whisper reassuring words. *"Relax, my love. You will not be hurt."*

Her scream turned into a choked gasp as my ethereal essence slithered over her beautiful dark skin before slowly penetrating it. Once again, I struggled not to be overwhelmed by the blissful sensation of a part of me taking root inside of her, anchoring me to my bride. But that wondrous experience was tainted by the growing stench of her terror. I would need to figure out what the fuck was causing this, but now wasn't the time.

Naima attempted to double-over in response to the

discomfort of this alien presence inside of her, but my arms held her up, tightly against me.

"Open the damn door, human, or you will face my wrath," I hissed at the foolish man. *"I will release her before I exit. You should know that I want her alive, not dead. She is mine, and I've achieved my goal."*

The older man hesitated and cast a worried look at my mate. For some reason, that pleased me.

"How can I trust you?" the fool asked.

The door I had closed suddenly burst open with three more agents storming inside the room. The older man raised his hand in an arresting gesture, preventing them from committing some regretful act that would have cost them dearly. I had no qualms draining every single one of those bastards. Then again, their emotions broadcast clearly that they didn't want to harm Naima and, oddly enough, they didn't want to harm me either.

"Your trust is irrelevant," I snapped. *"Make me ask another time, and I'll just burst your doors open. Do you really want the Mist roaming freely inside your building?"*

He must have sensed that I would do it, too. Yes, it would hurt, but I had enough energy to plow through. The biggest headache would be getting my mate to a safe place where she could comfortably spend the three days of the Mist. To my relief, he fished a remote control out of his pocket and opened the door behind me leading back to the corridor maze that still stood between me and freedom.

"Wise decision," I said tauntingly while gliding backwards through the opening.

To my surprise, the older man followed us at a safe distance. Worry and hope swirled within him, while near panic was taking hold of the other agents who followed in his wake. I couldn't help feeling a begrudging respect for the man. His almost paternal protectiveness—devoid of possessiveness—towards my mate pleased me. But so did their collective helplessness in controlling me.

"NO!" Naima shouted as we entered the maze. She stretched a desperate hand towards the agents.

"Hush, my love," I whispered, nuzzling her nape. *"I do not make promises I won't keep. I will release you before the exit. You will not be harmed."*

"What did you do to me? Where are you taking me?" she asked.

"I made my claim official," I said before lowering the zipper of her form-fitting leather top. The silly female jerked in my embrace, likely fearing I would molest her.

"Stop! What are you…"

Her words died in her throat when I slightly parted the collar of her top to show the dark swirls of my brand forming above her heart.

"This is me, my love, inside you," I whispered, my index finger briefly caressing my brand. *"I am a part of you, now. You are mine, forever."*

"Oh God," she whispered, horrified.

That stung instead of thrilling and empowering me. I should be swimming in a pool of euphoria right now, but all her reactions—perfect though they were—triggered the wrong responses from me.

Navigating backwards was awkward, but a swift glance over my shoulder confirmed that, at long last, the door was only a few meters away.

"Open the exit door, human," I ordered without slowing down.

A troubled expression crossed the older man's face. Guilt,

worry, and uncertainty warred on his features. His eyes rested on my brand on my mate's chest. Whatever internal debate he'd been having, my emblem seemed to help him reach a decision. Raising the remote control, he opened the door behind me.

The strength with which Naima's terror slammed into me left me reeling. I felt nauseous, hot, and cold all at once. A part of me wanted to move away from her while the other ached to appease and soothe her.

"You may go, my love. I will see you soon," I whispered before kissing her ear.

I released her with an odd mix of reluctance and relief. The latter echoed hers, although laced with a hefty dose of disbelief: she hadn't believed I would keep my word. That upset me more than it should have. But, to my surprise, the older man Naima had called Thomson didn't express relief but something akin to triumph and hope as he pushed my mate behind him. I would need to find out what the fuck was going on in this place.

I flew into the Mist, welcoming its cool and invigorating embrace, but lurked by the door long enough to make sure it properly closed behind me to keep my woman safe. I needed to hunt to replenish the energy I had expended breaking that massive glass and gain even more while waiting for my bride to go to sleep.

And then, the real fun would start.

CHAPTER 5

NAIMA

My right hand clutched the burning and throbbing mark branded on my chest. The other latched on to Thomson as he herded me back inside while multiplying the apologies. I couldn't focus on his words. My head spun, and my body tingled with a foreign energy that pulsated outward from my brand. My chest felt so constricted that I couldn't seem to get enough oxygen in my lungs.

He didn't hurt me. He didn't hurt me...

I had to keep repeating those words to myself or else I would lose it. Another wave of panic almost overwhelmed me as we navigated around the broken glass of the holding cell before exiting that room.

Images of the reinforced glass wall shattering then his shadow tentacles grabbing me started replaying in a loop in my head. In that instant, I'd believed my final hour had come. Seconds from my body slamming against his, I'd expected Zain to drain me with the same voracity he had siphoned Jared and that Cthulhu Beast.

After that dreadful night, I'd dream of a similar scene for

weeks thereafter. The Mistwalker would bash in my bedroom window, then pin me to my bed with his tentacles to feed on me. As I lived alone, it would have taken a few days of me not showing up to work and not answering calls before someone came to check up on me. They would have only to found the dried-up husk that remained of me. The growing intensity and vividness of those nightmares had eventually driven me to seek therapy.

He hadn't hurt me. He'd even tried to comfort me. That might have worked, even just a little, had he not put whatever that thing was inside of me. What was that even doing to me, right now?

"Am I going to turn into something like him?" I asked as Thomson ushered me inside a room in the middle of the corridor we'd been treading.

I blinked at the excessive brightness within, realizing it was some kind of infirmary. A pretty female with brown skin and long, silky black hair—likely of Indian descent—came to me with a concerned look in her eyes.

"No, Ms. Connors," Director Thomson said in a reassuring tone. "No harm will come to you from this. I will explain everything to you a little later. For now, I'd like Dr. Chandra to give you an exam."

"An exam for what?" I asked, suddenly feeling on the defensive. "For that thing?" I tapped on the marking on my chest which continued to throb and appeared to grow darker and more defined with each passing minute. "And no, I don't want to wait until later. I want to know *now* what the fuck is happening to me."

Dr. Chandra slowly approached me, wisely stopping at a non-threatening distance. "Ms. Connors," she said in a soothing voice and a gentle smile that did help a little. "You have just gone through a traumatic experience. You are extremely agitated—with good reason—but I fear you are about to start hyperventilating. You are a psychologist. I do not need to list the symptoms to you."

I swallowed hard and hugged my midsection. The rational part in me knew her words to be true, but the other part didn't give a damn. I closed my eyes and inhaled deeply before exhaling slowly.

"Very good," Dr. Chandra said in an approving tone.

I repeated the process a few more times until my head began to clear. Opening my eyes again, I glared at Director Thomson. He held my gaze, not with defiance, but with the calm acceptance of someone in the wrong determined to fix things.

"What is this thing?" I asked through my teeth. "Can you take it out?"

"That is the brand that anchors him to you," Thomson explained in a gentle voice. "Unfortunately, it can never be taken out. Even if Zain dies, his brand will remain on you. This was what I had asked you about earlier. When a Mist-walker touches a human, he can choose to implant a part of him in that person as some sort of beacon."

"A beacon for what?!" I asked, bewildered. "Clearly, he already knew how to find me, both eleven years ago and today!"

"Yes," Thomson conceded in an irritatingly soft voice. He was trying to calm me so that we could talk rationally, but I just wanted to break something. "However, he could only do that during the Mist. Once the portals open, and he enters our realm, as his creator, you shine bright like a beacon that he can easily go to. But once it recedes, he is completely in the dark, unless you are asleep."

"And now?" I asked, dreading where that was headed.

"Now, he can contact you at any time, even after the Mist has ended."

"WHAT?!"

"BUT that brand doesn't give him access to your house," Thomson quickly added, before I could freak out again. "He cannot enter without your express consent, as is currently the case with all Mist Beings. Furthermore, there is a cost to him using this connection. As long as he is in the Mist, if you aren't dreaming, contacting you through this link will be extremely costly, energy-wise. But if he's here in human form, then being anchored by his creator becomes necessary for him to be able to stay for extended periods of time."

The expression on his face, the intensity in his eyes, and the way he pronounced those last words gave me a cold shiver as understanding dawned on me. I took a step back, eyeing him with horror.

"You *wanted* this to happen," I whispered, feeling betrayed.

Had I been so gullible? Had he been playing me from the start? To my complete shock, he didn't even try to deny it.

"Yes, Ms. Connors. I had wanted you to anchor him to our world," he admitted without the slightest hint of remorse. "But not like this. I had hoped it would not only be consensual, but that *you* would be the one to offer it to Zain as an incentive for him to join our cause."

I gaped at Thomson, speechless.

"Ms. Connors," Dr. Chandra intervened, "Just like Alfred... I mean, Director Thomson, I have been with the Fourth Division pretty much since its inception, fifteen years ago. We have *never* seen a Mistwalker as powerful as yours. Never. The glass wall has been tested under hundreds of scenarios with both Beasts and Walkers. None of them ever even managed to make a dent in it. We didn't trick you."

She took a shuddering breath and clasped her trembling hands before her. The sight of the woman visibly struggling to control her emotions and maintain her composure made me forget part of my own anger and distress as confusion settled in.

"Six years ago, my baby brother died to a Nightmare named Morgan," she said with a shaky voice. "His creator was the sweetest woman you could ever meet. An artist whose biggest crimes had been slightly going over the speed limit and not properly sorting her recyclable wastes."

Like I had done previously, she hugged her midsection.

Thomson gave her a commiserating look before continuing in her stead. "Dr. Chandra's brother, Rajiv, was one of the agents assigned to eliminating that abomination. He and far too many of my other agents died, not to mention countless innocent civilians. If such a nice woman as Jade managed to involuntarily conjure up that abomination, imagine what the real monsters and sociopaths out there have been unconsciously unleashing on our world through their own Nightmares?"

I felt my blood drain from my face. "Are you saying that Zain—"

"No," Dr. Chandra stated forcefully. Having regained her composure, she lifted her chin with determination. "Your Nightmare is not a monster like Morgan, or Darryl who is out there currently killing people. That mark is the proof," she said when I opened my mouth to argue. "The killers rarely brand their creators. But the few that do make sure it's as painful and excruciating a process as possible."

"Why?" I asked, confused.

"Because the anchor mainly serves to allow a Walker to stay here without the need to siphon others," Thomson said. "Which in turn also means they have to be careful since not doing so keeps them weak."

"Whereas Nightmares don't need an anchor since they coldly go out and gorge on as many victims as they can to become as powerful as possible," I concluded, understanding dawning on me. They both nodded in acknowledgement. "But Zain craves power."

"He craves your approval more," Dr. Chandra said. "When Director Thomson first came up with the idea of this project, I thought he was crazy, and told him as much. But I don't think so anymore. Your Zain has the power to turn the tide and prevent the death of more innocents like my brother. I know this is not what you thought you were signing up for, but we *need* you to see this through."

I swallowed hard, feeling like I was getting conned into something that I would live to regret. But I'd already gone down that rabbit hole. The throbbing on my chest alone was a reminder that, like it or not, that ship had sailed, and my sorry ass was on it.

"So, what happens now?" I asked, feeling somewhat dejected.

"I'm going to give you a quick check up to make sure you didn't get hurt," Dr. Chandra said. "Then, Thomson will take you back to your quarters where dinner will be brought to you."

"Before you go to bed, you will have some decisions to make," Thomson said, looking slightly embarrassed.

"What now?" I asked, tensing up.

"There is no doubt in my mind that Zain will lure you into

the Mist while you sleep," he said cautiously. "Don't worry! You will be safe."

His face heated when I gave him the 'Are you fucking kidding me?' look.

"After the shattered glass incident, I fully understand you doubting my word when I say you'll be safe," Thomson conceded, rubbing the back of his head with a sheepish expression. "But it is true. Your body will remain safely tucked in bed. He will lure you to the Mist in your sleep. The difference is that instead of being a passive actor in your dream, this time, you will be fully aware and making conscious decisions."

"So, you're saying that I'm going to be wide awake inside my dream," I said, looking at him like he'd eaten one funky mushroom too many.

He snorted and smiled. "I know it sounds weird."

"This entire fucking evening has been nothing but a weird fest," I snapped.

Dr. Chandra bit the inside of her cheeks to repress a smile, while Thomson nodded.

"Take the next few hours to digest all that has happened," Thomson said. "I hate doing this to you, but time is of the essence. The selfish part in me is glad for this brand as it forces us to move faster. But another part of me had hoped to have more time to prepare you. You cannot hide anything in the Mist. Zain will be able to read your mind like an open book. If you do not truly wish for him to crossover and fight for our cause, he will know."

"He can read my flipping mind?" I asked, flabbergasted, then threw my hands up in despair and aggravation when he nodded.

"In our world he can only read your emotions, but in his,

he can read everything," Thomson confirmed with a sympathetic expression. "However, so can you."

I perked up at that comment. My eyes locked with his, I eagerly waited for him to continue.

"It will not be instant," he cautioned. "The more time you spend in the Mist, and specifically the more time you spend with him, the stronger the connection between you will be. Eventually, you will be able to read him as clearly as he does you."

That was a small consolation, but it was better than nothing. With time, it could prove a very useful tool. He didn't have to go into further details for me to know I would have my work cut out for me.

After he answered a few more of my questions, I reluctantly submitted to Dr. Chandra's exam—or Anika as she insisted I call her after Thomson left the room. I didn't need her to tell me that I wasn't hurt. Aside from that wretched brand on my chest and the alien energy coursing through me, I was totally fine. Now that panic and terror no longer controlled me, I had to admit that Zain had been gentle in his handling of me. The disconnect between what he was and how he acted was screwing with my head.

After Anika gave me a clean bill of health—although mentioning my iron was a little low—she released me to the good care of her boss who escorted me to my quarters. It required us to pass in front of the room with the broken holding cell. My jaw dropped at the sight of a full construction crew hard at work. They had not only already replaced the broken glass wall, they were now busy reinforcing it with a second layer. How the heck they got here with the Mist was beyond me.

Along the way, Thomson showed me the training room,

the cafeteria, as well as the access to a giant holding area where various Mist Beasts—like that seahorse fairy they had used as bait earlier—were held captive. The idea of caging creatures bothered me. However, knowing they weren't sentient but as apathetic as that fairy had been, made me feel better.

My room blew my mind. Huge and spacious, everything boasted light shades of grey, beige, and white. The modern but minimalistic décor gave it a very Zen feel. Everything screamed quality, from the King-sized bed, to the plush comforters and puffy pillows piled on top. A designer desk with sleek lines and a cushioned desk chair faced the wall left from the door. A giant screen covered the entire side wall in front of the seating area further left from the desk. It currently displayed an exotic wilderness scenery, creating the peaceful haven that I needed right now.

But it was the delectable aroma of the three dishes covered on the small, two-person table next to the seating area that retained my attention. My stomach growled from a hunger I hadn't really felt creeping in with all the insanity of the past few hours.

Hours... I couldn't believe how much my life had completely changed in such a short time. I uncovered the first plate and stared in disbelief at the huge, bone-in ribeye steak sitting on my plate. Since the Mist had nearly wiped out the herds of many farms and breeders, the cost of meat had skyrocketed. Everyone could still afford most cold cuts, bacon, and offal. Everything else had become a treat for the common folk. Thankfully, research and improvement of plant-based meat over the past decade had greatly helped compensate. Furthermore, fish and seafood having been spared by the Mist Beasts—who didn't go into the water—had taken a much bigger place in the world's diet while remaining affordable.

But that single ribeye in my plate would easily cost a little over two-hundred dollars. I didn't doubt for a minute that they had given me a bone-in steak so that there would be no question it was the real thing. I barely touched the all-dressed baked potato—delicious though it was—or the accompanying collard green salad. A smart decision, too. By the time I finished the meat, even sucking the bone, my belly was close to bursting. It would have been a crime to have filled my stomach with the sides and wasted such a divine gift. I washed the whole thing down with the glass of red wine on the tray before bringing the whole thing to the tray slot outside of my room for one of the staff to pick it up.

After locking my room, I showered in my private bathroom and changed into the nightgown I had brought in my overnight bag. Before leaving his office to go see Zain, Thomson had it delivered to my room.

Thankfully, it was still too early to go to bed. A part of me dreaded that moment. For a second, I wondered if I should have taken Anika up on her two offers. But I didn't want to take any drugs to calm me or help me sleep. Once I faced Zain—and I didn't doubt I would soon—I needed to have all of my wits about me. And the second option of sleeping with their cameras monitoring me in case I became excessively agitated so one of them could wake me just felt too creepy. I didn't want some stranger observing me while I slept.

But the truth was that I'd subconsciously wanted that confrontation. I hadn't known how things were going to play out, only that they could allow me to put to rest the unresolved trauma that had been my constant companion for the past eleven years.

I hesitated for half a beat then settled in front of the desk. A laptop on a closed network had been left for me. It opened on an internal wiki that contained the answer to every question I could possibly have about the Mist—well, almost—the Mistwalkers, Nightmares, murders, and the Fourth Division's initiatives.

I skimmed through a number of pages that covered things I already knew from both speaking with Thomson and reading conspiracy theory websites. It was disturbing how accurate they had been. I was disappointed not to find confirmation if the world governments were responsible, but that was fine. I was more interested in Nightmares, Walkers that had crossed over, and the waves of serial killers over the past decades.

Realizing that this phenomenon was occurring all over the planet floored me. It should have been self-evident but hearing about it happening in the countries with the lowest crime rates in the world, such as Finland and New Zealand was mind-boggling. It turned out that variations of the Mist Squad Project were being developed in every country. The wildest ones included some kind of robot-cops while others relied on some kind of mechanical armor, like Tony Stark's Iron Man.

The latter seemed like a good idea, but remembering how easily Zain had smashed the bulletproof, reinforced glass wall, I believed that a strong enough Nightmare would turn anyone wearing those suits into a heap of junk.

"No fucking way!" I whispered in disbelief when I reached the page with all the stats on the recorded demographic of Mistwalkers that had crossed over.

According to the chart, there were in excess of 128,000 Transients worldwide—the Walkers that had been reborn in a human body. The US alone accounted for 26,000 of them. Our own state had nearly 1,000 with twenty-eight in Cordell County where I lived. Thankfully, only 1% of them were Nightmares. However, that percentage had been 0.01% only six years ago; a 100% increase on an exponential curve.

I shuddered at the thought that over 1,200 freaks like the Thornhill Killer were on the loose, with more of them being born every Mist. Knowing that each of them could be as strong—maybe even more—than my Zain wiped away any hesitation I still held on to. The prospect of dealing with my Nightmare still terrified me, but I only had to remind myself that he had branded me and not harmed me.

With a newfound resolve, I headed to bed.

It was divine, the mattress swallowing me like a cloud. I'd expected to toss and turn for hours, my wretched brain torturing me with the darkest scenarios. However, the moment I rested my head on my pillows and closed my eyes, I instantly felt myself falling into a dark, endless void.

I landed with a thud on a mossy hill before rolling down the slope. Despite the impact of the fall, I hadn't felt any pain. I came to a stop in a thick forest filled with leafless black trees with twisted limbs raised towards a dark sky in an imploring gesture. The uneven ground was covered in a slithering blanket of fog. The scent of wet dirt and rotten leaves stung my nose.

My heart nearly jumped out of my throat at the sound of a terrible roar in the distance, breaking the otherwise eerie silence. My head jerked to the right as I tried to see through the Mist limiting the range of my vision. Two large, white beams hovered almost above the tree line in the general direction from whence the roar had resonated. Paralyzed with fear, it took a moment for my brain to understand what was approaching. The Beast reared, and its giant praying mantis front limbs slashed down the trees in front of it with the ease of a scythe cutting wheat.

Its white eyes zeroed in on me. Even from the distance, and despite the Mist, I watched in horror as the facial tentacles of a Cthulhu Beast stretched in a lethal grin.

I ran.

CHAPTER 6

ZAIN

I felt the moment my bride closed her eyes—at long last—to enter the realm of dreams. Normally, I would have waited endlessly for her to finally cross the Veil once she'd conquered her ever elusive sleep. But not anymore. My brand on her acted like a lifeline that I could simply yank to bring her to me the minute she surrendered to the lure of the Veil.

I had gorged on many Beasts on my way back to my domain inside the Mist Plane. It was odd to be here while the portals to the other side were opened. However, it was the only way for my mate and me to play without jeopardizing her safety.

I watched her running, terror etched on her face. I inhaled deeply, savoring the taste of her fear. Fuck, how I had missed it! Even though my body buzzed with an insane amount of energy, each delectable wave of her despair only fueled me further. For the first time, I didn't care about the power my woman was giving me. The scent of her fear no longer reeked and repulsed me like it had earlier.

Upping the ante to enhance her experience, I made the

terrain before her even more uneven, with knotted roots and brambles to make her trip. For a moment, I considered making the ground sticky, or muddy to make it even harder for her to advance, while accelerating the speed of the Beast, but it felt like an overkill. Still, a bit more spice was needed to truly push her over the edge. First, I thought of making the trees come to life and attempt to grab her: a classic that never got old. Then I thought of creepy shadows with glowing red eyes cutting her path as they emitted a haunting, inhuman laughter. And then I got it: a decomposing swarm of seahorse fairies nipping at my Naima while the Beast closed in on her.

And then I would yank her to safety, seconds before the Beast would get her.

This time, she will want me to console her.

As much as I loved and got off on her terror, the intimacy of appeasing and comforting her after the fact had always been my favorite part of our encounters. After today's trauma in the real world and the one I was currently subjecting her to, Naima would inevitably ache for consoling. And I would gladly give her all she needed. I never quite understood why my mate's subconscious had stopped wanting those tender moments while demanding darker encounters. I had disliked that path. But now was our chance to get back on the proper track.

Naima once more stumbled on a gnarled root, but this time, she fell to the ground. The Beast roared again and picked up the pace. Just as she was scrambling back to her feet, zombie fairies screeched in the distance. Lightning crackled between the radioactive specks of their pixie dust.

Instead of screaming and trying to run in the only two directions that temporarily offered an escape route, Naima froze, trembling in a complete state of shock. I frowned at that unusual reaction. My bride was stronger than this and a fighter. Had she weakened over our years apart?

She looked at her surroundings, and an odd sense of calm descended over her. More confused than ever, I explored her emotions. All that I got from her was a peaceful certainty that everything would be all right.

What the fuck is going on?

"ZAIN! HELP ME!" Naima suddenly shouted.

My brain froze. I was her stalker, not her rescuer. Why would she ask me to aid her? In the eighteen years since I'd become self-aware, shortly after her thirteenth birthday, Naima had never consciously called me to her. She'd always tried to push me away while her subconscious insisted that I relentlessly pursue her. I'd felt bipolar at times trying to juggle her twisted desires.

"ZAIN!" she called out again, snapping me out of my daze.

I didn't know how to respond. A part of me was exhilarated to have her consciously wanting me. Yet, another was terrified. If she no longer feared me, she would also no longer need me, whether to chase or comfort her. I would lose her, become no more than an abandoned dream, wasting away, until I became insane.

I hesitantly came out of my translucent state, allowing her to see me from the distance I'd been observing her. A relieved and happy smile stretched Naima's lips, and her beautiful, hazel eyes shone with a joyful glimmer that took my breath away. The wave of emotions that slammed into me had never been more powerful... more delicious. Images of me killing her boyfriend in the Mist then dispatching the Cthulhu Beast that had ensnared her flashed through Naima's mind.

Reeling, my instinctive urge to rush to her was crushed by

a little voice in the back of my head, keeping me locked in place. I was her stalker, not her rescuer as she appeared to start believing. She needed me to feed her fears, not appease them. Naima's love for me was bound to my ability to terrorize and punish her for her wrongdoings, then comfort her so that she could face another day. I couldn't lose her.

"Zain?" Naima whispered questioningly when I failed to come forward as the Beast and the fairies closed in on her position.

"Run, Naima!" I said tauntingly, although the words felt bitter in my mouth instead of exhilarating as they normally would. "They are catching up!"

My bride's face fell with the sudden realization that I wasn't going to protect her. Naima shook her head in denial and took a step back as if she couldn't tolerate being in my presence. The betrayal on her face and the hurt she broadcast towards me cut me to the core. A pain like I'd never felt before, in this realm or hers, flooded directly into me through my brand connecting us. It felt like acid eating me from the inside out.

"Fuck you," Naima hissed almost in a whisper filled with pain, tears rolling down her cheeks. The look of hurt and disillusion on her beautiful face struck me like a thousand daggers. "I'm not playing your stupid games anymore." She angrily wiped the tears glistening on her cheeks with the back of her hand. "You want your monsters to kill me? Then enjoy the show, you sick fuck!"

Turning her back to me, Naima spread her arms wide, tilted her head back, and closed her eyes while waiting for death to come claim her.

Terror, a feeling I had never experienced before, slammed into me at this reckless display. I raced towards my mate, while summoning countless trees before the Beast. It had gone into a hungry frenzy as he carved himself a path to Naima, now that she had surrendered her life to him. With a wave of my hand, I dispelled the zombie fairies that had been less than fifty meters away from her.

I swooped in and snagged my bride before flying away in all haste. Naima yelped in surprise and fear, thinking I was one of the creatures stalking her. She then instinctively wrapped her arms around my neck, shock and confusion visible on her face. The Beast roared in fury, having been denied his prize with less than twenty meters to go. It gave us chase, but I was too fast for it as I flew through the defensive walls that defined the perimeter of my domain in the Mist. The wall would kill the Beast if it attempted to trespass.

Even now that she was safe, my head spun with the over-whelming lingering fear that still wanted to choke me. At the same time, anger at my female's recklessness bubbled inside me with the need to erupt. I landed in the empty clearing that surrounded the immediate vicinity of my wall. Putting Naima on her feet, I gripped her shoulders in a bruising hold while glaring at her.

"What the fuck do you think you were doing?" I shouted, furious.

"Refusing to be a puppet in your twisted mind games," Naima hissed, lifting her chin defiantly in a way that left me speechless. She'd never stood up to me in the past, always cowering in fear instead. "You wanted to see me get eaten by a Beast. I was giving you satisfaction while getting out of this farce. Why are you so upset? Unhappy your prey didn't want to play by your rules," she added in a mocking tone.

"What you did," I hissed back in her face, "was nearly commit suicide! That Cthulhu Beast was not a summoned illusion like the fairies. It was a real Mist Beast I had lured here."

"So what?" she retorted with an irritated expression. "This is a dream. MY dream. The Beast kills me, I wake up, and I'm out of this bullshit scenario!"

"NO, YOU STUPID FEMALE!" I shouted, giving her a single shake. "This is *not* a dream. You are *not* sleeping. You are walking *awake* in the dream world. When you sleep, a sliver of your consciousness crosses the Veil. On its own, the human mind isn't powerful enough for a full walk like you are currently doing. That's why you don't remember your dreams in the morning. That's why you can die in your dreams. But when you do, that part of you in the dream *dies*! Your people usually awaken before it, but the few times you don't, a part of you is lost forever. There's a reason humans say that if you die in your dream, you die in the real world."

Naima froze, a horrified expression descending on her features. "Are you saying I would have died in the real world if that Cthulhu had eaten me?"

I heaved a sigh and let go of her shoulders. "I'm saying that the part of you that is here with me right now would have died. Unlike us, humans cannot do a full transfer of consciousness unless their body dies. There is a fraction of you left in your body in the Mortal Plane. Had the Beast killed you here, only that tiny fragment of you would have remained. You would have technically been brain dead, stuck in a coma that you would never awaken from."

"You exposed me to true death to play your sick games?!" she said in an accusatory tone, while taking a few steps away from me.

"I created the thrilling experience you crave," I argued defensively. "How the fuck was I to know you would do something so reckless? You always ran! You've always loved being hunted down."

"I hated it! I hated it then, and I hate it even more now," she shouted back, taking a menacing step towards me. "I spent two years in therapy to learn to stop being a victim, to learn to block *you* out. I've been at peace for the past nine years, and I'm not falling down that rabbit hole again. You're done getting your rocks off by terrorizing me."

Every single one of her words cut me like a blade. I had felt her slipping away from me during those two years. It had been painful. But the last nine years had been sheer agony. She had not called for me, not dreamed of me. I would see her in the distance as she sparked new Wishes that didn't involve me. I'd been so enraged, felt so betrayed that I'd killed them all.

"I gave you what you wanted," I said.

"I never wanted to be terrified. *You* imposed your will on me," she snapped.

"No, Naima. YOU dictated what happened during our time together," I countered. "Your conscious mind may have said no, but your subconscious shouted loud and clear that you wanted pain, that you wanted to be punished for destroying your home. But you did not respond well to pain so, *I* chose to give you terror instead. And *that*, you couldn't get enough of."

Naima gaped at me for a second, and a strange expression crossed her beautiful features. She shook her head and looked at me with discouragement before running her fingers through her puffy, curly hair. It had felt so soft beneath my touch when she rested her head on my shoulder as I consoled her after I'd 'punished' her. How I hungered for those moments again.

"Those were the twisted reveries of a heartbroken child,"

she said in a sad and tired voice. "My parents were constantly fighting. And when they did, it escalated quickly. They never hit each other, but Dad would throw things at the walls, and Mom would break dishes and whatever else she could get her hands on. And whenever it started getting out of hand, one would try to physically stop the other, which usually ended up with Dad pinning Mom against the wall, and Mom trying to bite him to break free. So, he would hold her tightly by the neck until she calmed down." Naima hugged herself and exhaled a shuddering breath. "Eventually, Mom would break down crying. Dad would then hug her and tell her he loved her, and they would apologize to each other."

She turned her back to me and walked a few steps inside the clearing surrounded by a wall of Mist that we were standing in.

"My parents adored each other, but they just couldn't live together. They thought having me would help fix their issues, it only made things worse." She shivered, then turned to face me. "All those years ago, the little girl that sparked you wanted someone to punish her for destroying her parents' happiness with her complicating presence. But she was wrong. She was never to blame. *I* was never the cause."

A part of me had known this but refused to face that truth. Acknowledging it also implied acknowledging that my entire existence had been premised on a lie. I refused to accept that and what it could mean for us going forward. The few hours since I had at long last reconnected with Naima had felt like an eternity. And my addiction with my creator—my obsession even—had returned with a vengeance. I would destroy anything and anyone that would stand in the way of me finally having a life with my bride.

"Is that why you always wanted me to strangle you all

those times you wished me to play the slasher-stalker?" I asked, my chest constricting with an unpleasant emotion I didn't want.

"Did I?" she asked, slightly stunned.

"Yes. You wanted me to chase you, and at the end, pin you down on the ground or against a wall, then strangle you while speaking evil things."

Naima snorted then shook her head again with a sad expression. "If I were to psychoanalyze that response, I would say that I was obviously reproducing what I'd seen in my own home. But, Zain, while the confused little girl unconsciously wanted to be punished, what I'd really wanted from you was what my Dad was doing to my mother."

"And what was that?" I asked in a whisper.

"Showing her that he loved her. No matter how angry he got, even when she tried to hurt him, holding her neck was his way of saying 'I will not let you hurt me, but I'm also never going to hurt you.' Instead, I conjured up one nightmare after another, then repeated the same pattern in real life. The boyfriends I ended up with that liked pinning women against walls and holding their necks, also liked leaving bruises everywhere."

I watched her slowly approach me, her determined gaze boring into mine. The pain in my chest expanded. I braced for the next words she would speak. They would hurt, badly. But I wasn't letting her go. She needed me as I needed her.

"I don't need fear or abuse in my life," Naima said in a firm and unyielding tone.

"You need me," I said just as firmly.

"I don't need someone who takes pleasure in my pain and misery and goes out of his way to put me in potential danger," she continued, as if I hadn't said a word.

"You need me!" I reiterated more forcefully.

"No, Zain. I don't need a Nightmare haunting me."

Silence settled between us, so thick I could almost touch it. I felt faint with pain. I could feel her emotions and clearly read her thoughts in my realm. She meant it.

"You created me, but you no longer want me," I whispered.

It didn't make sense. In two more days, after the Mist ended, we were supposed to be reunited once I'd crossed over. Had I spent all those years becoming what she wanted—what I believed she needed—only to be cast aside now? Even if I wanted to—not that I did—I could no longer change who or what I was.

"No, Zain. I do want you," Naima said in a soft voice.

A bolt of fire exploded in my chest. I gazed at her with disbelief to have finally heard the impossible words I'd so often dreamed would one day spill from her mouth.

"BUT I do not want you the way you *think* I do," she specified.

I glided forward, invading her personal space. She didn't step back, didn't flinch, and didn't appear scared or worried.

"How *do* you want me, my Naima?" I asked in a whisper.

She lifted her chin defiantly. "I want you the way you have been the three times we have physically or consciously met. I don't want you to be my Stalker, but my Savior."

I recoiled, taken aback by such an unexpected request. "Your Savior?" I asked, utterly confused.

"When Jared tried to kill me, you saved my life," Naima said, her voice becoming more pressing. "When that Cthulhu Beast was hypnotizing me in the Observatory, you tore it to shreds. And just now, you spared me from true death."

"But such instances will be extremely rare," I argued.

"There's no fucking way you're leaving me in the shadows again only to be called upon once every blue moon."

"Not anymore," Naima countered. "Nightmares are taking over my world in human form. They are leaving a trail of death behind them. No one is safe anymore. *I* am not safe anymore. At the end of every Mist, more of them enter our world and grow insanely powerful by feeding on my people."

Naima cupped my face in her hands, hope shining in her beautiful hazel eyes. The warmth of her touch sent the most exquisite shiver down my spine. She had never voluntarily laid her hands on me in such gentle fashion. I barely repressed the moan of pleasure rising in my throat.

"You are a psychopath, *my* psychopath, hungry for the fear of others, for power, for dominance. You can kill without hesitation, without remorse, and even derive pleasure from it," she continued. Her voice was not only devoid of condemnation but also filled with an excitement that awakened a sense of thrill within me. "I don't want to change that in you. I want you to use your powers to stalk those Nightmares who threaten humans. Cross over and become humanity's champion."

CHAPTER 7

ZAIN

My head spun. Of all the things my woman could have said, I never saw that one coming. My mind raced, cycling through the events of the past few hours. All the signs had been there. I'd known from the start that they wanted something from me, but this?!

I pulled away from her touch and slowly glided around the oval shape of the clearing. The intense gaze of my Naima weighed on me. As much as I loved her attention, I felt grateful for her silence while I sorted out my thoughts. Too many of them were simultaneously firing inside my head.

I had already intended to cross over. Despite my careful planning, as a newborn in that world, I would be vulnerable, exposed, without a penny to my name. I'd observed so many Transients die during their transformation due to their poor choice of location for their mortal birth, getting devoured mid-shift by Beasts or other Walkers. I'd heard tales of others dying of exposure, starvation, or insufficient energy to sustain them until they could bind their creator.

With her blessing to cross over, I wouldn't have to deal

with any of these non-negligible inconveniences. Better yet, I wouldn't have to change who I was. I could still hunt and dominate lesser Walkers. Those Nightmares would be the ultimate prey. A true challenge at last. There was nothing more boring than hunting a Spark. In spite of the crazy abilities their creators gave them, Beasts were usually too stupid to use them in a truly terrifying and tactical way. Sentient beings were the most fun quarry, especially Nightmares. Unlike Wishes, who were usually sweet and peaceful, Nightmares and Dark Desires were predators. I already relished the sound of their cries of agony, the scent of their fear, and the taste of their ethereal essence as I gorged on their lifeforce.

As an added bonus, in the Mortal Plane, I could amass an endless amount of power… with the humans' blessing… and with my creator to anchor me.

My Naima… I could finally bind her to me and claim her as my true mate.

But what if it's a trap?

Based on my observation of other Transients, it took hours for the human shell to form, hours during which they were completely vulnerable. If she or that shadow organization wanted to permanently kill me, I would be helpless to defend myself. Assuming I made it through that phase, after my birth, I would have lost at least a third of my current power—maybe even a bit more. I could be easily controlled or coerced.

Yet, even as those thoughts crossed my mind, I dismissed such deception from my mate. That did not mean that the Thomson male wasn't using her to get to me and others like me.

I glided back to my Naima. She stared at me expectantly. Although she attempted to look nonchalant, I could feel the tension bubbling inside of her, and her strong desire for me to say yes. That did strange but wonderful things to me. Who would have thought that being wanted could be more intoxicating than being feared?

It was my turn to cup her face with both hands as I pillaged the memories of her interactions with Thomson. Even though she disliked the intrusion, my bride didn't balk. Then again, I could see from her memories that Thomson had warned her that hiding anything from me in the Mist would be futile.

Unfortunately, the information I thus gathered only confirmed what Naima had said, and her genuine desire that I accept. But it didn't validate Thomson's honesty. When I had branded her, then demanded Thomson open the door to set me free, his concern for my mate had been genuine. But had it been out of worry for her welfare or for the bait he intended to lure me with?

It stung that Naima wanted me for what I could do for them, but not for what we could be together. No matter, I would make her love me. Deep down, she already did. I would simply make sure she acknowledged it. My bride had given me a taste of what it felt like to be wanted by her, and I was already addicted.

"Tell me, Naima," I said in a sensual voice, my hands slipping down her cheeks in a gentle caress, along the gentle curve of her shoulders, then down her slender back. "Are you my reward for dispatching those evil Nightmares?"

Naima's breath caught in her throat when I pulled her tightly against me. She placed her palms on my chest as if to push me back but, interestingly, she didn't. There was no guile or deception in her compliance. That turned me on.

"No," my female said in a whisper. "I am not your reward. Being the apex predator in both our worlds will be. But if you cross over, as your anchor, you and I will spend time together."

"As mates?" I insisted.

"No," she said in a firm but gentle tone.

"How then?" I challenged, annoyed by her conviction and yet excited at the thought of breaking down her walls.

"I will be your coach, your mentor to help you learn the ways of my people," Naima said. "You know little of the rules of our world. From what I've read about Transients, learning to adapt to human life, and especially the realities of a human body, can be challenging to figure out alone. Living in society can also be quite mystifying."

Her excitement at that prospect was contagious. I tightened my hold around Naima's slender waist. Her eyes widened again as I leaned forward. She thought I was going to kiss her. I almost did. But I pressed a kiss at the corner of her mouth then brushed my lips against her soft skin all the way to her right ear.

"When I cross into your world, I will claim you as my mate," I whispered in a voice full of promise.

She shivered, her hands on my chest tightening their grip. I straightened to stare her in the eyes. My right hand on her back slid up to wrap around her neck. Her lips parted in a soft gasp when I slightly squeezed.

"You will want me to," I added, drawing her face towards mine by the hold around her neck. "I will drive you crazy for me."

I crushed her lips in a searing but brief kiss. She stiffened at first, but once again didn't fight back. A sense of triumph soared within me at the confused, inner tug-of-war and sliver of arousal I perceived from her. Yes, I would make her love me.

I released her and glided a few steps away, feeling bereft now that I no longer basked in the warmth of her body. She touched two fingers to her lips, visibly shaken by her conflicting emotions.

"Go back to sleep, my mate," I said at last. "No Nightmare will further haunt you this night."

Her eyes widened at my unexpected comment. "What? Wait! What does that mean? Will you come? Will you do it?"

I smiled in a non-committal fashion. It wasn't fair as she couldn't really see my ethereal features, but she could sense my responses.

"You will find out soon enough. Sweet dreams, my love."

Without giving her a chance to argue, I sent her consciousness back to her body, only hanging on to a sliver of it, which I forwarded to the safety of a pretty memory of her youth. Naima often dreamt of that camp she'd gone to with her parents—one of the few times where they had simply been happy. No arguments, no fights, just a loving family spending quality time together. I would have her well-rested when next we meet.

For now, I had someone to talk to.

I crossed my protective wall, leaving the safety of my territory then opened my senses. With my great power, it took me seconds to locate my target. I sighed in annoyance realizing how far his host's territory was located from here. I could teleport and be there in a blink, but I didn't want to expend that much energy. It would only be a ten to fifteen-minute flight from here. Naturally, I munched on some easy prey along the way; Sparks too unaware to play tourists in the Mortal Plane while the portals were opened.

It struck me then that my days of feeding on Wishes might come to an end. I didn't need Naima to tell me that they would be off-limits. For shame. Humans and their compassion were a mystery I hoped never to comprehend.

The thick walls of Risul's domain crackled with their lethal warnings. They looked like rolling thunder clouds, rippling with lightning. Their intensity increased as I made my approach. I hovered at a safe distance, admiring with begrudging respect the defenses erected by a Wish. Risul had always been a careful and quiet one. He had built his power over the years, lurking in safe areas, feeding on apathetic Sparks while he fortified his lands. Then, in an unexpected twist, the lucky bastard had saved his creator from committing suicide in the Mist. Since then, she had given up mortal life to move permanently here in the Mist.

Having his creator willingly come live by his side in our realm had made Risul incredibly powerful. So much so, he no longer needed to hunt to maintain his tremendous energy level. Thankfully, he was a Wish and not a Nightmare. Had he continued hunting, he might have become as unkillable and god-like to us as that Darryl had become to the humans.

A bright light flashed as the lord of the domain crossed his defensive walls into the no man's land outside where I waited. Risul came out in his wraith form, his shadowy tendrils already out, crackling with impressive energy. I smiled at this deliberate display of power. The Wish was peaceful but wouldn't hesitate to kill to protect those he cherished.

"These lands and those within are not for you to hunt," Risul said as sole greeting. "You will leave my lands and not return."

"I am not on your lands, nor do I wish to enter them," I said smugly. "But I do wish to have a word with your guest. Would you be so kind as to call him out?"

"You will not harm or threaten my father-in-law," Risul hissed, advancing slightly in a menacing fashion.

"I have no such intentions," I said with a dismissive wave of my hand. "You can read me, *Wish*," I continued with a sliver of disdain in my voice as I stated his classification. "There is no lying in the Mist. You know what I seek. Bring him."

I felt his consciousness brush against mine as he assessed my intentions. He scrunched his face as if he'd bitten into something sour.

"I do not command him," Risul said with obvious reluctance. "I will forward him your message. He will choose whether or not to address you. If he declines, you will leave at once and never return."

I acknowledged his comment with a stiff nod. The Wish flew back through his wall. Seconds later, I was shocked to see Thomson walk out of the dark clouds, stopping a few steps from their protective embrace. His eagerness, and the visible displeasure of his son-in-law hovering behind him, majorly flattered my ego.

"Greetings, Zain," Director Thomson said to me.

He didn't shout, and yet his words reached me loud and clear, despite the great distance between us. With that alone, the human was making a statement, establishing that despite being a foreigner in our lands, he had mastered some of the Mist's quirkier features—something that could only be accomplished with many years of experience.

"Risul tells me you wished to see me," Thomson continued. "Or should I say, that you wished to read me?"

I didn't answer, too busy flipping through his thoughts and memories. The smugness of his broadening smile aggravated me. I hated that he had already anticipated that this night might play out this way. He had expected my visit. Being predictable didn't sit well with being a predator. However, he held no deception either. Worse still, Thomson was laying all of his hopes on my shoulders. He truly believed I was the answer to the Nightmare—both literally and figuratively— that was plaguing his existence. Even though I didn't give two shits about dead humans, past and future, his hope in me being their savior, their champion, stroked my massive ego.

"Time is of the essence for both you and us," the human said once he accurately guessed I was done reading him. "Should you choose to join us, you should aim to initiate your birth in the next ten to eighteen hours. It takes anywhere between six to twelve hours for your kind to form a human vessel. If something goes wrong, you want to complete the process long before the Mist ends so that you can safely make it back home before the portals close. As for us, you know the urgency of our situation. But it matters for you as well. With every passing day, Darryl grows stronger."

And that was the biggest concern. I couldn't let him become too powerful, or I might not survive the encounter. I wasn't embarking on such a journey only to get my butt handed to me right at the start.

"I will think on it," I replied, trying to sound bored.

His barely repressed snort pissed me off. He knew he had me the minute his son-in-law had gone in to announce my presence. I would find the appropriate time to knock him down a notch or two in the not-so-distant future.

"Should you wish to join us, simply come back to the same door you entered earlier. A safe birthplace will await you."

I gave him a stiff nod, then spun around and flew away. I needed to hunt one last time before I left this realm.

CHAPTER 8

NAIMA

I woke up feeling ridiculously well-rested and refreshed. My eyes popped at the sight of the time. I rarely slept in, considering it a waste of daylight. Normally, my running shoes were hitting the pavement by no later than 6:30 for my morning jog. But here I was, sprawled in the divinely comfy giant bed in my quarters well after 9:00 AM. I hopped out of bed with a spring in my step before heading to the bathroom for my morning ablutions.

Whatever dream Zain had thrown me into after our little confrontation had been wonderful. I hated that the details eluded me. I couldn't even remember what it had been about or where it had taken place; only that it had made me happy. And yet, every single moment and conversation during my time in the Mist with my Nightmare—or Darkest Desire as he labeled himself—was crystal clear in my mind.

Zain both confused and fascinated me. There was no question he was a psychopath. And yet, as much as he enjoyed terrifying others—yours truly included—and taking the lives of those he considered lesser, he didn't actually want to hurt me. He terrorized me in order to please me, not realizing his actions had the exact opposite effect. Zain wanted my approval, but his understanding of what I wanted was twisted by the lenses through which he saw the world.

The lenses *I* gave him.

Zain believed himself to be in love with me. Obviously, that wasn't the case. He didn't know me, only the tortured version of me that he had dreamed up. Navigating his expectations would be tricky, especially since he could read my thoughts.

As I brushed my hair, I tried to analyze my own feelings towards him. I didn't really know how to think of him. He wasn't really a person, not in the traditional sense. The virtual world he evolved in had skewed his perception of right and wrong as well as of pleasure and pain. The lawless, dog-eat-dog ruleset of his realm, further fueled by my own 'dark desires' that had shaped him as a psychopath, would make it insanely challenging for him to fit in this world.

All these years, I'd been incredibly terrified of him. Now, I saw him as an exciting project I couldn't wait to get started on. What an amazing psychological study he represented. This was a once in a lifetime opportunity. One that could also save countless innocent lives.

I finished dressing and slipped my feet into my ankle boots, mentally kicking myself for not having brought more casual footwear. Then again, I hadn't believed I would have made it this far. I picked my access card then headed to the cafeteria.

The construction crew that had been working on repairing the destroyed glass wall were nowhere to be seen. With the door into that chamber closed, I couldn't tell if they'd completed the task. However, considering how swiftly they'd progressed last night, I assumed they were done.

The large doors to the cafeteria swished open before me. The delectable aroma that invaded my nostrils had my stomach instantly rumbling with hunger. The imposing, oddly shaped room had a dozen rectangular tables wide enough to accommodate six to eight people. However, only a handful of them were occupied by clustered groups of agents, with the odd man out, eating by himself in the back corner of the room. My eyes widened when I recognized Riley.

I made a beeline for him, excited to have someone who could relate to what I was currently experiencing. It didn't hurt that we'd instantly clicked as well during the ride here.

"Hey! You made it!" I exclaimed, stopping on the other side of the table from him.

"Naima! There you are! I was wondering when I was going to see you!" Riley replied with a beaming smile.

"When or if?" I asked, slightly taken aback.

"When," he said, matter-of-factly. "You were the talk of this whole circus last night after the agent escorted you to that corridor, not to mention your badass Nightmare."

"Right, I can see that," I said scrunching my face.

"Go grab some food, and then I can spill the tea about what you missed while you eat," Riley said in a conspiratorial tone that had me burning with curiosity.

I headed towards the buffet. It was quite the impressive spread with a hot and cold section. Trays with scrambled and hard-boiled eggs, ham, sausage, bacon, steaks, hash browns, and sautéed vegetables sat near the pancakes, porridge, and oatmeal. Next to them, a variety of breakfast cereals, yogurts in ice bowls, muesli, and fresh cut fruits transitioned into the final section with breads and pastries, from sweet to savory, with a selection of cheeses, cold cuts, smoked salmon, jams, and other spreads. The decadent abundance on display was simply mind-boggling. The cost of the food laid out before me would easily add up to my annual salary of the next couple of years, including the yearly bonuses.

Not being one to look a gift horse in the mouth, I picked up a tray and shamelessly piled on the meat. Being a sucker for hash browns—and potatoes in general—I squeezed a small amount of it on my plate, then filled a bowl with fresh fruits to give me good conscience. As I was putting the spoon down, the sudden appearance of a hand on the other side of the freshly cut vegetables startled me. I realized then that what I had believed to be a set of mirrors at the back of the buffet was in fact a row of food trays catering to a completely different group.

I crouched and was shocked to see a whole other cafeteria with a much larger group. I recognized the faces of some of the candidates that had traveled with me yesterday or that I had seen in the Observatory. It first struck me as odd, but in light of all the things that had happened to me last night, I could see why Thomson wouldn't want me openly talking with others who had not made the cut.

Which means Riley also has a Nightmare.

That got me all the more eager to hear what he had to say. After a short detour by the beverage station to get a cappuccino and a tall glass of orange juice, I hastened back to Riley's table. He burst out laughing at the sight of the mountain of food on my plate. I scrunched my face in embarrassment, and my cheeks heated.

My appearance was quite deceiving. I was six feet tall with not an ounce of fat on me except where you wanted a bit —boobs, hips, and butt. However, if I put my mind to it, I could probably eat my own size. Growing up, my friends had hated me for my crazy metabolism. I settled down across from him, relieved to see he still had some food left on his plate. It would have been a little awkward to have him just watching me stuff my face.

"Tell me everything!" I said while digging in.

"Your Nightmare devouring that Beast naturally had everyone talking," Riley said with an almost boyish excitement, his light brown eyes sparkling. "We were all dying with curiosity after the agent took you through that door no one else had. Then everything got boring for a bit. Most of the Mistwalkers were just hovering there, looking stupid. A few of them followed some of the candidates, but they were quite subdued. They reminded me of lost puppies looking for a home."

"Sparks and newly awakened Wishes, I'm guessing," I said pensively before stuffing a chunk of spicy beef sausage in my mouth.

Riley nodded. "A few more people got escorted out. We all expected to get the boot. Then this one Nightmare came charging in, just killing everything. That freak was making a show of it and enjoying every moment. All the sentient Walkers and Beast hauled the heck out of there."

"Oh wow!" I whispered.

"Wow, indeed," Riley said with a troubled chuckle. "It was quite a disturbing sight. But then, when there was nothing left to kill, he started stalking Julia, one of the other candidates."

My eyes widened, and I instinctively looked around the room for any signs of a civilian woman, but only saw a couple of female agents.

Riley chuckled again. "She's not here, yet. Julia did go through the same door you and I did, though."

"She probably slept in like me then," I said before taking a sip of my cappuccino. "What happened after that?"

"Once Julia's freak was gone, the Mist Beings came back," Riley said with a contagious enthusiasm. "That's when my Merax showed up. He was badass and killed a huge Beast in front of us. It wasn't as big as the one your Nightmare devoured, but it was still impressive."

I laughed and shook my head. "You know, listening to you talking, I could see people holding Beast fights the way they do dog and cock fights."

My smile faded at the troubled look that descended on Riley's face.

"Those already exist," he said grimly. "There's some crazy shit happening out there. Beast vs. Beast is fine. The problem is when they start throwing humans in an arena with those creatures and take bets on how long they'll survive, and which Beast will get to them first."

I covered my mouth with my hand as I stared at him in horror. He snorted and gave me a sad smile.

"Some humans are the real monsters," he said dejectedly. "But that's a conversation for another time. Anyway, my Merax did his thing then started stalking me, trying to get me to come to the window near him. I got in that corridor, while he followed me."

"Did they pull the seahorse fairy stunt on you?" I asked with curiosity.

He shook his head. "No, Julia told me her Nightmare ate it. I got a Pegasus Bambi."

"Aww! He must have been soooo cute!" I said with a smile.

Riley chuckled. "He was... Until Merax ate it."

I gasped, and my companion burst out laughing at my shocked expression. "Your Nightmare ate Bambi?" I exclaimed, flabbergasted. "You didn't try to stop him?"

He shrugged in a 'What can you do?' kind of way. "I tried. For a second, I thought he would listen, but in the end, the temptation of an easy meal was just too great."

"Doesn't that frighten you?" I asked, troubled to find him still so excited—almost proud—of his Nightmare's uncontrollable urges.

"No," Riley said with calm conviction. "Merax is the sum of all my fears. I'm a gay man who was raised by devout Christians. I conjured Merax to punish me for my sinful desires and impure thoughts."

"They're not sinful," I said with a frown. "There is no shame in being who and what you are."

Riley smiled gently and with an inner peace that made me realize I had misinterpreted his current feelings about his sexual orientation.

"I have learned that since," Riley said. "But at the time, Merax embodied all the bullies and haters that had made my life hell growing up. All those who had rejected me over the years... When I realized who he was, I panicked. I literally wanted to run out of here and go back home. If not for the Mist, I might have done just that."

"I know exactly what you mean," I said with commiseration. "I almost fled the minute we arrived. I had *not* prepared myself to look at the Mist again."

"Again?" Riley asked, his curiosity piqued.

I told him the story of Jared's death, and how growing up in a dysfunctional family had spawned Zain.

"But he didn't kill the fairy," I said with undisguised pride.

"Which puts you in the driver's seat of this entire operation," Riley said without bitterness or jealousy, but with an enthusiasm laced with curiosity.

I recoiled at that comment. "What do you mean?"

Riley opened his mouth to answer, but something behind me drew his attention. He suddenly smiled and waved. Looking over my shoulder, I saw a woman with a slight limp come towards us. Blond with green eyes—although her dark eyebrows hinted that she was really a brunette—the female appeared to be in her early forties. Despite her limp, she walked straight, with determined steps and had a commanding aura about her.

"Julia," I guessed.

"Yep," Riley said.

After some quick introductions, Julia went to get some food then came back to join us.

"So, I hear your Nightmare upstaged mine," I said to Julia in a friendly tone.

She snorted and shook her head. "Hardly. Your Nightmare kicked some serious butt with style and ease. Mine was just an elephant in a china store. He's a bully. He made a show of slaughtering the weak ones to scare the others into thinking he's stronger than he truly is. Your Zain would make mincemeat out of him. If your boy is willing, mine is in need of a spanking."

Riley and I burst out laughing at her dejected expression. She smiled, but I didn't miss the sad glimmer in her eyes.

"You think he's unredeemable?" I asked in a sympathetic tone.

She shrugged. "I'm not sure, but I wouldn't be surprised if

it was the case. My Letho is a little too much like a man's Nightmare."

I recoiled at that comment, while Riley narrowed his eyes.

"What do you mean?" I asked.

"Haven't you noticed the high percentage of female candidates?" Julia asked. I stilled and scanned my memories, indeed remembering thinking that there was a disproportionately high number of women. "There's obviously a reason for it. Men's Nightmares tend to be the real deal, the true extreme. They can't be reasoned with. They're like Jason, Michael, and Freddy Kruger: single-minded and relentless in their bloodthirst. Whereas women's Nightmares tend to walk the fine line between psychopaths and Dark Desires."

I nodded slowly. "Beauty and the Beast. Women often fantasize about the villain falling in love with them."

Riley snorted, drawing our attention. "I was in love with my biggest bully in school."

"There was no love involved in what spawned my Nightmare," Julia said grimly. "Unlike both of your Nightmares, Letho hasn't been haunting me since my youth, but since the past six years. I'm a former special op. My helicopter went down over a contested area. Only two others in my unit survived. We were captured and tortured. My comrades were maimed, crippled, and eventually killed. As for me, well... you know what happens to women."

My heart broke for her. I wanted to reach out and hug her, but the professional in me recognized she didn't need it and wouldn't welcome it. I couldn't help but admire her strength. There had been no tremor in her voice, no physical tell of denial. She had faced her demons and learned to cope with them instead of letting them control her.

"So, there are definitely no dark desires between my

Nightmare and me," Julia continued, "No Stockholm Syndrome either. Letho is the embodiment of my pain, my hatred, my rage, and hunger for revenge. He's a wild and an uncontrollable animal, a beast… a demon."

"A demon that you now must tame," I said, matter-of-factly, although she understood my underlying meaning.

"Yep, *again!*" Julia said bitterly before shoving a mouthful oatmeal with dried fruits in her mouth.

Why she'd chosen all the 'lamest' things from the buffet baffled me.

"So, your Zain created some excitement last night," Julia continued. "Everyone pretty much pissed themselves when the alarm went off. Thomson told us—meaning only Riley and me—that your Nightmare broke through the protective glass."

"He told you!" I exclaimed, flabbergasted.

They nodded. Beyond my shock upon hearing this, my respect for the program director went up a notch. His 'failure' to protect me had shaken my confidence in the organization. But the transparency he displayed throughout the process so far certainly inspired trust. This was a new, experimental process. Of course, accidents would happen.

"Is it true that Zain branded you?" Riley asked. "Thomson says if we proceed with the project, we will need to let our own Nightmares mark us as well."

"It's true," I said before lowering the collar of my shirt to show my brand. It still throbbed, but it was thankfully no longer tender to the touch. "There it is."

They both leaned forward, examining it with fascination. Oddly enough, I didn't feel self-conscious having two strangers all but staring at my boob.

"Did it move?" Riley asked, awe filling his voice.

I nodded. "Yeah. Well, it's more like the lines waver a little, the way smoke does," I corrected.

"What happened?" Julia asked.

I gave them a quick rundown of everything that had happened, from the crashed window, to Zain dragging me to the Mist.

"Oh my God, you already asked?!" Riley exclaimed. "Did he accept?"

I frowned and pursed my lips, unsure how to answer. "I don't really know. Part of what he said, when he was hitting on me, implied that he was going to do it, if only to have me. But another part hinted that he wasn't ready to commit yet and wanted to think about it."

"He's going to cross over," Julia said with a certainty that took me aback. "He spent too much time building up his reserves to bail at this point, especially now that you want him to come. I think he's mostly trying to decide if he wants to do it under his terms or following ours."

"That makes sense," I said nodding slowly. "But—"

"Thomson's here," Riley suddenly said, interrupting me.

My head jerked right to look over my shoulder. The beaming smile with which the older man addressed me had me perking up with curiosity and something akin to excitement.

"Good morning, everyone," Thomson said, stopping next to my chair. "I'm pleased to see you're making each other's acquaintance. Hopefully, in the upcoming days, you will become the first handlers of the Mist Defense Squad."

I felt silly for being so stoked about it. I hadn't trained to be some sort of superhero handler. Seeing the same thrill reflected on the faces of my companions made it all better.

"Riley, Julia, I'm stealing Ms. Connors from you,"

Director Thomson said, pointing at me with his chin. "Belinda will be here shortly to discuss the next steps with your respective Nightmares."

They both nodded and waved me goodbye as I rose to my feet.

"Don't worry about it. I'll take care of it for you," Riley said when I leaned forward to pick up my food tray.

I gave him a grateful smile and, complying with Thomson gesturing for me to proceed, I headed towards the door. It bothered me that he had addressed both of them by their given names when he still called me Ms. Connors.

"I'm pleased to see that you are well rested," he said in a friendly tone, while holding the door open for me.

"Yes, thank you, Director Thomson," I said graciously.

"You can call me Alfred, although most people simply call me Thomson."

I smiled, relieved to have been afforded the same courtesy as the others. "Only if you call me Naima," I replied.

"Naima it is," he said with a grin. "Your little Zain paid me a visit while I slept last night."

I stopped dead in my tracks and gaped at him with bulging eyes. "He did?!"

"Mmhmm," Thomson said with a nod. "He wanted to know if our offer was genuine, or if I was manipulating you in order to lure him into a trap."

My jaw dropped further. I should have accounted for that possibility, but it never even crossed my mind. Clearly, I had much to learn about spy games.

"Were you able to convince him?" I asked, my stomach knotting with apprehension.

"Come see for yourself," Thomson said with a mischievous grin.

My heart leapt in my chest as he led me to a door similar to the one that had led to the first holding cell that Zain had destroyed. The door opened onto a larger room but with an identical layout. A desk sat a few meters in front of a large glass wall. This one had been doubled. The backdoor, which no doubt opened onto the tunnels to the exit was sealed. The Mist swirled inside the room. However, it was the whitish cloud streaked with lightning right below the surface that held all of my attention.

Laid down on some kind of camp bed, it clearly had the shape of a very tall and broad human male. The barely defined limbs and features could have passed for those of a partially melted wax statue.

I ran up to the reinforced glass wall and pressed my palms against its cool surface. "He's crossing over!" I exclaimed in an awed whisper.

"He is," Thomson said with undisguised excitement in his voice. "Zain came in four hours ago. He's so damn powerful, he's forming at an accelerated pace. Most Transients whose births we've managed to record took between six to eight hours just to achieve this level of development and nearly twelve to fully form. At this rate, your Nightmare could be awake in the next couple of hours."

My head jerked towards him in shock, the reality of what was about to happen finally sinking in. What if *Zain* had been the one playing us? What if he'd seized this opportunity to benefit from a safe birth only to destroy us from within? Granted, in his human form, he could easily be dispatched with a well-placed bullet or two—as long as he was still weak from birth. But what if he played along until he grew strong enough before showing his true face?

"I see your wheels turning," Thomson said with an

approving smile. "It is good to question the intentions of a potential threat. One can never be too prudent when dealing with the unknown. But, for the time being, Zain is not a threat."

I clamped down on the relief that wanted to wash over me, refusing to rejoice too early. "What makes you say that?"

"My son-in-law, Risul," Thomson said, matter-of-factly. I blinked in confusion, and his smile broadened. "My daughter is married to her Wish; except she has chosen to live with him in the Mist."

"Are you shitting me?" I exclaimed, immediately embarrassed by my lack of self-control.

But who could blame me for having my mind blown by such a comment? Thankfully, Thomson chuckled, not offended in the least.

"No, I'm not. But that's a story for another time," Thomson replied in a friendly tone. "I always spend the three days of the Mist with them, either in our world or in theirs." He turned to look at Zain's body still forming with a wistful expression on his face. "The minute he branded you, I knew he would come for you in your sleep, and that he would read your mind. I had hoped you would convince him enough for him to come seek validation."

Thomson turned back to gaze upon my face with an expression I couldn't define. Yet, hope and gratitude seemed to be part of the mix.

"Remember what I told you about being able to read minds in the Mist?" Thomson asked. I nodded and hugged my midsection. "The same way Zain was able to read you, Risul was able to read Zain. The absence of ill-intention from him was the only reason my son-in-law allowed me out of the safety of his domain to speak with Zain. According to Risul, your Nightmare is naturally obsessed with you, but he's also crazy in love with you."

I shook my head in denial. "He believes he's in love with me because I programmed him that way."

But even as I said those words, the warmth that spread in my chest troubled me. His obsession with me should worry me, not please me.

Thomson smiled in the paternal way of the wise who knew better. "Walkers do not 'convince' themselves of things that aren't there," he explained in a gentle tone. "They are very binary when it comes to their emotions. They love or they don't. Zain *loves* you. He will never love another but you, even though he doesn't necessarily understand the concept of love. You didn't create him that way. But he will never hurt you, because his existence is defined by the need to please you."

"He stalked me because that's what he thought I wanted," I said with a nod, although my mind still reeled from his statement.

"That's correct. Understand, Naima, that Zain is absolutely a psychopath," Thomson warned. "He would have no qualms killing every single person here and on Earth if he thought that would please you."

I felt myself pale at the realization of what he was saying. That, too, I hadn't taken into consideration.

"He doesn't have morals the way we do. He has no compassion or empathy. He craves power and dominance and doesn't care who he must trample along the way to achieve it… except for you. And he wants to kill. He gets off on the terror of his victims. That will *never* change," Thomson said, his gaze boring into mine as he tried to drive his point home. "Even if he wanted to, and no matter what you might try to do, he will always remain a cold, bloodthirsty killer. But handled correctly, Zain can still become one of humanity's greatest protectors."

"You're afraid I have unreal expectations," I said, tilting my head to the side.

"I want to help you manage your expectations," Thomson corrected. "But I also want you to understand exactly what you are signing up for. Zain will want to claim you as his mate. He will relentlessly pursue you to become his wife."

I snorted at what I considered an absurd concept. Who the fuck married a dream? The hard glimmer in Thomson's blue eyes sobered me. I fought the urge to squirm, remembering his own daughter had married one. I hadn't meant to insult him.

"I'm sorry. I—"

"No need to apologize," Thomson interrupted in a calm, but slightly cooler tone. "It is a difficult concept for most people to grasp unless they've been around a Transient. You will understand once you meet Zain in the flesh. But my point is that in an ideal world, you and Zain would become a couple."

"WHAT?!"

"Calm down," Thomson said, raising his palms in an appeasing gesture. "I said 'in an ideal world.' I'm not ordering or even pressuring you to do so. But understand that if you enter a romantic relationship with anyone else, Zain will want to kill him."

"Killing the person I love would hurt me," I argued. "You said yourself Zain places my happiness above all else."

"And he does," Thomson concurred. "But as long as he shares this world with you, he won't be able to tolerate another man touching you. Zain won't hurt you, but he might choose to eliminate the source of your potential sorrow to keep himself from doing the irreparable."

"He will kill himself," I whispered, understanding dawning on me.

"Once again, I want you to go into this with your eyes wide open so you don't get blindsided," Thomson said in an apologetic tone. He turned to look at the desk behind us. "I have left an agenda here for you, with notes on the training program you are to put him through. These are his temporary quarters. He has a full, private bathroom through that door at the back, and clothes in the closet next to it," Thomson added, pointing at the two doors at the back of the glass cell. "You may let him out of this room to perform all the activities in the schedule. But he is *not* to go *anywhere* without you by his side."

"Naturally," I said with a nod.

After a few more instructions, Thomson left me to go over the information he had provided me in a tablet. I settled behind the desk, suddenly feeling like the weight of the world rested on my shoulders. Despite that, anticipation bubbled inside me as the muscular shape of my Nightmare grew more defined by the minute.

CHAPTER 9

ZAIN

C ool air over me pulled me out of the endless void where time and space had lost any meaning and in which I'd been roaming. I felt heavy, pinned down to the soft cushion beneath me by an invisible force. Although fairly warm, the wall of flesh around me constricted my sense of freedom in the most disturbing fashion. But its outer layer, that fragile tissue called skin, felt unpleasantly cold.

The silence of my ethereal senses crippled me. I hated not instantly perceiving the presence of others on a wide radius, even through walls. This feeble nose detected no particular scent of either threat or ally. The only thing clearly tugging at me was the pull of my bride's brand anchoring me.

I lifted my eyelids only to close them immediately as a blinding light stabbed at my overly sensitive eyes. I batted my eyelashes a few times while those stupid human eyes watered, further blurring the vision I was trying to clear. Eventually, the damn things settled allowing me to see the high, white ceiling of a large room. At first glance, it seemed similar to the one I'd entered the previous day.

Turning my head to the side, a strange sensation exploded in my chest at the sight of my woman, head bowed, reading something on an electronic device. I felt hot and cold all at once, a strange fire awakening in the pit of my stomach. I attempted to lift my head, but the wretched thing weighed a ton. I lay it back down and began to contract the numb muscles of my limbs, getting them to awaken for the first time.

As thrilled as I felt to have my bride nearby, this wasn't how I had wanted to first present myself to her: weak, pathetic, and uncoordinated. The next time I lifted my head, I heavily leaned on my elbows to push my torso up, then on my palms to get me into a seating position.

"Zain! You're awake!" Naima exclaimed as I was struggling to turn my body and get my feet down so that I could sit at the edge of the bed.

With a Herculean effort, I eventually succeeded, my hands resting on the bed on each side of me to help me keep my upright, sitting position. I lifted my eyes to look at my female. She had come to stand by the glass wall that trapped me within this space. I couldn't resist smirking at the awe in her eyes as she gazed upon the beauty of my human vessel. She had fantasized often about this body, and I had made every effort to reproduce it exactly as she'd envisioned it. She tapped something on the tablet in her hand, and the sound of a fan resounded in the room. I realized she was evacuating the Mist that had lingered in the room to ensure my safe birth.

"How are you feeling?" she asked with a hefty dose of worry in her voice.

I liked that… a lot.

I attempted to answer her through mind-speak as I usually did, but I couldn't find my psychic voice.

"Okay," I said in a rough and scratchy voice from lack of use.

Fuck me, even talking demanded effort. What kind of lame ass vessel did I get conned into entering? I swallowed back my frustration and silenced the blossoming anger that threatened to rise to the surface at feeling so helpless.

"You must be feeling extremely awkward and weak right now," Naima said in a soothing voice. "That's perfectly normal. But it will only last a few minutes. Flex your arms and legs a few times to help get them going."

An odd mix of anger and pleasure swept over me. I hated that she had to babysit me because of my current state, but I loved having her care for me. I began contracting my muscles again, but Naima frowned and shook her head.

"No, not like that. Hang on," she said.

To my utter shock—and complete delight—Naima opened the double reinforced doors that kept me locked inside this space. There was no fear emanating from her as she approached me of her own free will. Even the tension in her eyes didn't stem out of any worry I might do something to her, but out of concern for me. I loved that, and yet it stung. Did my weakness trigger this absence of fear or had she finally accepted that, as her Darkest Desire, I couldn't harm her?

She sat next to me—although a little too far for my liking—in a position similar to mine.

"Lift your legs like this," she said, lifting her knee to her chest before putting her foot back down, then repeating the same process with the other leg.

I tried to imitate her but felt myself on the verge of falling off the bed and onto my face. I immediately lowered my foot back down, gripping the cushion to keep from making a spectacle of myself. Naima's hand flew to my shoulder to hold me back. It was as if lightning struck me where her hand made contact. An inferno burst to life in my groin and spread like wildfire throughout my body. A strangled moan rose in my throat.

Mistaking my moan of pleasure for one of pain, Naima jumped to her feet and came to crouch in front of me. Her beautiful hazel eyes filled with concern, and she cupped my face in her hands as she examined my features. Another moan escaped me, and my eyes all but rolled to the back of my head from the intense pleasure of her touch. How could such a pathetically weak vessel be so fucking responsive to the feel of my woman's skin against mine?

My blood rushed to my groin while the fire in my nether region intensified, and a dull throbbing manifested itself.

"Zain! Zain! Stay with me! Focus on me!" Naima said forcefully, trying to hide the fear in her voice.

That fear, born out of concern for me, smelled delicious. I inhaled deeply, savoring her distressed energy. My ethereal self, which I had felt disconnected from upon waking, stirred to the front to feed on her emotions. They coursed through me, giving my foreign limbs the jolt of power they had needed. I opened my eyes, my gaze boring into hers, then I covered her hands with mine. I exhaled before taking in another deep breath to fill myself with her.

"Yes, Zain. That's good, breathe in and out, and focus on me. You're going to be fine," Naima said encouragingly. "The dizzy spell will pass. Don't push yourself too hard."

"It's you, Naima, not my awakening," I said in a rumbling voice that had goosebumps erupt all over her deliciously dark skin.

"What?" she asked, confused.

Letting go of her hand on my right cheek, I wrapped my palm around her neck and drew her face a hair's breadth from mine.

"You're the one making me dizzy, my love," I said in a purring tone. "Your touch is like liquid ecstasy."

Shock, disbelief, and outrage crossed her beautiful features in quick succession before she pulled away from my touch and straightened. Naima glared at me, looking like she was fighting the urge to slap me. I would have preferred for her to bite me or rake her nails all over me...

"You sick fuck!" she hissed. "You had me worried something had gone wrong with your birth, and you were busy playing mind games?!"

I smiled and tilted my head to the side. "I wasn't playing any game, Naima. Your touch genuinely made my head spin. It set my entire body on fire. This vessel may be awkward and fragile compared to my ethereal form, but it fucking loves your touch."

Naima gaped at me, speechless, while I held her gaze unwaveringly. I recognized the moment she realized I wasn't lying. The rollercoaster of emotions that flashed across her face would have been hilarious under different circumstances, but I was too fascinated by her beauty and the lovely expression of embarrassment that settled on her face. My mate was troubled to be flattered by my response. The poor woman had no idea how crazy I would make her for me.

"Right," Naima said, looking a little flustered. "Well, you need to go slow and flex your legs to—"

Before she could finish her sentence, I pushed myself up and stood on my feet. My female's eyes all but popped out of her head. Then the suspicious expression returned on her features.

"I couldn't stand earlier," I said preemptively, in a taunting voice. "Your sensuous touch and those tender emotions of concern you feel towards your mate have given me the strength I needed."

She opened and closed her mouth a couple of times, looking for an appropriate reply. "I'm not your mate," Naima mumbled before giving me a furtive once over.

I nearly burst out laughing when her gaze slipped over my crotch only for her to do a double take. She stared in disbelief laced with another emotion I couldn't define. Suddenly catching herself, she abruptly averted her eyes and jerked her face left. Although her darker complexion hid it, I knew beyond any doubt that she was blushing.

"We need to get you dressed," she said a little too loudly.

Turning on her heels, she made a beeline for a set of doors on the left wall of the room. It opened on a wardrobe with a number of black and grey outfits dangling on hangers. On the left side, folded clothes filled a series of shelves, with a few pairs of shoes at the bottom.

"Why?" I asked, watching Naima with amusement while she busied herself picking out my clothes. "Don't you want to admire your greatest fantasy in the flesh?"

I spread my arms wide, relieved not to feel myself waver on my feet, and glanced down at the gladiator body Naima had wished. It had drained a ridiculous amount of my energy to create, but the effect it was having on her made it all worthwhile.

"You're such an ass!" Naima said in a clipped tone. "Cut it out."

"I am what you made me. And, right now, I want to do all kinds of unspeakable things to you," I said, letting my gaze roam over her in a suggestive fashion. "Touch me, Naima."

She clenched her teeth and glared at me.

"Why are you upset?" I asked, genuinely confused as to why she would deny herself the pleasure of enjoying what was hers, created for her, and according to her wishes. "Do you not like what you see?"

"It's inappropriate," Naima said, extending a pile of clothes towards me while keeping her eyes averted.

"Inappropriate?" I asked. "Inappropriate would be you drooling over another male. But I am yours. Created *for* you, *by* you. No other female but you gets to see and touch this," I said, taking a couple of steps towards her, while sliding my right hand down my muscular chest and chiseled abs.

The soft feel of my own hand on my skin reignited that pleasant flame in the pit of my stomach. It was further fanned by the sweet aroma of her arousal, dampened though it was by my limited human nose.

"Did I get it right, my mate?" I asked, in a purring tone. "Tall, muscular, tanned skin, with firm and round butt cheeks, and a massive cock small enough to fit, but big enough to make you feel like you're on the verge of getting split open with each thrust."

"ZAIN!"

Naima's outraged shout barely registered. My brain had tilted the second my hand had closed around my partially erect cock to flaunt it to my mate. Fuck, it was sensitive! I gave it a couple of strokes, and my knees nearly buckled from the intense pleasure it gave me.

"Zain, cut that out immediately," Naima hissed.

Closing the distance between us, she grabbed my wrist and forced my hand away from my cock. I opened my mouth to argue, but the words died in my throat. While my body undeniably attracted her, and despite the lingering scent of her arousal, the anger Naima felt right this instant exceeded the pleasure its sight gave her. I didn't like the slimy feel that specific emotion of hers gave me one bit.

Confused, I took the clothes from her. She appeared relieved and pushed me towards the other door left of the closet.

"Go in the bathroom to get dressed," she said before casting a nervous look at the top left corner in the front of the room. "And don't come back before you're presentable."

Intrigued, I glanced at the same area, and saw the small surveillance camera I hadn't previously noticed. My head jerked back towards Naima, my eyes widening with understanding.

A pleasant, warm, and fuzzy feeling spread over my chest. "You're upset because others are watching what's yours!" I said, with a blossoming grin. "Apologies, my mate. I had not been trying to make you jealous. I will rectify this situation at once."

"Oh God! Help me with this one," Naima whispered to herself, while covering her face with her palm.

She was cute and confusing. But no matter. I loved her being possessive of me. After glaring at the camera for their shameless voyeurism, I walked into the bathroom and placed the clothes on the counter while closing the door behind me. I didn't like this small, confined space. It made me feel trapped. I didn't much like the room I'd been born in, but at least, the glass wall gave the illusion that the room was far more spacious, less claustrophobic.

I made quick work of donning the dark grey shirt with a silver-colored, stylized logo of the letters M, D, and S. I didn't know what it stood for, but presumed M was for Mist. It was a very snug fit. Thankfully, the stretchy fabric didn't make it uncomfortable. A quick look in the mirror actually pleased me. While I didn't care much for clothes, the way this one hugged every curve of my chiseled abs, strong chest, and the bulging muscles of my arms were bound to make my female drool while hiding my nudity from others.

I eyeballed the long, black, stretchy pants she had given me and then the dark-grey, form-fitting shorts she had also included. While the long pants would give my dangling parts more room, the tight shorts would hold them more snuggly, on top of hugging the curves of the fantastic ass my mate had wished upon me. Wanting to seize every opportunity to break down the silly barriers Naima might erect between us, and eager to see her mad with lust for me, I chose the shorts that fit me like a second skin. I certainly didn't complain about the way the fabric outlined the thick shaft of my cock.

Pleased with my appearance, I opened the door to the bathroom. Instead of the appreciative expression I expected, Naima rolled her eyes, and her shoulders sagged in discouragement.

"Where are your pants?" Naima asked, as if addressing a particularly difficult and slow child.

"You gave me a choice between shorts and pants," I said, somewhat offended. "I chose the shorts."

She sighed and shook her head as if I was a hopeless case. "Okay, my bad. I guess I should have been more explicit," she conceded. "I'm realizing now that certain things I take for granted may be foreign to you. These are not pants but underwear. You're supposed to wear the pants on top of them. As you can see, these shorts are too... revealing of your private parts."

"Are you fucking kidding me?" I muttered with a sliver of

annoyance. "Clothes on clothes? That has to be incredibly uncomfortable."

"Stop whining and go put your pants on," Naima responded without an ounce of sympathy. "Anyone who doesn't need to wear a bra has absolutely no ground to complain about layers of clothes and, more specifically, underwear. Now, go, chop-chop. We have a lot of things to do today."

Scrunching my face in displeasure, I went back inside the bathroom but didn't close the door as I slipped on the garment. At least, the appreciative glance she stole at me soothed some of my aggravation.

"Much better," Naima said in an approving tone when I finished putting on the wretched garment.

This time, she wasn't so skittish in admiring the view. I instinctively puffed out my chest, basking in her attention. She gave me the 'you're so hopeless' look, but her emotions only broadcast amusement and an undeniable attraction.

To my shock, Naima then gave me a shameless once over, pursing her lips in a critical fashion. "Yeah, you're not bad," she said in a nonchalant way. "I've got good taste."

I snorted, a smug smile stretching my lips as I opened my arms wide.

"No, I'm not touching you, and you're not getting a hug," Naima said in a tone that brooked no argument. "Here's a pair of socks and shoes. Put them on so that we can go feed you."

Walking up to me, she shoved the items at me. I took them reluctantly, annoyed by the way she so easily shut down her desires to switch into full business mode. I'd need to cure her of that bad trait.

My feet also didn't appreciate this double confinement.

However, the soles of my feet appreciated the pleasant cushion of the running shoes.

"Before we leave, this is your bathroom," Naima said in a factual tone. "The human body needs maintenance that your ethereal form doesn't. This is your bath and the separate shower. Baths take longer but are great to relax. Showers are faster. You will do either one or the other, once a day. Some people prefer to shower in the morning, I prefer to do it at night so that I don't carry to bed the filth from the day that just ended."

I stared, feeling somewhat bewildered as she showed me how to operate the shower and the bath.

"The towels, washcloths, soap, shampoo can be found here. Careful not to get soap or shampoo in your eyes. It's not a pleasant feeling. Rinse until it stops stinging," Naima continued, visibly amused by my dismay. "Once you're done drying yourself, you will want to use this. It's antiperspirant. Roll it under your armpits like this. Otherwise, you're going to stink like a mofo. That's the best way to make sure everyone will flee you like the plague, especially the ladies. As a matter of fact, you should put some on now since I'm going to have you sweating like a pig in not too long."

Naima spoke in a taunting, and slightly suggestive way that made me itch with the urge to put her across my knees and spank her.

Begrudgingly taking the bottle from her, I brought it to my armpit only to have her immediately stop me.

"No, silly goose. Not on your clothes! Directly on your skin," Naima exclaimed. "You don't have to take off your shirt, you can just lift the hem."

I ground my teeth but complied. As I was switching hands to apply some of the wet, but clear gel under my other armpit,

I caught the way my female was eyeballing my exposed torso. Instead of expediting the process as I'd previously been doing, I slowed down and contracted my abdominal muscles to give her even more of an eyeful. She bit her bottom lip, her hazel eyes darkening, while the scent of her arousal tickled my nose.

Naima suddenly realized I had stopped applying the antiperspirant and was just staring at her drooling over me. She looked up at me, embarrassed to have been caught red-handed. However, she lifted her chin defiantly at the sight of my smug grin.

"I wouldn't be human if I didn't enjoy the eye candy," she said dismissively. "Close the bottle, and fix your shirt."

My smile broadened. I was going to enjoy playing this little game with my mate. She indicated for me to put it on the corner of the counter. The domestic feel of it all amused me. Naima then opened a drawer to pull out some device with a tiny comb at the tip.

"That's an electric razor," my mate explained with a shit-eating grin that told me I wouldn't enjoy what followed. "This is to shave the hair that will grow on your face."

My jaw dropped. "I don't have facial hair," I argued. "You didn't want facial hair."

"That's correct," Naima said with a nod. "But the fact that you don't have any *now* doesn't mean it won't grow. In fact, your beard and mustache are quite likely growing as we speak, but it won't show for a number of hours. Make sure your skin and the shaver are perfectly dry before you do it. When you're done, you'll need some aftershave to keep your skin from developing a bunch of bumps. And don't forget to clean the shaver before the next use."

"Are you shitting me?" I growled.

"Nope, not in the least," Naima said in a sing-song tone. "Speaking of which, the toilet is going to become your new BFF," she added, playfully pointing at it with her index finger. "You will visit it at least once a day, but probably more like three or four times to evacuate waste from the food you eat and beverages you drink."

She walked over to the toilet and lifted the seat.

"Very important lesson: men pee standing up. When you do, you *lift* the seat, grab your little birdy, and *aim* in the center. Not on the edge, not on the floor, not on the walls. In. The. Center. *Capisce?*"

"It's not little," I grumbled, to which she waved a dismissive hand. "What does *capisce* mean?"

"Understood, in Italian," she replied. "And when you're done, *put the motherfucking seat down.*"

The aggravation with which she said that sentence made me believe there was some sort of story there. But she didn't give me a chance to question her about it.

"For a number two—meaning the solid wastes—you will sit on the toilet, do your business, then wipe with this," she continued. "In either case, when you're done, flush like this, then go wash your hands with soap. Any questions?"

"I'm not doing any of that nonsense," I snarled.

"Oh, you will," Naima said with conviction. "Otherwise, you'll be walking around swimming in your own filth. And believe me, that stench by far exceeds that of a sweaty armpit."

"If you're trying to discourage me from pursuing a human life, you're doing an excellent job," I grumbled.

"Are you saying that the Mighty Zain is unable to handle basic hygiene functions that even the weakest human performs without blinking?" she asked, her eyes wide with fake disbelief.

I bared my teeth at her, and she burst out laughing, completely unfazed.

"This is me giving you a heads up so that you won't be caught with your pants down... literally," Naima said in a teasing voice before sobering. "Kidding aside though, do pay attention to what your body tells you. There will always be a sign. Heed it before it's too late. That is true not just of your bladder and bowel, but also hunger versus overeating, the good pain from training versus the one from an injury in the making. The human body constantly speaks to us. You will need to learn to recognize what it's trying to tell you."

I nodded, feeling slightly overwhelmed by how much more complex this transition was turning out to be. No wonder so many of the Transients who crossed over on their own didn't make it past a few days, in some cases not even a few hours.

"Come, I've traumatized you enough with this," Naima said, this time with something akin to compassion. "You must be starving. Let's go feed you."

I wasn't starving but knew of hunger and the weakness that accompanied it. My stomach was hollow from having never received food before. My ethereal energy was enough to sustain me right now, but I didn't want to unnecessarily waste it. Human food would be welcomed to continue fueling my vessel.

I followed in her wake as she escorted me out of the room and into the long hallway I hadn't been able to enter the first time around. It was wide with a few doors on each side. A couple of agents conveniently happened to be standing a few meters away from us, 'lost' in an intense discussion. I smirked in a provocative fashion as Naima and I walked past them. Although they did a remarkable job of keeping a neutral expression on their faces while holding my gaze unwaveringly, the delicious scent of their fear wafted to me. Countless violent images flashed through my mind of all the ways I could dismember them, smash their heads against the wall, painting it and the hallway with blood and gore. If only my female would allow it...

"Behave," Naima hissed, drawing my attention back to her.

Her frown, and the disappointment laced with worry emanating from her wiped away my predatory smile. Although it didn't go away, my bloodthirst dampened, doused by my female's disapproval.

We entered the cafeteria at the end of the hallway. Once again, a couple of armed agents conveniently happened to be there. Their emotions clearly broadcast they'd been expecting our arrival.

"They're not fooling me," I muttered.

"Nor are they trying to," Naima said matter-of-factly, while gesturing for me to take a seat at an isolated table surrounded by a few carts laden with food. "They are here to ensure my safety and that of the other people in the facility. While we believe you will behave, we can't be too cautious with human lives. Unlike you, death is permanent for us. There is no going back to the Mist to rebuild our energy."

Although her bluntness took me aback, I appreciated the honesty. The only games I liked to play were those that involved hunting down prey or seducing my mate.

We settled at the table, and Naima spent the next eternity shoving all kinds of food at me, from sweet to savory, mild to spicy, sour to bitter, and everything else in between. She took an almost malicious pleasure at my dismay whenever I tasted something I considered foul. Naima's sadistic streak was fucking sexy, despite it being aimed at me. It would have been an even bigger turn on if the rancid flavor of some of the repulsive dishes didn't still linger on my taste buds.

My woman didn't just sit there watching me eat, but shared my meal, often finishing the things I'd taken a single bite out of before cringing. Naima had a healthy appetite. While our tastes completely differed on certain things, her pleasure as she enjoyed our meal not only soothed me, it also fed my ethereal energy. No wonder my kind were so eager to connect with their creator in this Plane. Their mere presence was an energy battery constantly fueling us. It was strange to enjoy simply eating in my mate's company. I never thought I could find pleasure in anything that didn't involve stalking and killing a prey, or consoling my mate after 'punishing' her.

It turned out that I enjoyed food with strong tastes; sweet, spicy, and acidic. Crunchy food gave me an odd sense of power. I loved the sound of them shattering beneath my teeth. And meat... I loved meat, bloody... or rare, as my female called it.

"You have expensive tastes that you might not be able to afford," Naima said as I chowed down on a nearly raw piece of meat.

I smirked with shameless arrogance. "They'll give me the meat I want to keep spanking their runaway Nightmares."

She shook her head at me but didn't challenge my statement. My gut said she also believed it.

I stopped eating long before my mate. Those signs she'd mentioned about my body talking to me manifested themselves with a sensation of fullness in my stomach that threatened to become uncomfortable if I didn't stop. For a moment,

I feared that this vessel's limitations would also impede my ability to gorge on ethereal energy. But to my relief, my full belly didn't block me from continuing to feed from the emotions my mate projected.

By the time we got up to leave, I'd almost forgotten the presence of the other agents. That was reckless, especially for a predator. The minute you let your guard down, your enemies would get the jump on you.

That would not happen again.

CHAPTER 10

NAIMA

G ood Lord! Zain's human form was freaking insane! I
now better understood why so many humans ended up
in a relationship with their Wishes. We had dreamed up our
ideal partner. And boy, had I gone to town on mine! He was
tall and built like a bodybuilder. Not the overly bulgy ones
where they even stop looking human, but the perfect propor-
tions, and divinely well-defined grooves that made you want
to lick him up and down. Thank God I wasn't a man, or I'd be
walking around with a permanent hard on.

I'd never been a superficial type of woman. In truth, most
of the men I'd dated wouldn't have qualified as drop-dead
gorgeous. That I'd even think of Zain as a human right now
showed how hard I had fallen for his appeal.

When I embarked on this whole adventure, I'd
convinced myself I'd be safe because my Nightmare wasn't
a real person. He was just a fantasy that had somehow
managed to take a human appearance. But when I'd joined
him inside the bathroom to show him the basics, the only
thought that had played in a loop in my mind was how

badly I'd wanted him to pin me against the wall and fuck me senseless.

I no longer feared him. Whatever reservations I had about him being a threat to me had further faded away in his room earlier. As a psychopath driven by self-gratification, he shouldn't have stopped masturbating when I'd asked. In many ways, Zain was in a position of power. We needed him far more than he needed us. He knew that as long as he didn't cross certain lines, we would have no choice but to close our eyes to some of his more questionable behaviors. As long as he didn't try to force himself on me, I technically couldn't have forbidden him from enjoying his own body.

I couldn't begin to imagine what it was like for him to feel touch for the first time—real human touch. A part of me had ached to comply when he asked me to touch him. The way his face had dissolved into a mask of complete bliss as his hand had gripped his cock had been the sexiest thing I had ever seen. I had wanted to be the one giving him that kind of plea-sure. And that body... That ridiculous body, with its golden skin like melted caramel, and those arms and hands big enough to snap me in two without him breaking a sweat, had me weak in the knees.

I couldn't be thinking about him as a lover, but that's all my mind kept going back to. Pictures of his massive cock, impressive even as it was only half-erect, had me throbbing in all the right places. And yet, his need to please me had outweighed his own need for self-gratification. Thomson had been right. Zain was a weapon under my full control. I had to be careful about my own desires as he would act without hesi-tation, without remorse, without mercy to fulfill even my darkest of wishes. Even my hate could become a weapon of mass destruction.

As we entered the training room, I couldn't help but shake my head when my Nightmare's attention was immediately drawn to a couple of agents sparring in the boxing arena. The predatory grin on his face was both terrifying and the most incredible of turn-ons. Zain was the ultimate violent, heartless, bad boy. And he was turning me into a complete puddle. He was bad for me, like every other man I had desired before. My attraction to him was all the more dangerous that, this time, I knew I wouldn't get physically hurt as I'd been by the others in the past.

"No," I said when Zain made to go towards the two men sparring. "I'm not letting you anywhere near other humans right now, not until I know for sure that you have your more violent instincts under control."

Zain glared at me and scrunched his face as if he'd bitten into something bitter.

"You know, my bride, you are no fun. A little spanking would have helped keep them on their toes," Zain grumbled like a spoiled brat who had just been denied his favorite toy.

I chuckled and shook my head at him. "We're not putting you through anything overly intense right now, especially since you've just eaten. For the time being, we're just going to do some stretching and muscular exercises to help awaken your body and make you familiar with its strength and limitations. I don't want you hurting yourself by overextending your abilities."

I led him to the back of the room where we picked up a couple of bottles of water and a towel each. Opening the drawer as indicated on the instructions on my tablet, I retrieved a few wireless patches from it.

"Lift your shirt," I said to Zain, relieved that my eagerness didn't show in my voice.

His eyes widened in surprise before smoldering.

"Don't get any funny ideas, big boy," I said in a chastising tone. "I'm only going to place these monitoring devices on you to track your vitals while we're doing some exercises."

The slight disappointment that flashed over his features did funny things to me. What woman wouldn't feel flattered to have such a breathtakingly handsome man obsessed with her? Even now, I wanted to sink my fingers through his wavy black hair that fell to his shoulders. He was stunning, with a square jaw, plump lips on a wide mouth that was made to kiss, a proud nose and emerald eyes with long eyelashes that would make any woman jealous. They stood out against his bronze skin in the most hypnotic fashion.

Averting my eyes not to get swallowed up by their mesmerizing effect, I lowered my gaze only to have a bolt of lust exploding in the pit of my stomach at the sight of the bare skin of his chest. I swallowed hard, forcing myself to ignore the obnoxious smirk that stretched his lips as I placed the patches on him. It was only fair when he shivered, his abdominal muscles contracting every time my fingers brushed against him.

The slightly evil side I discovered in me whenever dealing with Zain surprised me. I made it a point to deliberately touch him but in a way that appeared accidental. It was ridiculous because his torture was also mine.

"You may lower your shirt," I said at last, the gravel in my voice giving away how much he was affecting me.

He complied without a word. When my gaze met his, my knees nearly buckled, and my stomach did a couple of backflips. He stared at me with an almost feral hunger. His parted lips gave me a glimpse of his teeth clenched in a snarl. With lightning speed, Zain's hand wrapped around my neck, and he drew my face close to his. My fingers instinctively closed around his wrist, but I didn't attempt to break free. Although his hold was firm, he wasn't choking me.

"Be careful, little Naima. You are playing with fire," Zain whispered, his lips a hair's breadth from mine. "When my fire ignites, it will be all consuming."

He released me and straightened, leaving me oddly disappointed.

I took a step back, startled to notice that the handful of agents inside the room had all stopped their training to stare at us. Judging by their stances, they'd been ready to intervene, thinking that Zain was hurting me. I discreetly shook my head to indicate that all was fine and elbowed my wretched companion in the ribs when he started grinning at them in a provocative way.

We proceeded to perform some warmups. Zain didn't see the point of any of this, even when I explained to him that it was to prevent injury. I was slightly concerned by the fact that it was becoming increasingly obvious that my Nightmare was disappointed by the extent of the weaknesses of the human body compared to the near invulnerability of his ethereal form. Still, he complied with my requests. Lifting weights actually met with his partial approval. He liked being able to put a number on his strength, especially compared to others.

However, he once again quickly grew frustrated with the limits of his new vessel. Thankfully, his self-preservation instincts exceeded his need to display power. He paid attention to the pain his body felt when he started to overexert himself.

"How the fuck am I supposed to hunt that Nightmare of yours with this pathetic body?" Zain asked with a bitterness laced with a quickly rising anger.

"There's a reason we need you," I said in an appeasing tone. "You are now seeing the limitations that we are coping with. However, you have something we don't; your ethereal powers. With it, you can create a powerful armor that will shelter your human body from a tremendous amount of damage that would crush us. But it will also allow you to inflict an insane amount of damage to your target."

Zain perked up, the glimmer in his eyes telling me I had caught his interest. I almost smiled in triumph.

"For that lesson, you will need someone better versed in the Mistwalker powers than me," I continued. "And this is why what we're doing right now is so important. You need to understand this body in order to know when to protect it and how much shielding is required based on whatever situation you will be facing. Preserving your energy will be vital moving forward since you can't walk around shielded around the clock."

He nodded slowly, his entire demeanor changing, and his frustration melting away. He looked at his body with new eyes and then at the various training equipment around us.

"Train me, my mate. I will master this body," Zain said with a determination that had me instantly hot and bothered.

I should have corrected him for calling me his mate, but the moment passed and, truth be told, I didn't really want to correct him.

Time flew while Zain pushed himself with the relentlessness and the discipline of an Olympic athlete. I couldn't help the feeling of pride that washed over me as the other agents looked on with both admiration and awe. Thomson walking in put an end to our training.

Although he kept a calm and friendly expression on his face, the program's director bubbled with an excitement that even I could feel. I didn't need to read his mind to know he was as thrilled as I was to see Zain so fully cooperating. Granted, that cooperation was driven in large part by my Nightmare's hunger for power. But as long as our respective goals aligned, we didn't care about his motivations.

"Hello, Zain," Thomson said in a warm tone. "I am pleased to see you adapting so quickly to your new body."

"Did you expect any less?" Zain responded with an insufferable amount of arrogance.

Rather than being annoyed, Thomson seemed amused by my Nightmare's ego.

"I had expected to be impressed," Thomson conceded, "but I'm happy to see you exceed my expectations."

Zain puffed out his chest and gave me a sideways glance. I grinned and shook my head at him. To my shock, he gestured at me before turning back to Thomson.

"I also happen to have the perfect coach," Zain added.

Thomson's face reflected the shock I felt. Psychopaths didn't normally hand out compliments unless it benefited them somehow. He had nothing to gain from acknowledging my efforts. Should he have chosen to act like a complete douchebag, I would still remain by his side training him because the survival of the population of this city depended on it.

The program director gave Zain an odd look before smiling. "You are correct," Thomson said. "Naima, too, has exceeded all that I could have hoped for. Much and more depends on the two of you."

To my surprise, Zain appeared pleased by Thomson complimenting me. Then again, I shouldn't have been. As he considered me his mate, his possession even, a compliment to me was a compliment to him. It confirmed the superior quality of something directly associated with him and, there-fore, a part of him.

"But you have trained enough for the time being," Thomson continued. "I want to show you exactly what it is that we would like you to face on our behalf."

He gestured for both of us to follow him. Zain and I exchanged a curious gaze before falling into step with him. He brought us to a room I had not visited yet, located along the corridor on the right side of the cafeteria, halfway to the personal quarters located further back. It was a small audito-rium able to seat about a hundred people. We sat down a few rows from the small stage, and a curtain opened revealing the giant screen at the back.

"Some of the scenes you're about to see are quite disturb-ing," Thomson warned the both of us although his gaze remained on me. "These are some of the recordings captured all over the city of the attacks performed by Darryl on unsus-pecting innocents. This is so you understand precisely why every day, every hour is of the essence. His power grows exponentially by the minute. If this project is to succeed, we need you to confront him in all haste."

A wave of unease washed over me, and my protective instincts came to the fore. Zain was still a newborn. He had just started familiarizing himself with his new body. Although his performance had been impressive in the gym, there was a huge difference between lifting some weights and facing off against a bloodthirsty predator who already had over six months of rampaging throughout the city, unstopped and unchallenged. Suddenly, my belief in Zain's ability to bring Darryl to heel began to waver. How could he ever catch up to that Nightmare?

But the video footage playing put an end to my dark

musings. I watched in horror as a rather handsome blonde man walked inconspicuously in a parking lot before making a sudden dash towards another person just as they opened the door of their vehicle. A number of cars still filled the parking lot, but there was no one else in sight. The limited angle of the camera gave the impression this was some sort of factory where an employee was leaving just as the late-night shift was beginning.

I couldn't tell the gender of the victim. Even with the zoom in, the grainy image made it hard to tell. However, a stamped text at the bottom of the image stated Robert D. I could only presume that to be the name of the victim. In a way, it was a blessing that I couldn't clearly see the features of that poor soul. Darryl had moved at supernatural speed, crossing close to two hundred meters in the time it took his prey to open the door, throw in a bag to the passenger seat, and put a foot inside the vehicle. Shadowy tentacles shot out from around Darryl and wrapped around the victim's waist, before they yanked him back.

Robert struggled as Darryl turned him around so they'd be face to face. My stomach churned as he brutalized his victim, punching him and clawing at his face. Darryl was enjoying Robert's terror and pain. I was grateful for the absence of audio. Seeing was already too much. Only when his prey stopped fighting did Darryl finally begin feeding. Well, to drain Robert's lifeforce would be more accurate. There was no question in my mind that he had previously been feeding off of his distress. The same kind of electric waves flowed from his mouth into Darryl's as Robert's body quickly deflated. Once done, the Nightmare threw down the unrecognizable remains of his prey, and then he casually walked away. To my utter shock, he entered his victim's vehicle and drove off.

I shuddered, swallowing back the bile that wanted to come up. A sideways glance at Zain made me even more uneasy. His eyes glowed with a sadistic glint that made my blood run cold. A gleeful grin stretched his lips as he raised an eyebrow in a way that spoke of approval, if not admiration.

"Smart and effective," Zain reflected out loud. He looked at Thomson who was staring at him with a slight frown. "He made maximum use of the energy his prey had to offer. It is a smart move. Why settle for the lifeforce alone when you can also have the fear?" Zain added with a shrug. "That Nightmare is clearly focused on building his strength. This was not merely a hunt for pleasure, although he did get that as well."

"He's been getting plenty of it and growing exponentially bolder in his attacks," Thomson said in a grim tone. "I will spare you the dozen other murders similar to this one that we managed to capture. However, this will give you a true sense of how powerful he has become, or rather how powerful he was five days ago."

Clasping my hands on my knees, I braced for what would follow. I was shocked to see the feed from a camera inside a shooting range. Surely, the Nightmare wouldn't be so bold as to go hunt in a place filled with 'prey' armed with live rounds that could kill him?

The same handsome blonde man we had seen in the previous recording walked into the range area, and casually strolled towards one of the empty lanes. Instead of entering it, he continued until he reached the last stall. He then grabbed the man busy shooting there by the back of his collar and yanked him back with enough force to send him crashing against the back wall.

Half-stunned, the poor man scrambled to his feet and aimed his weapon at Darryl who just stood there with a malicious grin. Opening his arms wide, he appeared to dare the man to proceed. His target mouthed something that I couldn't hear, but that I guessed to be a warning to step back or get shot. And then Darryl's ethereal shadow began swirling around him. The man made the sign of the cross, no doubt praying to a higher power to save him, then opened fire.

The bullet bounced harmlessly off the thin layer of shadow surrounding Darryl. The Nightmare suddenly rushed his victim and began draining him. He was almost done when another one of the shooters finally noticed something abnormal was happening. All of them had been deaf to the victim's likely screams due to their ear protectors, and the loud noise of the weapons being fired at the targets down the lanes.

That second man yelled and pointed his weapon at Darryl who ignored him as he casually finished his 'meal.' As the man drew the attention of the people in the neighboring stalls separated by full-height, black partitions, Darryl discarded the dried-up husk to turn towards his next victims. The person in the lane next to him had still not noticed the unfolding drama. Darryl's tentacle shot out and nabbed him. The others didn't dare to shoot for fear of harming the Nightmare's second prey. But as he began feeding off of that one as well, they realized they had no choice but to intervene.

They opened fire, but once more, the bullets appeared to hit an invisible wall. Darryl didn't flinch, in appearance completely immune.

"How the fuck does he do that?" Zain whispered to himself with awe laced with greed.

But even as he continued feeding, Darryl moved towards

the other people, his victim partially serving him as a meat shield. They started to back away while shooting. Darryl merely increased the pace. As soon as he was within ten meters of them, he deployed his tendrils, pinning the arms of four targets against their bodies, immobilizing them. Four more people came running in, having undoubtedly been alerted by the security camera feed. But faced with the horrible spectacle that welcomed them, a couple of them ran back out while the other two joined forces with the remaining three shooters that had not been caught by Darryl yet.

It had been the moral choice, but a deadly one.

One after the other, the Nightmare syphoned the people held in his shadowy grip, discarding the corpse only to grab another victim, all the while feeding on one of those he still held. The last two shooters made a run for it once they finally understood there was no hope. When he had finished the slaughter, Darryl gathered the bodies, lining them up against the wall then standing between them. He placed his arm around the desiccated shoulders of one of the two female victims before taking a selfie. He then turned to the camera, winked, then waved with the tip of his fingers before walking out, his tendrils resorbing into his body.

"Smug bastard," Zain whispered with a chuckle.

I recoiled and gave him a horrified look. Zain's head jerked towards me. He must have sensed my repulsion at his statement. His smile faded, and he gave me an assessing look.

"I am what you made me," he said in a neutral tone, although his expression was slightly reproving.

I swallowed hard and averted my eyes. He was indeed the result of my fears. I couldn't fault him for liking what he did. But that further underlined what a powder keg I held in my hand.

"You are indeed," Thomson conceded. "However, I would ask you to make every reasonable effort not to display your pleasure at the sight of violence against humans, especially in front of the agents. The victims you just witnessed were police officers in training. This was retaliation because agents had prevented him from slaughtering the resident of a retirement home. One of the officers happened to be visiting his mother and recognized Darryl coming in from the APBs."

I shuddered again and hugged myself, my right hand rubbing my upper arm in search of some comfort.

"I see," Zain said in a non-committal tone. "I will try to remember."

Thomson clenched his jaw but didn't argue, understanding as I did that this was the most honest answer—and the extent of the commitment—that Zain could give him on this front.

"How did he resist the bullets?" Zain asked.

"By protecting himself with an ethereal shield," Thomson said, standing to face us. "It is the next training we are considering giving you."

Thomson sat on the backrest of the seat in front of him in the auditorium. Zain leaned back in his seat, his long body appearing almost to be lying on an inclined bed.

"Only considering?" Zain challenged, raising an eyebrow.

"I have no intentions of training someone that might go out there and do more of the same," Thomson said in a firm, but non-threatening voice. "We plan on using every means to help you succeed in defeating that monster and any other that might rise from the Mist. But for that, I require a commitment from you."

"I'm here, aren't I?" Zain said with an insolence that made me want to smack him a good one.

"First and foremost, you're here because you want

Naima," Thomson retorted, his voice hardening slightly. "You're also here because we gave you a safe rebirth location and an easy start for a first time Transient. You're here because you hunger for power and dominance over a new world as yours has grown stale for you. You are not here to save humans. I want this to become your top priority, and for you to commit to see it through."

Zain's face closed, and my stomach dropped at the sight of the hard glimmer in his green eyes.

"That will never happen," my Nightmare replied in a tone that brooked no argument. "I do not give two shits about the lives of humans. I will not hunt them, because my bride does not wish it. Your cause will never be my priority. My female is, and always will be. I do not need your aid or blessing to achieve the power I seek."

"Zain, what are you saying?" I asked, my voice slightly shaking with fear and disbelief.

My Nightmare turned to look at me with an unreadable expression. He examined my features as if attempting to read my mind.

"Merely what I just said," Zain said matter-of-factly. "I want you above all else. I do not care about this cause. I will take it on because it pleases you, my mate, and because I will derive great pleasure from the hunt, not to mention the power. But my *commitment*, as he calls it, is to you, and to making you mine." He turned back to look at Thomson. "So no, Director Thomson. Unless you wish me to lie, I will not commit to making your cause my priority. So long as you keep my woman devoted to this project, you shall have my aid. But the minute she walks away, so will I."

A thick silence settled in the room. I didn't know how to feel about any of this. The weight of the responsibility that now rested on my shoulders overwhelmed me. Naturally, I wanted us to help the Fourth Division eliminate this threat. However, I didn't believe myself strong enough to stomach the horrors that came along with it. The images from the videos would haunt me for a while. But more importantly, I feared I would grow repulsed and even terrified by the monster Zain might become as he fell down the rabbit hole of greater power—and potentially complete dominance—in our world.

As the silence stretched, and the weight of the stares of the two men on me intensified, I realized they were waiting for me to make a statement. I licked my lips nervously and swallowed hard. Locking gazes with Zain, I placed my hand on top of his. He stiffened, his eyes widening ever so slightly before they darkened. His gorgeous face took on a sensuous expression that made it harder for me to concentrate.

"Zain, I understand why your priorities are what they are," I said in a soft tone. "You are indeed what I made you. And while your nature is troubling to me as a human, I do not fault you for it. All I know is that you are the key to making me and my people safe. I've been honest with you about your expectations for us. I will not make you false promises any more than you did to Director Thomson. But I promise that I will at least stand by your side as a friend and ally as long as you fight for us. Whatever the future holds for you, for me, for all of us, I can never be happy as long as I know that my fellow humans are being terrified and hunted by monsters. If you truly want my happiness, please help us."

He wrapped his hand around my neck, and his thumb gently caressed my pulse there.

"As long as it makes you happy, my Naima, I will help

you," Zain answered. "And I can already tell you what the future holds. You will be my mate."

To my surprise, he released my neck to brush his fingertips against my lips. Then, bringing them to his own lips, he kissed his fingers where they had touched mine. My stomach did a backflip, and my nipples tingled. I found that incredibly sexy.

Thomson's intense stare on my Nightmare then on me, made me squirm. He didn't need to remind me of how he hoped things would evolve between Zain and me. And while he didn't pressure me in any way, I felt incredibly pushed towards something that could only be terribly wrong for me. And that made it all the more appealing and irresistible.

"You have your answer, Director Thomson," Zain said casually. "But in order to face your monster, you will need to feed me far more than that human food you provided earlier. Are you willing to give me some of your agents to protect the greater numbers?"

"Zain!" I exclaimed, flabbergasted, realizing he was only half-joking, if at all.

"No. I will never feed you my agents," Thomson said in a harsh voice. "However, we have been luring as many Beasts and Sparks as possible in our holding areas. We were planning on giving them to you once we'd reached an agreement," he continued, casting a sideways glance towards me.

"It seems that we do have an agreement, correct?" I said, turning towards Zain.

"We do," Zain said. "However, unless many of your Beasts are high level, their lifeforce will never suffice for me to compete with the one siphoned from a human—or in his case, from countless humans. Surely, you have some criminals that can be sacrificed to the cause?" Zain asked with a greed that made my blood curdle. "Don't you have people on death row?"

I stared in horror at Thomson's face as he narrowed his gaze and studied my Nightmare's features while pondering his response. That he hadn't immediately said no told me he was actually considering it.

"Death row convicts are no longer electrocuted or given lethal injections," Thomson said at last.

He pinched his lips as Zain lifted an inquisitive eyebrow, leaning forward with a predatory grin.

"And what do you do with them?" Zain pressed. "Go on, Director Thomson. Your secrets are safe with me."

Thomson looked as if he was feeling nauseous. "They are cast out into the Mist on the last day," he admitted with reluctance.

I covered my mouth with my hand and stared at him with horror. I'd never been one to follow much about death row. Most states had abolished it over recent years.

"Feed them to me," Zain ordered in an imperative tone.

"Zain, you can't feed on humans!" I exclaimed before turning to Thomson and looking at him with pleading eyes. "Tell him! You don't want to open that Pandora's box."

"And what do you prefer, my mate?" Zain challenged me. "That Darryl feeds off them and gets even stronger before I can confront him? That another Nightmare in the making grows fat on them? They are dead men walking anyway. If they die, shouldn't it be so that innocents may live?"

"But they are people," I argued pleadingly. "You're here to kill monsters, not people."

"Was Jared not a monster?" he countered.

That robbed me of words. Jared had indeed been a monster. I didn't believe in taking someone's life as punishment for a crime. And yet, I felt no remorse, guilt, or empathy for the fate that had befallen my ex-boyfriend. He had sought to murder me just for the pleasure of watching me suffer and be destroyed by abominations. With the massive judicial reforms that had taken place a few years back, mistakes that had previously occurred were no longer an issue. Only the truest, and most unredeemable monsters were now condemned to death row. Still, it was one thing to see your personal tormentor get his comeuppance, but another one altogether to coldly plan the death of a stranger, no matter how horrible he may have been.

"I do not have control over the handling of prisoners," Thomson said, while eyeing me warily. "They are under the jurisdiction of a different branch of the government."

"I don't give a shit," Zain said dismissively. "Figure it out but give them to me. Now, I'm ready for that shield training," he said rising to his feet.

I instinctively followed suit, disturbed by the not-so-subtle shift in power that had just occurred. Once again, I wondered if we weren't creating an even greater monster than Darryl.

CHAPTER 11

ZAIN

That pathetic vessel that served me as a human body once again showed its weaknesses and inconveniences. Between a full bladder, the need to pause at regular intervals to feed, and now the fatigue that demanded I turn in for the night, there was always something. Granted, the release of peeing was quite agreeable, and some of the food served to us was very tasty. Too bad I could only intake a limited amount of it. Those videos proving what a formidable killing machine this deceptively feeble body could become once shielded by ethereal energy had been thrilling. If not for them, I would have grown quite disheartened by my female's obsession with protecting a bunch of strangers. Were their roles reversed, those fuckers probably wouldn't lift a finger to reciprocate.

To my annoyance, Naima escorted me back to my birth room rather than to her personal quarters. I intended to be with her in a far more intimate fashion tonight anyway. She knew something hot and passionate would happen between us the moment we lay in bed. Her avoidance was silly. But I played along and followed.

I hated how much she had closed herself off to me following my reaction to those videos and my request to feed on those to be executed. I sensed no deception in her when she said she understood why I liked the things I did. But similarly, I could sense her inner struggle with coming to terms with it. The way she went from lusting after me to fighting her fear of me was all but giving me a whiplash. Humans were too complicated. Things didn't have to be so convoluted with vague concepts of morals, compassion, and laws. The only law that really mattered was that of the strongest, of the fittest, and of the fiercest.

Naima waved me into the bathroom. I gave her a teasing nod and entered. She followed in and showed me another obnoxiously annoying hygiene step she had omitted earlier: dental care. I rolled my eyes so hard I could see the back of my head. My mate burst out laughing and didn't stop the whole time I brushed my teeth. The damn paste kept foaming and dripping all over my jaw, the brush, and even my hand. She then had the audacity of asking me to brush my tongue, which had me gagging to the point I thought I would regurgitate my evening meal.

I couldn't even be furious, because her mirth was so intoxicating. I wanted it to endlessly cascade over me, even if it was at the cost of this frustrating torture. When she had me do the dental floss part, I nearly lost my shit. But then Naima started doing it on herself to show me. For some inexplicable reason, doing such menial activity with her gave me the strangest sense of intimacy. It was… pleasant.

"Do you remember how to operate the shower?" Naima asked.

I nodded.

"Perfect." She stepped outside for a second, and I heard

the wardrobe door opening. She returned moments later. "Here are your pajamas for the night, and clean undies," my female said, extending the small pile to me. "You can dump your dirty clothes in that little basket in the corner," Naima added pointing at it. "I'll be outside at the desk wrapping up the lovely little report I need to write about your progress, which was quite impressive I must say," my mate said in a gentle tone.

"Thank you, my love," I smugly replied to her compliment.

"I will wait until you're done to tuck you in bed like the big boy you are," she added tauntingly before strutting out and closing the door behind her.

I smirked, fighting the urge to catch her and spank her for her insolence. Maybe I should just walk out buck naked once I finished showering. But I discarded that thought as soon as it crossed my mind. While I didn't mind being naked, I didn't want any potential female seeing what only belonged to my Naima. And I had no doubt that at least one or more agents were observing us through that wretched camera.

I lifted the handle of the shower, and the water immediately began raining down. Swiftly stripping out of my clothes, I threw them in the wicker basket my mate had indicated then, enticed by the white plumes of vapor swirling around the shower, which reminded me of the Mist, I stepped under the water.

It no sooner came into contact with my skin than a roar of pain rose from my throat. I jumped away from the scalding water, and my wet feet slipped on the tiles covering the floor. My arms milled around in an instinctive attempt to maintain my balance, but I lost both the battle and my footing. The room spun around me as I fell and landed with a loud thud on the cold, hard surface of the floor. A lancing pain at the point of impact—my right butt cheek—quickly spread through my right leg and my back.

"Motherfucking son of a bitch!" I shouted, rolling to my left side to rub the sore spot.

It was in that less than glorious position that Naima found me, as she came bursting into the room.

"Zain! Are you—?"

Her words died in her throat seeing me sprawled on the floor. Her eyes went from my face, to my hand rubbing my butt, to the shower still raining boiling water, and then to my chest, which had reddened from the burning slap it had received. The worry plastered on her face quickly faded, and Naima bit the inside of her cheeks, visibly fighting the urge to burst out laughing. I was embarrassed, humiliated even. While my brain understood the comical aspect of the situation, I didn't take well to being the butt of a joke—no pun intended. And yet, the emotions emanating from her seeing me this way were soothing and delicately pleasant.

It then struck me, with a clarity I couldn't explain, that this very human mishap made me more approachable and endearing to her. Maybe I shouldn't fight so hard those weaknesses of my new vessel and use them to my advantage to seduce my mate.

"I am starting to believe you are attempting to murder me," I grumbled.

This time, Naima didn't stop herself from laughing.

"No, silly goose," she said, helping me up. "I did ask if you remembered how to operate it. You had to go all macho man on me and say of course you did. See what it got you? If you ever get to drive and get lost, don't start doing the tough guy routine. Stop, and ask someone for directions. There is no shame in asking for help. It won't emasculate you, I promise."

I wondered what the fuck driving had to do with anything, and why human males would have an issue with asking for directions.

"This is obviously *way* too hot," Naima explained. "Before you step under the water, always make sure you've tested the temperature by waving your hand under it. Then adjust the heat until it feels comfortable to the touch. There, this should be good," she said after turning the knob and touching the water once it had stopped smoking.

"You're going to shower?" I asked.

"Of course," she said, matter-of-factly. "Like I said earlier, I like to shower before bed. I'll do so as soon as I'm done here."

"You should shower with me," I said, my voice dipping lower. "You can make sure I do it properly. I mean, I could drown. We wouldn't want that, right?"

Naima snorted and rolled her eyes.

"You can't drown in a shower, silly man," she said crossing her arms over her chest while giving me the 'nice try' look.

Despite that, I didn't miss the subtle once over she gave me, admiring the view of my naked, slightly wet body.

"Oh, my love," I said in a purring voice, taking a step closer to her, "you have no idea all the things I can achieve when I set my mind to it."

She burst out laughing and pressed her palm to my chest to keep me from moving any closer.

"Nice try, pretty boy. But for now, the one thing I want you to set your mind to is getting cleaned up properly without turning yourself into a lobster. I have a few more things to do before I can go take care of my own stuff. So, get busy and get your tush to bed."

I scrunched my face, pretending to be hurt, although I had expected that response from her.

"You could at least stay and direct me while I experiment with this torture device," I said in a pouty tone. "As an added bonus, you get a free private show."

"You're hopeless," Naima said, throwing her hands up in despair. "Be swift," she said in a commanding voice before walking out and closing the door behind her.

I grinned as I stepped under the water. I was enjoying this unexpected playfulness in myself and how my woman responded to it. Despite her annoyed display, my mate had also been entertained by our little banter. I was realizing that humor seemed to trigger positive responses from Naima. Even more so than fear—of the good kind. I would need to keep that in mind going forward in my efforts to seduce her.

To my surprise, the effect of the water raining on me at this slightly hotter than lukewarm heat proved quite pleasant. The sensitivity of this body had its perks. In the Mist, all these nuances from taste, to smell, and sensations were significantly dulled in comparison. We didn't realize it because we didn't know otherwise. To us, what we felt in response to any type of interaction was based on what we imagined it to be. But the human body gave no wiggle room. It was very binary. Something was either nice or unpleasant, each on a varying scale from very mild too insanely extreme.

In this instance, the water pummeling my skin gave it a gentle massage on impact and a subtle caress as it trickled down my body. The comfortable heat soothed my muscles deep within and gave me an overall sense of well-being. This hygiene ritual wasn't so bad after all. I could see myself doing this frequently, not so much for maintenance of my vessel but purely out of enjoyment.

Washing my back and my face, however, reminded me that everything in this human world always had to throw you a curveball in one form or another. I nearly scratched my eyes out trying to rinse out the aggravating soap that just wouldn't stop stabbing at them. Next time, I'd remember to soap my face last. Furthermore, no matter how much I contorted myself, I could never quite reach a certain spot between my shoulder blades. I gave up in annoyance.

Tending to my cock certainly lasted far longer than it should have. But fuck me, its sensitivity was off the charts. And my soapy hand stroking it made the movement even smoother. I had never felt such an intense pleasure simply from touch. The thought of Naima's hand on me instead of my own had me so hard my stomach cramped painfully with need.

I hadn't meant to pleasure myself, but I simply couldn't stop.

Naima's face floated before my mind's eye while a pool of lava swirled in the pit of my stomach. A burning fire spread throughout my nether region. My abdominal muscles contracted spasmodically, and my skin became feverish. The water on my skin felt like a million tiny kisses and the gentle caresses from my mate. I came with a sharp shout, followed by a rumbling groan as my mortal seed shot out in blissful spurts. My legs shook, and I had to rest one palm against the textured white tiles of the shower for support. I continued to caress myself until the last of my seed was spent, slowing down the movement, and tightening my grip with each stroke to squeeze out every drop. It slightly hurt but in the most wondrous way.

Yet, even as I had just found release, a part of me wanted another round, but this time with my mate. I'd always known myself to be insatiable. It pleased me to see this body also possessed a healthy appetite. Pushing down those thoughts to the back of my mind, I made quick work of finishing my shower and of drying myself.

I had no idea how much time had gone by since I'd started, but I suspected that my mate knew what I'd been up to. She had probably heard it, too. If so, what thoughts had crossed her mind? Had she been aroused? Had she regretted not staying to bear witness and savor the view of what was hers, and what would soon be inside of her? Had she fantasized about what our first time together would be?

I picked up the pajamas she had brought me. With a slight annoyance, I slipped on the underwear first and then the pajama pants. I eyed the top and decided to rebel. My 'modesty'—which was frankly quite nonexistent—was sufficiently covered. Pushing the door open, I stepped back into my room. I found Naima sitting at the edge of her desk outside the glassed-in section that constituted my quarters.

An unreadable expression lingered on her face as she observed me. I had expected some sort of comment for the absence of a shirt, but she didn't seem upset or displeased in any way.

"Antiperspirant?" she asked as sole comment.

I rolled my eyes in annoyance, having forgotten about that step. Turning on my heels, I went back inside the bathroom and took care of it. To my surprise, rather than waiting for me outside, Naima walked into the bathroom, slightly pushed me aside, and then opened the bottom drawer of the vanity. She pulled out a device that looks like a strange gun, although I knew it not to be. She plugged it into the wall then sat on top of the counter before gesturing for me to approach.

Intrigued, I complied.

"You should not go to bed with your hair wet. You'll find it mightily uncomfortable," my mate said.

She spread her legs so that I could stand between them. I eagerly did just that before resting my hands on her thighs. Naima gave me a warning glance. I smirked, biting back the taunting remark that burned my tongue. This was the first time she was voluntarily initiating such proximity between us and choosing to touch me. I wouldn't risk alienating her.

The loud noise of the device startled me as it began blowing hot air.

"This is a blow dryer," Naima explained, holding it up for me to see. "It takes care of that problem in no time at all. Turn around."

My eyebrows shot up, but she held my gaze, a smug smile on her plump, kissable lips telling me to comply. I grimaced and once more obeyed. The feel of her soft hand on my bare shoulder guiding me back closer to her had my abdominal muscles contracting with pleasure.

Picking up the comb on the counter, Naima proceeded to dry my hair. It meant something that she was doing it herself rather than merely showing me how to do it on my own. I couldn't say what though. A part of me believed it was my female's need to touch me that had finally gotten the best of her. Another thought it was her nurturing nature expressing itself. In the end, I believed it was a mix of both, not that it really mattered.

The feeling of the comb gently scraping my scalp made me purr. Naima chuckled, the lovely sound enhancing that sensation of well-being. Yes, this feeble body indeed had many perks, and that hygiene thing was steadily growing on me.

"Turn around," Naima said.

Making no effort to hide my keenness, I obeyed, placing my hands on her hips this time and standing so close, I could almost feel the heat of her body. It took all my willpower not to slide her forward on the counter so that our sexes would touch.

Our gazes locked, and an electric current flowed between us. How she managed to continue drying my hair without her gaze ever wavering from mine was beyond me. At one point, it was no longer the gentle scraping of the comb that I felt, but her fingers slipping through my curly locks.

I pushed her hand aside, wrapped mine around her neck, and drew her face to mine. The loud sound of the blow dryer died, and Naima's fingers still weaved through my hair tightened their grip. Blood rushed to my groin, and my shaft throbbed. The heady scent of her arousal wafted to me, making me even hungrier for her. Her nipples pebbled, their hard tips pushing against the black tank top she was wearing, begging for my attention. Naima's lips parted, and her breathing shortened as she stared at me with an almost fearful anticipation. I leaned forward, our lips so close I could feel their heat against mine.

But I didn't kiss her. Instead, I pressed my lips to the side of her jaw, right at the corner of her mouth, before brushing them along her cheek to her earlobe.

"Thank you for taking such good care of me, my love," I whispered in her ear.

Pressing a gentle kiss on her shoulder, I straightened, and slowly pulled away from her. I repressed the taunting smile that threatened to blossom on my lips as she stared at me in shock and disbelief. Turning around, I headed back into the bedroom, this time allowing my smug smirk to stretch my lips. I hated that I couldn't read her mind in this realm as I could in the Mist Plane. But her emotions told me loudly enough that I had her exactly where I wanted. She *would* surrender to me tonight.

I sat down at the edge of my bed, and watched her make her way to me, her composed and neutral expression belied by the frustrated scent of her arousal still tickling my nose.

"As you can see, pillows and blankets have been added," Naima said in a 'friendly hostess' tone as if nothing had just happened—or rather nearly happened. "If you need more, you can find extra blankets and one extra pillow in the closet. I'll be here to pick you up at 8:30 sharp tomorrow morning," she continued. "Please be dressed and ready to go by the time I arrive. If you wake up early, you may buzz the intercom to call me, and I will come sooner. But don't call me at 5:00 in the morning, or you will *not* like my response."

The stern glance she gave me with that last sentence made it obvious she didn't believe me above such pesky tricks, merely to annoy her—which was quite accurate.

"You can turn off the lamp on your nightstand simply by waving your hand in front of it, or by pressing this button," Naima further explained. "Please, do not attempt to leave your quarters. There should be no reason for you to roam around the premises. If, for whatever reason, you believe it to be the case, contact me on the intercom."

I smiled in a non-committal fashion but didn't answer otherwise.

"Questions?" she asked, slightly confused by my submissive behavior.

I shook my head, the same obedient smile plastered on my

face. She narrowed her eyes at me, knowing I was up to no good, but did not comment further.

"Sweet dreams then, Zain. Welcome to your first night as a human," Naima said in a strange tone that seemed teasing and yet genuine in its welcome.

"Thank you," I said at last. "May you have memorable dreams," I added in a voice full of promise.

Lying down on my bed, a little narrow to my liking, I threw the cover over me and rested my head on the pillows, my eyes staring at the ceiling. Without a word, Naima left the room, locking the double reinforced doors behind her. Seconds later, the room was pitched in darkness aside from the glow of the lamp on my nightstand. I waved my hand in front of it to turn it off and settled comfortably to let sleep claim me.

No sooner did I close my eyes than the portal into the dream world that lay in the human consciousness shone like a glowing star in my mind's eye. I let myself float towards it, the call of the Mist growing stronger as I allowed myself to fall into its arms. The strange feeling of weightlessness followed by the impression of free falling was both unnerving and exhilarating. Halfway through, I found myself once more in my natural ethereal form. How I had missed the sense of freedom it gave me—no boundaries, no limitations.

I glided around the no man's land I had landed in situated just outside my domain. In the future, I would have to make sure that I returned into the Mist within the safety of my territory. No potential enemies or Beasts were currently lurking in its vicinity, but it wouldn't have been ideal to appear right in front of the gaping maw of a hungry behemoth.

Naima would take at least twenty to thirty minutes to fall asleep, between returning to her quarters, completing her hygiene ritual, and doing whatever other things humans—and in particular females—did before bed. That gave me a bit of time to hunt.

That Darryl was no joke. As exciting as the videos had been, they were also a major wake up call. He was powerful, probably way more than I had been before I crossed over, and definitely way more than I was now. Thomson promised I could feed off of the Beasts and Sparks they had gathered so far in their holding facility, but I doubted it would suffice. If humans had managed to lure them, then they were likely on the weaker spectrum. While any energy was welcomed, for the first time, I wasn't certain to be able to defeat a foe. In truth, I did not think I could. That messed with me in too many ways to count.

Failure was not an option.

If Darryl defeated me, I would have an extremely narrow window to escape back into the Mist before he could syphon my lifeforce. If I failed, it would mean permanent death. However, even if I succeeded in escaping, I would be so weak that it would take me months, maybe even years to regain sufficient strength to return to the Mortal Plane. Time was not an issue. As long as we had the drive and will to live, Mist Beings could live for eternity in this realm. But the way the Nightmare had escalated his attacks and the boldness with which he had entered the premises filled with armed policemen only proved the extent of his power. Darryl believed himself nearly unstoppable.

Soon, he would go on a rampage and no longer hide as he gorged on everything and anything in his path. I still didn't give a damn about humans. In his shoes, I would have done the same—assuming my creator had permitted it. But his relentless pursuit of self-gratification represented a direct threat to my mate and all that she cared about. For that alone, he needed to be stopped. Beyond potential harm to my Naima, fanatic creatures like Darryl would never stop unless someone put an end to their reign of terror. Once there were no more humans or living creatures for him to hunt in the Mortal Plane, he would come back to the Mist and obliterate whatever remained of our people. By then, no amount of joint efforts would suffice to destroy him.

That made Darryl a direct threat to *me*.

Roaming the no man's land at my highest speed without starting to burn energy, I fed on everything I could find. Well, on almost everything. It was stupid of me not to feed on the weak Wishes freshly awakened to self-awareness. They weren't humans, and yet my mate would consider them as such now that they had become sentient. It was all the more stupid that she would never know unless I told her. And yet, the mere attempt to do something I knew would displease her sufficed to give me that nauseous feeling I'd grown to associate with Naima's disapproval. Still, I relished their fear and gorged on their distressed emotions as I glided past them.

A tingle at the back of my head warned me of Naima's imminent entrance into the realm of dreams. I raced back to my domain, surprised by the amount of time it had taken her considering how much energy I had been able to harvest during that time. Tonight and tomorrow would be my last chances to do so as the Mist would end, leaving me with no other resources than my mate's emotions, those of the agents, and whatever Thomson had in store for me.

Beneath his gentle exterior, a hard man coexisted with the paternal father figure that genuinely cared for the welfare of my mate and of his fellow humans. He had no qualms giving me those condemned humans. And yet, his reluctance had not been a show to mollify my mate, clearly in disagreement. He feared I might develop a taste for it. In truth, I probably will. But Naima would keep me in line.

It was her that Thomson needed to worry about. If he were wise, he would limit her exposure to the less palatable means his organization was willing to take to achieve their goals. If Naima hardened and began to embrace these harsher methods, he wouldn't like how much free reign I would gain.

But this was a discussion for another time. Right now, I intended to claim my mate. The tall walls of my domain loomed on the horizon. My chest swelled with pride at the sight of the thick and impenetrable barrier crisscrossed with lightning, and the vaporous volutes of the dark clouds forming it. Anyone foolish enough to approach it without my consent would be obliterated.

Even Darryl?

I frowned at the unpleasant thought. Would he be able to breach it? I couldn't tell for sure. But if he did, he would be so drained that destroying him would become child's play— assuming I wasn't helpless myself.

A slight fissure parted before me as I made my approach. I glided through and was immediately struck by another surge of energy. While merely being in the Mist gave me a certain amount of energy, roaming within my own domain gave me even more. My walls constantly absorbed what they could from the daydreams and wandering thoughts of humans fueling the Mist.

I moved a little farther in, away from the defensive clearing surrounding my protective wall where I had first brought Naima. I invoked a gothic bedroom with cathedral ceilings and arched stained glass windows. A massive bed with black and purple satin bedding occupied the back wall.

Chains and shackles dangled from metal studs riveted to the finely chiseled darkwood head and footboard. Across from it, a giant candle chandelier hung from the ceiling above the seating area made of large cushions and pillows surrounding a giant fur carpet. It faced an imposing fireplace carved in stone. Candles burned all around the room, giving it an intimate and mysterious atmosphere.

My female had a thing for vampires. Although she would be getting me tonight, if she played nice, I might give her a nip just for kicks.

Pleased with my setting, I took on my human appearance, wearing nothing more than a black robe before summoning Naima to me. I watched with impatience and hunger as the glowing light of her consciousness appeared like a star in the Mist, growing in size and intensity as she fell towards me. She finally took form just as she passed through the ceiling, wearing a barely-there negligee I had wished upon her. She blinked, her eyes adjusting to this new environment as it became visible to her. Simultaneously, Naima's body tilted to the vertical, and she delicately landed on her feet a couple of meters in front of me.

My mate looked around the room, recognizing the setting of one of her frequent, naughty fantasies, inspired by a vampire movie she'd watched too many times to count. She cast a glance at the black, diaphanous negligee hugging the delicious curves of her slender body—the exact same model the heroine of the movie had worn. Hands on her hips, Naima glared at me.

"What do you think you're doing?" she asked in a stern voice.

I slowly prowled towards her, a smug smile on my face. "Finishing what you started, my love."

CHAPTER 12

ZAIN

She stiffened, a flash of guilt crossing her beautiful features. She averted her eyes and lost a bit of the right-eous attitude she'd been broadcasting.

"That was a moment of weakness. I apologize," she said in a defensive tone. "You made the right call by walking away."

"I didn't walk away," I said, continuing my advance. Naima began backing away. The wondrous mix of fear, desire, and confused anticipation emanating from her further turned me on. "I simply didn't start what I knew we couldn't properly finish with an audience spying through the cameras. Our first time together would never happen in that closet you call the bathroom. It is not an appropriate setting for my bride."

Naima's lips parted with a mix of shock, arousal, and another emotion that I could only interpret as her being flat-tered at me showing that consideration towards her. And yet, I could hear her mind racing to come up with an argument that might convince me to not pursue what she knew to be inevitable, and that she secretly desired in spite of all her denial.

"I appreciate your restraint when I failed to display the same," Naima said. "However, what I told you earlier still stands. There is no us. I am here to be—"

A gasp escaped her when her back met the footboard of the bed. The expression of a trapped animal that descended onto her features sent a jolt of lust and excitement straight to my groin. My predatory instincts roared to the forefront. Judging by the panicked way Naima began to look for a place to flee, the emotions her reaction had awakened in me must have shown in my face.

"Why are you fighting this?" I asked, my shadowy tendrils emerging, ready to kick into action and catch her should she attempt to run. "I can read your mind in this realm, remember? You want me as fiercely as I want you. You ache to touch me just like I am starved with the need to touch you, to taste you, to make you mine."

Naima faced away from me, unable to hold my stare as she prepared to spew the lies forming on her tongue.

"Your expectations for us are unrealistic," Naima argued. "You are my Nightmare, not my mate."

"I am your Darkest Desire," I snapped back, slightly angered by her continued denial. "I hear the ridiculous thoughts you're trying to use as a shield to deny us both."

"They're not ridiculous!" she exclaimed, seizing on to her outrage to give herself the strength to resist in a battle lost before it had even begun. "What would you know about—?"

"About what?" I interrupted, invading her personal space. "About those intangible and repressive concepts that you humans call morals? Virtue? Being a proper little lady?" I asked, my voice dripping with contempt. "What crime are you committing by yielding to what you want? We're both consenting adults, burning with desire for each other, unattached to any other partner, and shielded from wandering eyes by the privacy of my domain. So, what the fuck is the hold up?"

"Being *able* to do something doesn't automatically mean that you *should*," Naima countered harshly. "Choices have consequences. Acting on an impulse, especially in response to our baser instincts, often leads to people getting hurt!"

"And refusing to act on what you know can never cause you pain is hurting the both of us," I snapped.

"You spent your entire existence terrorizing me!" Naima exclaimed.

"Because it's what you wanted!"

"*I* never wanted this!" she shouted, slapping her chest angrily.

"Your subconscious did because, deep down, you thought you deserved it. And *I* can only ever do to you things that you *want* me to," I retorted, just as heated. "You dated all those fucked up boyfriends looking for *me*. I can fulfill any of your fantasies, however dark, however twisted, or however innocent, no judgement, no condemnation, no boundaries. And I will *never* go beyond what you want or can tolerate, because it is physically impossible for me to harm you or go against your will."

"And yet, here you are trying to force me into something I repeatedly told you I didn't want," Naima snapped back.

I placed my hands on top of the footboard on each side of my female, caging her in. She leaned back, away from me, holding my stare unwaveringly.

I tilted my head to the side and gave her a smug smile. "Yes, I am. Because you *want* me to. You want me to give you the arguments that will allow you to yield to your desires without guilt or fear. And deep down, you know it."

The expression on my woman's face was all the confirmation I needed. I leaned forward and brushed my lips against hers. Naima placed her palms on my chest and tried to push me away with a complete lack of conviction.

"Zain..." she whispered pleadingly, while the last of her defenses collapsed.

"Consent, my mate," I whispered, against her mouth before biting her bottom lip. She shivered and inhaled sharply through her parted lips when my hands slipped under the diaphanous frontal panes of her negligee to wrap around her waist. "Consent, Naima. I *need* your permission. I ache for you."

I captured her lips in a searing kiss. Naima didn't fight it. Her hands resting on my chest slipped under my robe, parting it before she pressed herself against me. An approving growl rose from my throat, and my tongue invaded her mouth like a conqueror, demanding her complete surrender. She yielded willingly, responding to each caress of my tongue in kind, while shivering in my embrace.

The sweet sound of Naima's moan in my ear had my cock throbbing with need. Breaking the kiss, I fisted her curly hair at the nape, and my gaze bore into hers, unyielding.

"Say yes, Naima," I commanded in a tone that brooked no argument.

A glimmer of confusion flashed through her hazel eyes, darkened by desire. Technically, I didn't need her to say the words. Both her conscious and subconscious minds had given me their blessing. But I wanted her to acknowledge it out loud so there would be no question where we stood as I eventually led her to a full bonding over the upcoming days or weeks.

"Say it, my mate," I ordered, this time in a more pressing tone.

"Yes," she breathily whispered, so low I barely heard it.

I was about to demand she repeat it louder, but a sudden shift took place within Naima. It was as if a switch had been turned on. With an air of almost angry determination, my female stared me straight in the eyes.

"Yes," she said, loud and clear, a challenge in her voice.

Naima violently yanked wide open the panes of my robe exposing my naked body to her. My blood rushed to my groin, and my cock jerked in response to the almost feral hunger with which she feasted her eyes on me.

"For me. By me," she whispered to herself while her hands roamed over my chest. "I consent."

My mate no sooner spoke those words than she lunged for me, her lips immediately closing around my left nipple. I hissed with pleasure, my hand fisting her hair tightening as she laved my little bud before sucking on it. Naima raked her nails down my back while she covered my chest and my neck with kisses. Her hands and lips left a blazing trail in their wake, driving me mad with lust.

I hastily discarded my robe. She yelped in surprise when I picked her up and walked around to the side of the bed. I laid her down at the edge, intent on feasting at last on what was mine, but the wretched female seemed determined to keep challenging my dominance. Instead of remaining on her back, her legs dangling at the edge of the bed, Naima promptly sat up and closed her delicate fingers around my cock. A strangled cry escaped me as she stroked me with both hands. The blissful caress was quickly accompanied by the inferno of her mouth closing around me. I hissed again, liquid fire running through my veins as my female greedily bobbed in front of me.

I threw my head back, tortured moans dripping out of my mouth while my hips gently thrust with a will of their own in counterpoint to my mate's movements. Between licks, and nips, Naima took me all the way to the back of her mouth and then grazed her teeth along my length as she pulled me out. I thought I would die with pleasure. Considering my girth, she shouldn't be able to take so much of me, so deeply. Without realizing it, my mate had instinctively manipulated the Mist to adapt her ethereal form. As my creator, she had complete control over everything within my domain. She just didn't know it... yet.

As I neared the edge, it took every ounce of my willpower to pull away from her. While I always sought to sate my constant need for pleasure and gratification, this evening was first and foremost about seducing my mate and breaking down her last barriers to our relationship. I needed her to be the first to climax, many times over, before I allowed myself to yield to ecstasy.

When Naima tried to reclaim her prize, I caught her by the neck. She tried to resist, but I squeezed tighter and snarled menacingly. She gasped, her fingers closing around my wrist, but didn't attempt to break free. Her lips swollen and glistening, her eyes smoldering, she submitted as I forced her to lie back onto the mattress. Holding her pinned down by the neck, I parted her legs with a rough sideways swipe of my knee. Naima's pupils dilated, and her breath shortened into short gasps caused equally by her slightly constricted airways, her growing arousal, and the sliver of fear and excitement that my predatory expression awakened in her.

My mate's eyes widened when my shadowy tendrils

wrapped around her wrists and ankles, immobilizing her, spread in a vulnerable position. Leaning forward, one hand resting on the mattress next to her head for support, I released her neck and claimed her mouth in a possessive kiss. My free hand explored her body over her thin negligee, squeezing and fondling her breast while my tongue continued to plunder her mouth.

She moaned against my lips, a violent shiver coursing through her when my hand ventured lower, slipping under the tiny triangle of her thong. My fingers zeroed in on her engorged little nub, scissoring and massaging it while Naima writhed beneath my touch. I dipped two fingers inside her opening. My cock jerked with impatience at finding my mate already soaking wet for me—a need further fueled by the maddening scent of her musk. I pulled my fingers out and, breaking the kiss, I shoved them in my mouth, licking off my woman's essence.

Something snapped inside of me.

With a savage growl, I ripped her negligee to shreds, tearing if off her. Naima cried out in equal parts of fear and excitement. Her mind was shouting for me to ravage her, to take her like a beast. Every part of me was far too eager to comply. I buried my face in her neck, kissing, licking, sucking, and biting my way down her body. I paused only long enough to give one of her erect nipples a solid nip, hard enough to sting, keeping it just on this side of pain. Naima cried out, but her mind chanted 'yes' in a litany.

When my mouth closed on her clit, my mate shouted my name, her back arching off the bed. She struggled against my shadowy tendrils keeping her prisoner and at my complete mercy—none of which would be granted. An endless string of blissful moans dripped from Naima's lips, her hips gyrating under my relentless assault. Between my lips sucking on her sensitive nub and my fingers making love to her, my female's body quickly seized, swept away by a violent orgasm.

Normally, I would have wrested at least one more climax from her before I took her, but Naima's mind kept shouting for me to fuck her into next week. I was too eager to comply. I climbed onto the bed, dragging her with me closer to the center. While my tendrils kept her arms pinned down to the bed above her head, they set free her ankles. Naima immediately wrapped her legs around me as I rubbed my shaft over her exposed sex, covering it with her essence.

"Please," she pleaded in a needy whisper that resonated straight in my loins.

I always loved the sound of her begging me.

"You want my cock, Naima?" I asked, rubbing myself against her even more strongly, my lips a hair's breadth from hers.

"Yes," she breathed out.

"Then you shall have it," I replied, claiming her mouth at the same time I began inserting myself within the burning heat of her sheath.

She was delightfully tight, her inner walls' resistance to my invasion eased by how wet I had gotten her. Although her mind was spurring me on to ram myself home, caution be damned, I ignored that request.

Since my mate and I had finally spoken on a conscious level rather than through the semi-consciousness of her dreams, I had realized that what humans thought and believed was right for them sometimes couldn't be further from the truth. Complying with her request would actually harm her. Granted, this was the dream world, and no permanent damage would befall her. But I needed to define the proper rules of engagement between us going forward. In the real world, ramming myself home would have torn her up.

I considered cheating in my impatience to sate my own burning desire. With a simple thought, I could make her instantly accommodate my girth. However, remembering how much more intense sensations were in a human body, this would serve as my rehearsal in exerting self-control when in the throes of passion with my mate.

With slow thrusts, increasingly forceful, I eventually found myself fully sheathed inside Naima. Moving with deep and controlled strokes, I didn't give her much time to adapt. I hissed at the overwhelming pleasure of the exquisitely tight grip of her inner walls caressing my cock. I rapidly picked up the pace as a raging inferno roared in my loins and the pit of my stomach. As much as I hungered for my Naima's hands touching me, seeing her helpless beneath my body, having no other choice than to accept the punishing way I pounded into her, was driving me too wild with lust and an intense sense of power. The sound of her voluptuous moans, her strangled cries as I pummeled her sweet spot, the clapping of our flesh meeting, and the burning feel of her feverish skin against mine made me feel like a god.

Naima shouted as another orgasm came crashing down on her. Her inner walls clamped down on my cock, making me roar with the excruciating need to surrender to my own release. But no... not yet. Clenching my teeth, my tendrils released her wrists, and I pulled out of her only long enough to flip her onto her stomach. Before she could react, I drew her hips towards me, forcing her onto her knees, and rammed myself home in one powerful stroke. Naima cried out, throwing her head backwards. But even as I resumed my brutal assault, she moaned my name and began rocking back and forth, meeting my cock stroke for stroke.

Floating in an endless sea of pleasure, I leaned forward to caress her back, fondle her breasts, and rub her clit. As I sensed her nearing another climax, I summoned a standing mirror right in front of us. Fisting Naima's curly hair, I yanked her head back hard enough to make her gasp, but not harm her, so that she could see our reflection. Her eyes widened with shock, fear, and sinful excitement as she saw me behind her, still pounding into her. A dozen shadowy tendrils waved like dancing flames around me, my green eyes having turned a glowing red—including the sclera—and my mouth contorted in a vicious snarl as my fangs descended.

I didn't actually have fangs. However, in the Mist, I could become anything I wished—in this instance, anything Naima fantasized about. I wouldn't drink her blood—she had no real blood to give here anyway—but only give her the illusion I was. Letting go of her hair, I slipped my hand around her neck and forced her to arc back against me. My other arm wrapped around her midsection to give her support, I pressed my lips to her ear.

"You are mine, Naima. Body and soul," I whispered in an almost menacing fashion.

I didn't wait for her to answer and sank my fangs in the fleshy part of her shoulder. My woman's scream from the initial sharp pain—which I deliberately gave her before taking it away—turned into a blissful cry as a third orgasm swept her away.

This time, I didn't resist further, my roar of ecstasy mixed with her voice. I rammed myself deep, holding my mate in a bruising hold against me as my ethereal essence flowed into her, binding her to this realm. Even as I gave myself to her, I gorged on the powerful tsunami of energy and emotions that rushed out of my female and slammed into me. We collapsed on the bed, and I carefully gathered Naima in my arms. She held on to me as if fearing I would disappear. Her face buried in my neck, her breathing labored, she continued to tremble against me, shaken by the lingering throes of bliss.

I took her four more times that night. With my insatiable hunger far from being sated, I would have continued for countless more hours. However, both our human bodies required our conscious minds to shut down for a while in order to function at optimal capacity in the morning. With the challenge that awaited me, I needed to make the most of the next day of training before the end of the Mist.

With much reluctance, I sent Naima's consciousness into a pleasant and peaceful dream before allowing my own to drift away and dream of the day I'd bind her to me in the Mortal Plane.

CHAPTER 13

NAIMA

I stood in front of my mirror, repeating positive affirmations to give myself the courage to go out and face Zain. The vivid images of the previous night kept replaying in a loop in my head. I could almost feel his hands on me again, the heat of his body, his hard length wrecking me as I begged for more.

I pressed my palms to my burning cheeks, mortified. Worse still, shame burned in my gut as every inch of me ached for more. I didn't know that I could keep my hands to myself when I next saw him, especially since he would undoubtedly stake his claim the minute we met.

I'd been so stupid. Even now, as I tried to remind myself what arguments had convinced me to give in to my deepest and darkest desires, they now sounded hollow. I allowed myself to be convinced *because* I wanted to be, because of my unhealthy attraction to everything that was bad for me.

My intercom buzzed for the second time, startling me. Zain had good reasons to be impatient. Taking a deep breath, I pushed away from the sink and forced myself to leave my room. On my way to Zain's quarters, I passed a few agents who greeted me as they headed towards whatever duty called them. There was nothing different about their behavior, and yet, every stare felt like a condemnation, like everyone knew what sinful activity I had indulged in and was still craving.

So much for my immortal soul.

I found Zain sitting at the edge of his bed. His back stiff, his palms resting on his lap, he stared ahead with the stoicism of the Sphinx. He examined my features and my demeanor. The absence of any emotion or indication as to how he currently felt rivaled the most professional poker face. And yet, with a certainty I couldn't explain, I knew beyond any doubt that Zain was seething inside.

"Good morning, Zain," I said, proud that my voice came out friendly, revealing nothing of my inner turmoil.

"Naima," he replied as sole greeting.

"Sorry for being late. I'm afraid I slept in," I said sheepishly, hoping he'd attribute the trembling that had seeped into my voice to embarrassment and not fear.

"Understandable," he responded in the same neutral note. "You've had a rather... *eventful* night."

My face heated at the way he said eventful. Right this instant, I couldn't be happier for my darker complexion that hid my blushing cheeks.

"Indeed," I replied, nonetheless grateful by his discreet choice of words to describe what we both knew he was referring to. "Ready to go?"

"Yes," he said, rising to his feet. "But I would appreciate you showing me the functioning of the electric razor again. I believe I may have started damaging it."

"Of course," I said, eager to get busy with anything that would end the awkwardness.

I made a beeline for the bathroom. However, as I reached for the drawer, my hand froze, a dark suspicion finally piercing through my foggy mind. My head jerked towards Zain, and my stomach dropped at the sight of the angry, hard expression on his face as he closed the bathroom door behind him. I straightened and opened my mouth to say... I didn't even know what. But a frightened gasp escaped me instead as, moving with lightning speed, Zain pushed me against the wall. With one hand, he held both of my wrists pinned above my head while his hard body pressed against mine kept me trapped.

His free hand held my nape in a vise, forcing me to look up at him. Chest pounding, my breathing coming in quick, short bursts due to fear and—to my shame—sinful excitement, I stared at him with wary eyes.

"So, we're back to the denial game, are we?" Zain snarled. "Do you regret what happened between us last night? Do you?"

I opened and closed my mouth repeatedly, words failing me. I shouldn't have slept with him. Not so soon, and definitely not before I knew him better or where the hell this whole Squad thing was headed. And yet, it would be a lie to say I regretted the most amazing night of my life.

"You can't, because there is nothing to regret," Zain hissed. "Your body knows we are meant to be. Your subconscious begged me for more, even as I was sending you back to sleep. Why are we back to this? I may not be able to read your mind in the Mortal Plane, but even now I can smell your arousal. You secretly want me to tear off your clothes and fuck you senseless, right here, right now against this wall."

"Sex isn't everything!" I hissed back. "I can't let lust dictate my choices."

"It is more than just lust between us," Zain snapped back. "Tell me I'm not in your mind during every waking moment? Tell me you don't long for my presence every time we're apart? Tell me you don't enjoy our banter and our conversations when you forget to try to fit in the arbitrary mold you think you should? You can't because I, too, feel the same about you. I want to be with you, and you want to be with me. Nothing else matters."

"Humans aren't binary like you!" I exclaimed in a hushed tone, not wanting to alert whoever might be listening.

The fury that flashed through his face before it closed off gave me cold shivers.

"It's them, isn't it?" he asked, contempt dripping from his voice. "You fear what those insignificant humans might think about you getting involved with something like me?"

Yes. I shouldn't, but yes.

And that thought shamed me. How many times had I told my own patients not to live their lives according to others? Not to let their social network dictate what they can or cannot do, especially if that compliance made them miserable. So, why was I doing it to myself?

"Zain, I... I..." my voice trailed off, not really knowing what to say.

This was all happening too fast. In the nine years since I'd ended my therapy and begun my studies to become a psychologist, I'd believed myself recovered. But I'd also avoided men. Not because I was too busy or no good ones were to be found. There had been plenty of upstanding, eligible men, the type you brought home to Mom and Dad. And yet, I'd shunned all of them because the only thing I wanted were the wrong ones. I hadn't broken the vicious cycle, I'd just hidden from it.

Until I found the one bad man who could fulfil my fantasies and not hurt me in the process.

Our eyes locked, and some silent communication flowed between us. An odd sense of peace descended over me at the same time as his anger melted away from his gorgeous features. His hand moved away from my nape to tighten slightly around my throat. I didn't resist as he leaned forward, stopping close enough for me to feel the heat of his lips right in front of mine.

"I will allow it," he said in a firm but whispered voice. "I will allow you to hide our relationship from these weaklings, *for the time being*. But when we are in private, I will not tolerate you pretending you aren't mine, that you don't want this as much as I do. Understood?"

"Yes," I said breathily, shocked by my immediate response.

"Louder," he insisted.

"Yes," I repeated.

"Are you mine, Naima?"

This time, a few seconds passed, my eyes flicking between his as I came to terms with the decision I was making. I could drag this on, knowing the outcome was inevitable. He was asking for a commitment. That scared me beyond words and thrilled me just as much.

"Yes, Zain. I am yours."

An incredible sense of relief washed over me when those words left my lips. I had expected a triumphant grin, a smug smile, or a satisfied smirk from Zain. Instead, his face took on a soft, tender, almost vulnerable expression I had never thought to see on one such as he. My Nightmare released my neck and my arms, which had still been pinned against the wall above my head. He slipped one arm around my back, the fingertips of the other tracing my features like a blind man would to discover a face he had long wished to see. My hands settled on his waist, gripping his shirt.

"Do you have any idea how crazy I am about you?" he asked in a soft voice.

A brief, nervous laughter escaped me. "I... I'm starting to notice," I said, my voice choking on the last word.

Zain stared at me a moment longer before kissing me gently, slowly, with something akin to reverence.

"I am yours, Naima. All that I am always was, and always will be yours. You are my reason for existing."

The devotion in his words, in his eyes, and in the way he looked at me as if I was the greatest wonder in the world made my eyes prickle. I buried my face in his neck, my arms wrapping tightly around him. Zain gently caressed my back in a soothing motion, as one would to console another. In the arms of my Nightmare, I had never felt safer.

After a few seconds—or an eternity—Zain chuckled and pulled away to look at me with an amused smile. I eyed him questioningly.

"There are a few agents outside growing increasingly worried that something highly unfortunate has happened to you," he said with a sadistic grin.

"Of fuck!" I whispered, mortified.

Of course, they would be concerned. We'd been here for far too long, with a closed door at that. I also bet they'd heard a couple of raised voices from our earlier argument. Freeing myself from Zain's embrace, I made to open the door, but he stopped me. In response to my stunned look, he quietly fixed my hair and then the sleeveless shirt I was wearing.

My jaw dropped in the face of such a thoughtful gesture. Zain wanted to cry from the rooftops that I was his. And yet, when my impatience would have involuntarily outed me, he protected me. When he'd given me his word that he would grant me some time to come to terms with my stupid fears of what others might think, I'd never expected him to go out of his way to ensure I indeed got that time. Talk about paradoxical for a psychopath.

"You are something else, you know?" I said with undisguised awe and gratitude.

"I know," Zain said smugly, returning to his insufferable asshole persona.

"Ugh, you're hopeless," I said, rolling my eyes.

He chuckled then opened the door, exiting first with a swagger clearly aimed at provoking whoever stood outside. That wretched man would drive me insane.

"Lost something, boys?" Zain asked in a taunting voice.

As I exited the bathroom, I saw Agent Tate and Agent Peters stretching their necks to look past Zain's imposing body with worried eyes. The obvious relief on their faces when they finally spotted me further increased my guilt and my urge to smack Zain across the back of the head. And yet, the subtle tension draining from his back made me realize my Nightmare—or should I say my boyfriend?—had gone ahead to be the one in harm's way instead of me if things went south. I was getting whiplash from being loved by a protective psychopath.

"Sorry, guys," I said, scurrying in front of Zain to keep him from further needling them. "It appears that having a woman teach a man how to shave was not the smartest decision. We're ready to go."

Although they weren't fooled in the least, both agents nodded, and stepped out of the way. Agent Tate held the door for us while we made our way to the cafeteria. I didn't know what thoughts had crossed the two men's minds, or what they presumed had gone on in there. It shocked me to realize I didn't care that they knew I'd lied. In retrospect, a part of me now wished at least one of them had shown disapproval to see if my reaction would have still been the same.

We entered the cafeteria to find Riley and Julia finishing their meal. Belinda—Thomson's right hand in managing the program—was also sitting with them. I waved at them then picked up some food from the buffet behind Zain who had already begun piling up some on his plate. But, as soon as he was done, he headed straight for the most isolated table in the room, making eye contact with no one. I hesitated then cast an apologetic look towards my fellow mentors. I hadn't seen them since that first breakfast together and wanted to catch up with them before we all split-up tomorrow, once the Mist ended.

Riley winked in a 'it's okay' kind of way, while Julia's gaze remained locked on my Nightmare with an unreadable expression on her face. For some reason, that made me uneasy. Catching up to Zain, I settled down next to him and gave him a stern look.

"What?" he asked, in a slightly grumpy tone, wondering what he had done this time.

"First, proper etiquette dictates that you're not supposed to start eating until everyone else is seated with a full plate in front of them," I said matter-of-factly, already knowing he would flip it the bird.

"Proper etiquette can go choke on a fat cock," he said dismissively. "Why would I sit there starving while my meal grows cold to wait on someone dallying? What's second?" he asked before shoving a mouthful of hash browns into his mouth.

I shook my head at his colorful language and hopeless-ness, all the while fighting the urge to laugh.

"Second, you need to work on your social skills," I said sternly. "You saw me waving at Riley and Julia. We could have joined them to—"

"No," Zain said, with a harshness that took me by surprise. "This is *our* time in public, just the two of us. The rest of the day, I have to suffer the presence of others I'd rather be hunting instead. So, no, Naima. I am not sharing you during meals."

I gaped at him, speechless. He held my gaze, daring me to argue.

"Whatever am I going to do with you?" I said, shaking my head again in disbelief.

The lurid expression on his face spoke volumes and made me squirm on my chair with a sudden throbbing between my thighs.

"Zain!" I hissed in a whisper, casting an embarrassed look around the room.

"You asked," he said with a shrug before eating the huge piece of steak on his fork.

Gesturing at my plate with his chin, he reminded me to start eating as well. I tucked in, and the rest of our meal was uneventful but pleasant. I escorted him to the gym, and while doing my personal morning workout, I watched him pursue his ethereal shield training with Agent Tate.

It had scared me at first when the agent had told Zain to block the blows that he would give him with a baseball bat. With his predatory nature, I had expected my Nightmare to attack Agent Tate the minute he struck him. But my man was extremely serious about this training, and I couldn't have been more grateful for it. The insufferable pest was growing on me. I didn't want to lose him now due to lack of preparation.

When the training ended, I was surprised to see Director Thomson come get Zain.

"I promised you some Sparks and Beasts," Thomson said with his usually friendly demeanor. "Our holding areas are full. Go ahead and gorge to make room so that we can catch a few more before the Mist is over."

"Gladly," Zain said with a predatory grin.

"It is best you do not come, Naima," Thomson said. "That area isn't safe. I will escort Zain alone. I trust he will behave in your absence until I can bring him back to you?" he added, looking this time at my Nightmare.

Zain slightly frowned, clearly displeased at the thought of us being separated. He stared at Thomson for a second before giving him a stiff nod.

"I will behave," he confirmed.

"Excellent!" Thomson said with enthusiasm. "Might as well start getting used to it now since he's going out hunting with Agent Tate and me in the morning. See you later, Naima."

I gave him a stiff smile, feeling bereft and oddly concerned while I stared at their receding backs. This time alone was actually a good thing. I wanted to catch up with Riley and Julia, and I needed to prepare to wrap up my own previous life before the Mist Defense Squad.

I had already signed the *very generous* employment contract with the Fourth Division. However, as a practicing therapist, I couldn't just dump all of my current patients. I needed to transition them over to a new specialist they would be comfortable with, which could take some time. Beyond being Zain's handler, I was also to provide psychological support to the agents, many of whom suffered from severe PTSD since the major increase of Nightmare invasions.

I'd begun poring over some of their files, and I was starting to suspect that many of the most violent Nightmares could actually have been created by agents. Considering the horrors they saw on a daily basis at work, it wasn't a big stretch. Their troubled and traumatized minds provided plenty of fuel for a Nightmare to flourish. I intended to dig deeper into that theory. If it proved true, helping the agents cope with the stress and trauma of their daily tasks would be essential to reduce the birth of extremely violent Walkers.

By the time I was done with my most immediate work and had packed my meager things for tomorrow, my stomach reminded me that lunch had been hours ago. I'd eaten a sandwich and a small salad while Zain had been gorging on Sparks and Beasts. Although Thomson stated they had four holding areas, they should have been done a while ago. And Zain was also human now. His body required sustenance that ethereal energy couldn't provide. They would have informed me of their return. Right?

Or did he get hurt while feeding?

Once that thought crossed my mind, it refused to leave, no matter how I rejected that idea. Zain had never hunted with a human body's limitations before. Did he get too cocky, and a Beast swatted him? If something had happened, surely, Thomson would have told me.

Trying to keep my fears at bay, I headed for the cafeteria to double-check. It was well past supper time, and Zain was the type of man that got hangry. He also wasn't one to wait for others when he needed to eat. Still, the thought that he wouldn't have sent for me when, this very morning, he'd been so possessive of our eating time together seriously stung. I opened the door to the cafeteria and stopped a meter in. My heart sank when my gaze scanned the room and failed to find him or my candidate buddies.

I turned around to leave and yelped when I nearly crashed into Agent Tate who had just come in from behind me.

"Oh, excuse me," I said, my palm pressed to my chest as if to hold my heart in.

Agent Tate smiled. "If you're looking for Riley and Julia, they've decided to eat dinner in the Observatory. They want to admire the creatures for the last time this Mist, and to see how my colleagues are luring them into the holding areas to refill them."

"Refill them?" I asked, perking up. "So, Zain managed to empty them all?"

"Empty them?" Agent Tate said with a snort. "Your Nightmare all but inhaled them. I've never seen anyone be such a natural hunter. He cleared those four holding areas in just a little over an hour. Your man is impressive. It's been a long time since I've felt this excited about the rounds on the day after the Mist. But, right now, I'm really looking forward to it."

I gave him a stiff smile, feeling guilty that, right this instant, I couldn't have cared less about his enthusiasm, even knowing how therapeutic it was for him to be able to express the secret fears he'd harbored.

"That's wonderful to hear," I said in a friendly tone. "Although I wonder why Thomson didn't tell me Zain was done feeding. Do you know if he's moved on to another training?"

"Oh no, he's not done feeding," Tate said, brushing his palm over the short strands of his hair cut in a military style. "Thomson has taken him on a shuttle to fly him over to the

State Penitentiary. They won't be back for at least a couple more hours."

My blood turned to ice in my veins as I stared at him in shock. My stomach knotted, and I swallowed painfully. I should have known. In fact, I subconsciously had known but once again buried my head in the sand.

Agent Tate's friendly expression faded, and his face hardened. A cold shiver ran down my spine.

"As a human, I can understand your distaste for this. But these condemned are no better than the Nightmares we're hunting," he said in a stern voice. "For all his power—and it is tremendous—Zain is nowhere near the level that Darryl has achieved over the past six months. Do I enjoy the thought of a Walker syphoning humans, even those that hardly qualify as such? No. However, letting the Mist Beasts have them will help no one, while giving them to Zain gives us a chance to save countless lives, including his and ours."

Tormented by the same fears, I hugged my midsection.

"I understand that. Really, I do. But what about Zain? What about his soul, or whatever animates him?" I asked in a tortured voice. "What if he develops an addiction for it?"

Tate shrugged. "I'm not worried about his soul," he replied dismissively. He held my gaze unflinchingly as I recoiled in disbelief, anger blossoming within me in the face of such callousness. "Yours is the only one that matters," the agent continued in a soothing voice. "In the end, *you* define what he will and won't do. And your reaction just now, confirms to me that, on that front, we have nothing to worry about."

Those words flattered and actually somewhat appeased me, while also adding the weight of the world on my shoulders.

"From your lips to God's ears," I mumbled, defeated.

Agent Tate snorted. "God has nothing to do with any of this mess." His face softened, and the friendly expression returned. "Do not waste your compassion on those monsters, Ms. Connors. Zain needs your support, not your condemnation or guilt. For now, I suggest you go enjoy the company of the other two handlers before the night is over. Chances are, you won't get to see them before their departure tomorrow. And they will not return here for another month."

"A month!?" I exclaimed.

He nodded. "Grab some food and hop on upstairs. I'm sure they will be happy to see you."

With a final nod, the agent went to talk to a few of his colleagues.

CHAPTER 14

ZAIN

My human vessel thrummed with an insane amount of energy that it was struggling to contain. No wonder Darryl had grown so addicted to feeding off mortals. The Warden had been a sadist. Instead of letting me simply syphon the inmates within their cells, he had released them one by one into the Mist for me to chase, while also dealing with the prowling Beasts.

It had suited me just fine.

Their terror as they fled through what I quickly recognized as a deliberately plotted maze had been beyond delicious. The exquisite taste of their lifeforce had given me such a hard-on, I believed I had leaked a little. While Warden Pritchett had taken Thomson to their watch tower so that he could observe us from a safe vantage point, I doubted the Director had realized there was more to this than met the eye.

The network of cameras along the maze, and the intense greed and excitement that had swirled around the Warden as he led me and the prisoners to the exit, convinced me some shady operation was ongoing. My gut said he had some kind of 'death race' betting going on, with customers watching the camera feed in real time.

I considered informing Thomson but thought better of it. I was having too much fun and gathering too much energy to risk some stupid moral rule ruining it for me—not to mention, I needed the power.

However, with the Warden releasing only one or two of the twenty-three condemned per round, the whole process lasted forever. By the time we were finally done, I could have eaten even Pritchett's ugly face to silence the ferocious hunger that gnawed at my human body. I devoured my long overdue meal, frustrated to share it with these wretched humans and their inane conversations instead of with my woman because we'd been here so long. According to Thomson, I'd benefited from an unusually high number of prey. Normally, each state only held one or two executions a month. However, after his unexpected request to the Warden, Pritchett had reached out to the other penitentiaries to have them transfer their dead men walking to his institution.

I'd welcomed the bounty. Good on him if he'd made some illicit profit from it. I'd play along and keep mum as long as he continued to feed me the power I craved—and in this instance, needed.

The return to the base seemed to drag on even more than our trip to the penitentiary. Thomson attempted to make conversation a couple of times before giving up. He was a nice enough sort. Principled, honest, loyal, devoted to the cause, to his men, and to his people as a whole, Director Thomson was everything I wasn't and would hate to be. He observed too many self-imposed, intangible boundaries. He was a smart man, but unless he wanted to discuss ways to make me more powerful or to get the upper hand on my enemy, I simply didn't care to socialize or make small talk.

The only voice I would never tire of belonged to my mate. My blood boiled with lust and anger just at the thought of my Naima. I'd had such plans for us tonight, now that she'd consciously surrendered herself to me. But, by the time we landed, it was already past midnight, and my female had turned in for the night.

My own vessel was struggling to keep its eyes open. Still, after Thomson locked me in my holding cell, I honored Naima's wishes of hygiene ritual with the shower, the wretched floss and brushing, and the antiperspirant.

Before I yielded to my own need for sleep, I let my consciousness flow through my mind's doorway into the Mist and immediately sought my woman. An angry snarl rose from my throat at the sight of the darkness surrounding the sliver of her consciousness that had crossed over. My mate was spawning a new Nightmare. A faceless evil that was stalking *me* this time, instead of her. Trapped inside a doorless stone house and looking out through a large window, Naima was banging on the unbreakable glass, screaming for me to watch out. Naturally, as nightmares would have it, her voice didn't come through to the other side as my stalker closed in on me.

As the end of the Mist approached, I had felt Naima's increasing concern for me. However, I had not realized it had grown to this extent.

I flew through the instance of her dream in my ethereal form and devoured the mindless Spark of a stalker. Gliding back towards my mate, I transformed the grim setting into the gothic bedroom we had been in the previous night.

"You are safe, my love. I am in no danger. Calm your fears, my Naima," I whispered, extending my arms to her.

She smiled with joy and relief, then came willingly into my arms. I carried her over to the bed where we laid down together, her head resting on the shoulder of my shadowy form.

"Sleep, my love. I will keep the darkness at bay."

Naima sighed with content, a dreamy smile stretching her lips as she snuggled deeper against me. My arm tightened around my female, and I erected a protective shield around her dream that would keep further negative thoughts from invading it. She wouldn't remember any of this, but she would rest peacefully. After gently kissing her lips, I, too, surrendered to the call of Morpheus.

Morning came too soon. Thomson woke me a little after 5:00 A.M. to get ready. Along with him and Agent Tate, we would be scouting the various locations throughout the city where the agency had recorded significant ethereal power surges, or where surveillance cameras had caught a Transient in the process of crossing over. As a Walker myself, I would immediately be able to sense if these newborns were Nightmares to be eliminated before they grew stronger or Wishes to be left in peace.

If everything followed the usual routine, the Mist would recede around 6:00 A.M. We needed to be on the move as soon as it did to avoid our targets wandering too far off from their birthplace. Other agents would also be scouting to track the Transients at the locations I hadn't visited yet until I could catch up.

I quickly dressed in the dark combat uniform Thomson had given me, including a bullet-proof vest. As reality set in, I couldn't decide if I was more excited than worried. That feeling messed with my head. I'd never been scared of anything. But I didn't trust this body. Today would truly be a baptism by fire.

I headed to the cafeteria with Thomson and Tate shadowing me in silence. This would be my third time sharing a meal with the program Director instead of with my woman. I hated it. He was a fine enough companion, but this was my special time with my mate. And, as much as I hated to admit it, I had really wanted to see her before heading out into the unknown.

I opened the door with a bit more force than necessary, my discontent manifesting itself through a certain level of aggressivity. I no sooner stepped inside than the tingling of my connection with my mate struck me. My head jerked to the back of the cafeteria, and my heart lurched at the sight of Naima setting down a tray filled with all my favorite dishes right next to hers.

"Naima," I whispered, a strange sensation making my chest burn with gentle emotions.

Abandoning my companions, I made a beeline for her. I couldn't tell whether she had sensed my approach or heard my footsteps, but my female raised her head and our gazes connected. Time stood still for a moment, then a soft smile stretched Naima's lips. I responded in kind as I approached her, touched more than words could express not only that she had gotten up so early to see me off, but also that she didn't seem to hold any resentment for the previous night.

"I took the liberty to pick food for you," Naima said timidly. "I hope it's okay."

"It is much appreciated," I said sincerely. "I was saddened at the thought of missing yet another meal with you."

A strange expression crossed her features. It was so brief that I didn't get a chance to get a sense of its nature.

"You had important things to do," she said in an understanding tone. "We all need you to be as prepared as possible."

My chest further warmed for my female. Naima hated everything about what I had done last night, but that she stood by me, knowing how essential it had been, meant the world to me. Fighting the urge to draw her into my embrace and kiss her, I merely smiled and took a seat next to her.

My companions wisely found a different table to sit and eat, granting my mate and me a few moments of privacy. Unfortunately, there was no time to relax and enjoy the meal in Naima's company. While we'd been gone to the penitentiary, the agents had gathered more Sparks and Beasts for me. I needed to syphon them before we headed out, and the clock was ticking.

Too soon, I rose from my chair, bombarded by the impatient vibes from the agents—from both my team and the others who would scout ahead of us. Naima followed us as we headed to the holding areas. To my utter shock, she took my hand and held it while we walked. My throat and my chest constricted. This damn human vessel was far too emotional. By their not so subtle glances, the agents took notice. But my mate lifted her chin defiantly. I gently squeezed her hand in approval, my head spinning with a mix of pride and affection for my mate to thus be publicly claimed.

We stopped in front of the reinforced doors with a huge 'restricted access' sign on it. Naima turned to face me. She slipped her fingers through the hair at the back of my head and pressed herself against me. The way she looked at me erased any doubt anyone might have still held that we were an item. Fighting the urge to roar in triumph, I wrapped my arms around her. How I had missed the feel of her in the flesh.

"You go and be a hero, and then you come back to me in one piece. Do you hear me?" Naima said in a stern tone, oblivious to the ten men and women surrounding us.

"I hear you, my mate," I responded.

Bending forward, I captured her lips in a deep and passionate kiss, yet controlled and restrained. My intimate moments with Naima were no spectacle for others to gawk over.

Breaking the kiss, I caressed her lips with my thumb. "I *will* return."

Putting on a brave face, Naima smiled encouragingly as she released me. I caressed her cheek with my knuckles then, with much reluctance, I entered the restricted area. Like the previous night, I made quick work of siphoning the Sparks and the Beasts that had been herded into the holding facility. Despite the limited amount of time, the agents had done a surprisingly good job of rounding up a respectable number of them. However, most of them felt weaker than the previous group. It didn't surprise me. By now, most of the sentient and higher-level creatures had returned to the Mist Plane, having sensed the impending closure of the portals. These weaker and mindless creatures would have been found in the morning turned into ash statues.

Although I didn't hear the city defense siren from within the thick walls of the base, I felt the very moment the Mist dissipated. As my connection to my homeworld was severed, I was struck by a wave of dizziness. Both the strength and energy the Mist had passively been feeding me stopped. For the first time, I truly felt vulnerable. The reality of my new situation as a human sank in at last.

As we headed for the vehicle, I assessed my current state and was reassured by the tremendous amount of energy thrumming within me. I could take a serious beating before I reached a dangerously low enough level that might keep me from piercing the Veil if needed.

We drove through the deserted streets of the city of Cordell. The other vehicles followed us for a while, having to navigate around an impressively large number of ash statues. A particularly striking one held my attention. Two beasts had been in the midst of a battle. One of them had been in the process of siphoning the other when the Mist retreated, immortalizing their last moments.

But even as we left the building, other agents, that weren't accompanying us on this scouting expedition, deployed throughout the city to start erasing these mostly nightmarish —but occasionally adorable—remains from the streets.

"Where is the population?" I asked as every single house and building we drove by remained shuttered.

I had expected that after three days of confinement, many would have been eager to witness the sunrise and get some fresh air.

"The siren hasn't gone off yet," Agent Tate explained from the back seat of the car. "The siren only goes off two hours after the end of the Mist. Officially, it's in order to make sure that no lingering Beasts had somehow survived a while longer or that the Mist had taken a bit longer to recede."

"And the unofficial version?" I asked.

"Unofficially," Thomson replied in his stead, "it is the short window granted to the Fourth Division to clean up as

much as possible, especially desiccated bodies, and to eliminate whatever Nightmares might have spawned."

"Clever and practical," I reflected out loud. "If things get
ugly, it will be good not having to worry about civilians."

"Exactly," Thomson said with a smile.

Blood started pumping in my veins as our vehicle closed
in on one of the dots on the map displayed on a screen
embedded in the dashboard. Those locations corresponded to
the massive power surges recorded by the Fourth Division's
surveillance systems, which were provoked by the birth of a
Transient. This specific spot left me a little perplexed as it
offered little protection from certain types of roaming Beasts.

We were in a residential area of the Thornhill borough, at
a white wooden house that could have used a bit of a facelift.
Nevertheless, the front porch was clean, and the lawn well
maintained. Although a light-grey picket fence surrounded the
house's perimeter—including the backyard—its gate wasn't
locked and didn't close properly. This meant any Mist Being
was free to come and go as they pleased on the exterior property without the negative effects of trespassing.

Taking the lead, I summoned my ethereal shield then
circled to the back of the house where the whispers of a
Walker beckoned me. Weapons in hand, my companions
closely followed. The spectacle that awaited stopped me dead
in my tracks.

A handsome young male, somewhat shaky on his legs,
was chewing on what appeared to be a tomato while taking a
long-sleeve shirt hanging on the clothesline. Tall and athletic,
in a lean and fit swimmer way rather than the massive and
bulging style of a bodybuilder—like me—he reeked of
kindness.

His head jerked towards us, having finally sensed our

presence. The cool morning breeze blew his long, blond hair out of his angelic face. His striking pale-blue eyes widened with surprise and then shock at the sight of my companions' weapons trained on him, but above all, at mine. Fear descended on his features as he clearly struggled to understand who and what we were. Beyond any doubt, he knew me to be a Nightmare. However, despite their menacing stance and the fear emanating from the agents, he would perceive no malice from them. So, what the fuck were they doing with one such as me?

The Transient swallowed the mouthful he had stopped chewing upon noticing our presence, and carefully slipped on the shirt he had taken to cover his nudity.

"I... I'm not here to cause trouble," the newborn Transient said in the type of pleasantly masculine voice that would have females feel weak in the knees.

"Zain?" Thomson asked with a slight tension in his voice.

I waved a dismissive hand. "He's one of those disgustingly gentle Wishes. He is no threat to your people."

Relief flooded my companions who holstered their weapons while approaching the Transient to speak with him. Annoyed, I turned on my heels and headed back to the car. I should be relieved. Not fighting today could be a good thing to give me time to build my power as I didn't truly feel confident with my current level—impressive though it was. However, with the end of the Mist, Naima would become my greatest source of energy, and only from her emotions. Would it be enough when Darryl was out there gorging on humans?

Just as the men were returning to the vehicle, another Fourth Division car pulled up in front of the house to pick up the Transient.

"That was a clever one," Thomson said as he sat behind

the wheel. "Not the sturdiest shelter, but he'd planned for everything."

I grunted in agreement, begrudgingly recognizing the merits of his birthplace selection. At a glance, he'd chosen the sturdy treehouse in the back which appeared to close with a large wooden plank that he'd likely secured once inside. Even though we were in the middle of summer, the morning air had a cold bite. The clothes hanging in the backyard—which also had a small vegetable garden—gave him a good head start on basic necessities.

"Where are they taking him?" I asked with genuine curiosity.

"Transient Immigration Center," Agent Tate said with a snort.

Thomson gave him an amused look through the rearview mirror. "I guess you could call it that," the Director conceded. "We have no quarrel with Wishes. We do not really intervene. However, to those like him who clearly have a chance of making it, we will provide basic clothes and legal identification so that they can function within our society. For everything else, they're on their own."

I stared at him for a moment, once more confused by this strange human trait called compassion. Why would they help us out in any way? He was implying they respected survival of the fittest to a certain extent, but clearly not enough if they gave them a leg up. Then again, with his personality and the fact that his own daughter had chosen eternal life with her Wish in the Mist, I could see why one such as he would feel a certain sense of duty—if not loyalty—towards others like his son-in-law.

Although he hadn't mentioned it, there also was a practical side to this assistance that I'm sure he'd accounted for.

His job was to keep our existence a secret. It would raise too much suspicion if a bunch of grown men and women kept popping up the day after the Mist with no identity and no history.

The next five Transients also turned out to be Wishes. One of them sadly didn't make it. Based on the ashen remains we found, he was drained either moments after his birth or close enough to finishing forming. The residual energy was vile. The victim had not been a Nightmare, but his killer had been.

We were pulling up to the next location when a loud scream nearly made me jump out of my skin. I barely waited for the vehicle to stop before jumping out and racing towards an abandoned store. It was located next to a women's shelter in the middle of a poor neighborhood. The wave of malice and evil glee that slammed into me nearly drowned the despair and panic of his victim. Wrapping myself in my ethereal shield, I ran to the side door in the back alley that appeared to have been broken years ago.

At a glance, the place regularly served as a squatting venue for homeless people. It would make sense for a newborn Transient to select this location as some of the makeshift beds and basic accessories used by its usual tenants were left available for her. Once the city reopened, she no doubt would have sought assistance at the women's shelter next door.

The female screamed again, and the sound of battle resounded from behind a cement wall covered in graffiti. Despite the darkness, my ethereal powers allowed me to compensate for the limitations of my human eyes.

"Release her!" I shouted, deploying my shadowy tendrils as I burst into the backroom where a number of dirty sleeping bags and mattresses filled the large open space.

Standing in the middle, a ruggedly handsome male dressed in rather fashionable grunge style, was siphoning a stunning female with waist-length, light-brown hair. Judging by the shredded state of the dirty shirt she had scavenged, and the angry welts on her arms and legs, the Nightmare had whipped her with his tendrils to feed on her terror and pain before finally starting to drain her lifeforce.

A few more minutes, and it would have been too late for her.

Overconfident, and too absorbed by his feeding frenzy, the Nightmare had not been on the lookout for potential intruders. That gave me hope that he was too stupid to make the most efficient use of his power, which was greater than mine.

His head jerked towards me with an evil grin, clearly thinking the poor human who had dared interrupt his meal would squeal in terror. But his grin faded, and his eyes widened in shock at the sight of my own tendrils. Recognizing the bigger threat in me, he shoved the female back, sending her crashing against the wall. Although battered, bruised, and severely weakened, she looked like she would survive the ordeal—assuming I won this fight.

"*My* prey!" the Nightmare snarled, advancing menacingly towards me. "Hunt your own."

I braced, ready to strike. However, the Nightmare suddenly froze, and terror crossed his features. He quickly hid it, but the scent of his fear lingered.

"Zain!" he whispered, just as Thomson and Tate were finally making their entrance.

I recoiled, startled that he should know me. I narrowed my eyes at him, obviously not familiar with his chosen human vessel. Extending my senses, I tasted his energy, and especially his fear. It was my turn to freeze as I recognized him.

"Little Weasel…" I said in a soft, almost whispered voice. "I thought you'd gotten your sorry ass siphoned at long last."

"My name is Tobin," the little vermin hissed. "You are a weak newborn on *my* territory. Here, you are no longer the apex predator. It is your turn to cower before me."

Tobin was the typical, fanatically mindless Nightmare. His insatiable hunger and cruelty guided his every move. But he was also a coward. He only ever attacked those he knew to be significantly weaker than him, that he had an unfair advantage over, or that he could land a sneak attack on.

He launched his tendrils at me—which I had expected. But just as I raised my own to intercept it, they suddenly veered to each side of me to target my companions behind me. I barely managed to swat them down while Thomson and Tate rolled out of the way. I groaned inwardly when my shadowy tendrils struck his. It felt like punching a cement wall with my bare knuckles. While the men got back on their feet, I used my own shadowy tentacles to whip at Tobin's human body only to meet the unbreakable wall of his ethereal shield. The way he laughed at my efforts proved I'd done more damage to myself than to him with those blows. And yet, they had weakened his armor.

Tate opened fire on the Nightmare, quickly imitated by Thomson. As much as I hated their intervention, Tobin was right. Despite all the gorging I had done, I was but a newbie Transient, still green in handling battle with this human body, and not yet powerful enough. Bullets were doing wonders breaking down the Nightmare's shield. Replenishing it meant divesting more of his energy reserves towards it, which would weaken him to a level more manageable for me.

The attack naturally enraged the Weasel. He once more tried to strike the two males with two tendrils towards each of them, which I blocked again. This time, however, I hung on to them. Simultaneously, I summoned two more shadowy tentacles, which I shaped like giant fists and pummeled him with them. Tobin roared in anger and, for the first time, in pain as the men resumed shooting. His armor was cracking, but I needed him weaker still.

The Nightmare tried to yank me to him, both to use me as a meat shield and to have me within striking range with his own fists. I resisted while he increased the force with which he was trying to pull back his tendrils that I still held. Then, I suddenly released him, immediately following through with an uppercut from my free tendrils. Tobin flew backwards, crashing against the wall.

The female, who had cowered into a corner, dashed towards us. Tobin tried to catch her with one of his tentacles. Before I could intervene, the woman summoned a wisp of a tendril, so thin it looked like a metal wire. Without slowing down, she swiped it in an upward movement, and the damn thing sliced clean through Tobin's shadowy limb. The severed section flopped onto the floor with a small thud, then turned into ashes within seconds.

He screeched in pain, quickly retracting his wounded tendril. I bitchslapped him with one of my own, resorbing into me the two extra ones I had previously summoned to punch him. Four tendrils were our default and didn't drain our energy. But each additional one we summoned put a strain on our reserves—a luxury I didn't have right now.

"You just got spanked by your newborn victim," I taunted, while the female scurried past the men to take cover behind us. "And I had to slap you like the little bitch you are to stop your crying. You were pathetic in the Mist. You're just as sad in the Mortal Plane. All these months feeding on humans, and this is all the power you garnered? You're a disgrace."

Right on cue, Tobin jumped back to his feet and made a show of displaying his power with a dozen tendrils waving around his back like a shadowy peacock's tail.

Yes! Burn away your energy!

But even as my companions resumed shooting, the Nightmare rushed me, forcing them to cease fire. This time, he didn't bother with the humans. Instead of attempting to tackle me to the floor, Tobin wrapped his tentacles around me and drew me to his body. I might as well have slammed into a brick wall when I collided with his chest. His hands flew to my neck in an attempt to strangle me while his tendrils held me in a vise. My own attempted to push back to prevent him from crushing me. I could already feel my shield cracking under the pressure. With the two of us so intimately intertwined, the agents couldn't shoot without risking hitting me instead.

Remembering the human self-defense and combat techniques Tate had been teaching me, I brought my arm down hard over his, close to his wrists, breaking his hold. I immediately followed by slamming my elbow against his jaw, and then struck him right under the nose with the bottom of my palm. Tobin shouted, his hold loosening around me as he held his face. Normally, considering the strength I had put behind the blow, that should have broken his nose, even smashed his face in. However, while his shield had protected it, being thinner around his face, it didn't shelter him from the pain.

Pressing my advantage, I broke free of his embrace and kicked him square in the chest, sending him flying back. But a couple of his tendrils caught me and dragged me with him. I landed on top of Tobin in a tangle of limbs. Before I could recover, the Nightmare rained blows on me with his fists and his tendrils faster than I could block or react. I couldn't tell if his human body or ethereal form was doing the damage, but he was on the verge of wrecking me. I'd never felt such debilitating pain. When a lucky blow struck the side of my face, my teeth rattled, and I nearly blacked out.

This fucking body was too damn slow.

I was losing this fight by trying to battle like a human. I didn't master my body. At this rate, it would soon die. But if I were to keel over, I was bringing this bastard with me.

I stopped trying to damage his much-too-well-shielded human vessel and reverted to my usual strategies in the Mist. Swallowing back the pain, I stopped my efforts to try controlling him and devoted most of my energy to my shield. Shifting back to my Mistwalker vision, I examined my opponent for signs of weaknesses in his ethereal armor. They shone like glowing fissures on the dark surface.

Thinking he had broken me when I remained almost still, Tobin roared in triumph, and relaxed his hold. To my relief, he stopped striking me with his tendrils, switching to punching and slapping my face. The fool wanted to humiliate me before going for the kill. He should know better than to toy with an apex predator. Waves of fear flowed to me from my companions who were also starting to believe I was being defeated. Their fear doubly served me by reinforcing Tobin's overconfidence and by allowing me to shamelessly feed on their emotions.

Perfectly timing my attack, I extruded my ethereal claws and turned the tips of my tendrils into blade. As soon as he pulled his arm back to swing at me again, opening himself wide, I stabbed at six of his vulnerable spots with both of my hands and all four of my tendrils. They pierced right through his shield and then sank into his vulnerable flesh.

Tobin's body jerked then froze, shock and disbelief replacing the smug and malicious joy on his face. As his brain registered the serious damage he had just sustained, the Nightmare shrieked like a banshee. He tried to back away from me, but I didn't let him. I bent the tips of my limbs inside him before yanking them out to cause maximum tissue and organ damage as they came out.

My prey screeched again and slapped his hands on a couple of his wounds to staunch the blood pouring out. He haphazardly batted at me with tendrils, but I didn't relent, targeting his other weak spots with my tentacles. It became too easy. Like most stupid Nightmares controlled by their basic urges, Tobin had never learned real battle strategies. In the Mist, he'd preyed on the weak and easy targets. In the Mortal Plane, humans had been no challenge for him. For the first time, the fool was feeling true pain, and it robbed him of the ability to think straight—not that he ever had before.

I pounced on him, pinning him to the floor. Straddling him, I began feeding on both his exponentially growing terror and his lifeforce. It was slimy with malice and bitter with fright—just the way I liked it.

"No! Noooooo!" he shouted, struggling vainly to free himself.

I grinned with evil pleasure the moment Tobin realized he was about to die. The terror on his face was blissfully delicious. In a desperate, last ditch effort, the Nightmare attempted to siphon me. I backhanded him so hard it dislocated his jaw and a few teeth flew out.

His remaining shield collapsed, and his eyes rolled to the back of his head as he struggled to remain conscious. I cursed inwardly, realizing my mistake. If Tobin passed out right now, his state of unconsciousness would give him access to his human mind's doorway into the Mist. The Weasel still had sufficient energy left to cross over... barely. Granted, if he succeeded, he would be as weak as a newborn Spark and wouldn't be a threat to anyone for a loooong time. But I *wanted* his lifeforce, first as my reward and second to help me defeat Darryl.

I siphoned Tobin with greater greed and speed, the electric glow of his lifeforce flowing into me bathed the dark and dirty room in a blinding light. His tendrils were the first to turn to ash. I held his gaze with malicious joy and watched with fascination the tears that trickled down his cheeks. Tobin's mouth moved but only a choked, gurgling sound escaped him as the last of his ethereal essence turned to ash around him. Only his wounded human body remained.

"You were pathetic," I said in a cruel and merciless voice. "I always said I would kill you someday. There shall be no rebirth for you. Goodbye, Little Weasel."

With these last words, I drained his human vessel, enjoying the sight of it caving in on itself like a deflated balloon. But his death was even more enjoyable than those condemned humans I had hunted yesterday. When they'd died, the core of their soul flew away, I had no idea where. But not Walkers. I devoured the last fragment of his essence. His death was like an electric shock at the back of my throat which then ran down my spine.

I released Tobin's remains and resorbed my tendrils into my body. My vessel thrummed with an insane amount of energy. But now that the rush of battle was abating, agonizing pain coursed through my entire body.

"He did it!" Tate whispered behind me with awe and joy.

"How are you feeling, son?" Thomson asked, his voice filled with worry as he carefully approached me.

Grinding my teeth through the pain, I got back up on my feet. Thomson flinched when I turned to face him. Although he quickly controlled his expression, it had been enough for me to know I looked as dreadful as I felt.

"Let's get you back to the base and have Dr. Chandra take care of you," Thomson said in a gentle voice.

I didn't argue, although all that I really wanted was to hold my woman in my arms. I turned my gaze towards the female, who was hugging her torn clothes close to her body. Although she didn't whine or complain, she was clearly freezing. Confusion and a bit of worry filled her eyes as they flicked between the three of us before resting on me.

Thomson and Tate cast an inquisitive look towards me. They already knew what the answer would be but wanted confirmation.

"Yeah, she's a Wish," I said in a tired voice before starting to walk towards the exit.

"Nightmare!" the female called out. I stopped to glance at her. "You saved me."

"Yes, and?" I asked, annoyed by this additional delay. I *really* wanted to get off my feet.

"Why?" she asked, confused.

"Do you wish I hadn't?" I snarled. "That can be rectified."

Her eyes widened with greater confusion, and she cast an uncertain look towards Thomson. He shook his head at her in a way implying she should just let it go. Wise advice. As I couldn't be bothered any longer, I just limped back to the car. To my surprise, four more agency vehicles had surrounded the location. The agents, weapons in hand, were waiting to ambush Tobin had he gotten the upper hand.

When they saw me coming out, quickly followed by Tate, Thomson, and the female, they began clapping. The happiness and relief on their faces, the wave of gratitude they broadcast my way did funny things to me. I always liked accolades, but this felt different. It was… nice.

Getting inside the car was excruciating. I could see Tate's desire to help me, but he wisely didn't. I would have smacked him. The other agents burst into action like an army of ants. One of them rushed towards the female to cover her with a warm blanket before escorting her to one of the vehicles. Others went in with some broom-like vacuums, no doubt to collect the ashes, while another went in with a body bag.

"The other sites?" I asked Thomson, dreading his response.

"There were only three more, and the men have handled them," Thomson said reassuringly. "There had been another Nightmare, but very weak. My men took him out. I doubt he had enough energy to go back."

I gave him a stiff nod, rested my head on the headrest of my seat, and closed my eyes. I didn't recall falling asleep—doubted I actually did, considering the amount of pain I was in—but the sound of the city's siren resounding startled me awake. I suspected I had in fact passed out. A number of shutters immediately started going up. Within minutes, I could barely recognize the streets near the base. They looked so different now with the houses unlocked and people starting to spill out of their homes.

By the time we entered the underground parking of the base, I felt feverish and nauseous with pain. Despite my pride, I nearly fainted again when I tried to get out of the vehicle. Drowning in an ocean of agony, I didn't react when multiple pairs of hands hauled my massive body out of the vehicle to lay me down on a stretcher. Although they did their best to be gentle, my human vessel's excessive sensitivity got the best of me. The room spun, and a veil of darkness descended before my eyes.

I welcomed it.

CHAPTER 15

NAIMA

I slapped my hand over my mouth at the sight of Zain being carried in on a stretcher. His face was black and blue, his right eye slightly swollen, and his bottom lip split. His uniform hid the extent of the damage his body had no doubt sustained. It took every ounce of my willpower not to get in the way of the men rushing him to the Infirmary. I wanted to touch Zain, call out his name until he opened his beautiful green eyes and looked at me.

Thomson tried to be reassuring, telling me Zain had been fine, walking to the car on his own and holding a coherent conversation. But that didn't mean he hadn't sustained a concussion or that he wasn't severely bleeding internally.

Anika and another medical employee I didn't know were waiting for us in front of the Infirmary. The female doctor directed the agents as to where she wanted them to put Zain before kicking us all out. Although the exam would take a bit of time, and despite Anika promising to update me as soon as she had something to share, I frantically paced outside the Infirmary.

Thomson gave me a summary of what had happened, going on in detail about how my man heroically rescued a female Wish and protected them from the repeated attacks of a Nightmare named Tobin. While his tale warmed my heart, I also knew he was hiding the more gruesome details from me. I swallowed the urge to press him on it. I was freaked out enough without causing myself more distress.

"You have no idea what an even more precious gift your man just gave me," Thomson said in a voice filled with emotion.

I gave him an inquisitive look.

"I know the creator of that female Zain saved," Thomson said. "Her first Wish, Donna, had died in a terrible car accident."

"Monica!" I exclaimed, my eyes bulging. "That female is Monica's Wish? Donna came back?"

"How do you know about—?"

"I've been reading the files on the Wishes living here in Cordell," I interrupted with a dismissive gesture.

"Ah yes, that makes sense," Thomson replied with a nod. "But no, Donna met her final death many years ago. You cannot 'resurrect' a Wish who died on the Mortal Plane and failed to return to the Mist. Faye—the female we rescued this morning—is a completely new Wish."

It took me a minute to digest that information.

"But… If Monica wished to get Donna back, will she want Faye?" I asked cautiously. I didn't want to even envision Zain's death. But should the worst come to pass, I wouldn't want a replacement.

"I've only had a few moments to talk to Faye," Thomson replied, "but from what little I've seen, I think she might be exactly what Monica wants and needs. Our wishes and desires evolve as we age. Monica wished Donna in her teens. It takes years for a Wish to become self-aware and then grow strong enough to cross over. Back then, Monica was self-centered, immature, and very much controlled by her father. She wanted a pet, not a partner, and had treated her Wish poorly. Donna's death changed Monica—for the better. She will want a more mature and more assertive woman in her life now; one that she won't be able to step all over. I believe Faye might be that female."

"I see... How is she going to get in touch with Monica?" I asked. "I understand the organization's policy is to basically let the Wishes fend for themselves."

"Correct, but we made an exception this time," Thomson conceded. "Monica is currently on her way here."

My jaw dropped as I stared at him in disbelief. "Okay, what's the catch?" I asked with suspicion. "I'm not buying that this is just you suddenly being in the mood to play fairy godfathers. What's in it for you?"

Thomson chuckled, a glimmer of amusement and admiration in his eyes.

"Actually, we owe Ms. Sheffield a favor considering the pain we put her and others through when one of our agents went insane six years ago," Thomson said, in a serious tone that caught my attention. "However, Monica also happens to be the heiress to the Sheffield chain of luxury hotels throughout the world. While we have no complaints about their operations, it isn't the case with many other chains. If we could 'recruit' her into our services, she could provide us a backdoor entrance or use her contacts to access other venues that hold questionable events in their hotels during the Mist."

"Why do I feel like I really don't want to know what kind

of 'questionable' we're talking about?" I asked, highly disturbing scenarios already playing through my mind.

"When it comes to greed, there are no limits to just how repulsively creative certain people—who do not deserve to be called human—can get," Thomson said in a grim tone. "It is one of the many things the Squad will be able to help eradicate if we—"

"YOU DARE!" Zain shouted.

I nearly jumped out of my skin at the sudden outburst. Although muffled, the vicious threat in his voice was unmistakable. I rushed back inside the room—Thomson on my heels—and found Anika and her assistant cowering away from Zain. Leaning on his elbow and holding his side with the other hand, he was snarling at the doctor with murder in his eyes. Had he not been hurt, I believed he would have made mincemeat out of her.

"Zain! Calm down!" I said, rushing to his side, while casting an inquisitive look at Anika.

"They touched me!" Zain hissed with outrage. "They were rubbing their hands all over me."

My brain froze for a split second. Surely, he didn't mean... Anika rolled her eyes like she couldn't believe he'd actually said that. A quick glance at his body showed Zain was still wearing his undies, and the white cream smeared on his chest matched the medical ointment in the container on the tray next to his bed.

"You mean they were putting this cream on you?" I asked. "That's... normal. They're trying to make you better."

Shock, outrage, and betrayal flashed over Zain's bruised face in quick succession.

"You are fine with another female touching what's

yours?" Zain asked me in a dangerously low voice, filled with a mix of hurt and anger.

"Oh, Zain," I said in a soothing voice. "Dr. Chandra isn't touching you in a sexual way. I *would* have a problem with that. But she's not." I pointed my index finger at the pot of ointment. "This will reduce the inflammation and swelling, and help your bruises heal faster. The only way to apply it is by gently rubbing it on your skin. I, and everyone else here, want you to feel better and not be in unnecessary pain."

Although my words somewhat appeased him, he kept glaring at the two medical professionals like they had stolen his lunch money.

"I don't care. No female touches me like that, but you," he grumbled.

This time, I couldn't help but smile. My man was being silly, but how could a woman complain about such a sexy beast wanting to exclusively belong to her?

"All right, then. I will apply it on you, and Dr. Chandra can supervise to make sure I'm doing it right, okay?" I said, glancing at Anika for her approval. She nodded.

"Yes," Zain replied, satisfied.

My chest tightened watching him clench his teeth through the pain as he lay back down. It was no wonder, seeing the network of black and blue stripes crisscrossing his chest and legs where Tobin's tendrils had whipped Zain. Other round bruises indicated where he'd likely been punched. It was a miracle he hadn't sustained any serious injury.

"How is he doing?" I asked Anika while beginning to apply the ointment.

"I was about to ask the same," Thomson said.

Zain emitted a soft moan that I assumed to be of relief as

the cooling effect of the cream no doubt slightly dulled the pain.

"He's in a remarkably good shape, all things considered," Anika said in a reassuring tone. "He has a mild concussion, whiplash and, as you can see, some severe bruising. Thankfully, there are no fractures or broken bones, and no indications of internal bleeding. I've given him some Tylenol for the headache and a muscle relaxant to ease some of the pain in his neck and upper back. The cream should be applied on the bruises three times a day."

She turned to look at Thomson with a stern expression on her face.

"Zain needs complete rest for the next few days," Anika said. "No physical exertion of any kind for him until I give the greenlight."

To my relief, Thomson didn't argue.

By the time I finished applying the cream, Zain had dozed off. We agreed to transfer him to my quarters so that I could take care of him. This threw a bit of a wrench in my plans. Aside from the mundane tasks of going home to open the shutters and water my plants, I needed to deal with my employer and my patients. It would all have to wait until tomorrow. Thankfully, as per the law, the day before and after the Mist were official holidays to allow people to go to their safe house before the curfew began, and to return to the city for those who sheltered in remote places.

For the remainder of that day, Zain slipped in and out of consciousness. A part of me believed that he was sleeping so much to enter the dream world where he was stronger and healed faster. However, now that the Mist had ended, Zain was almost like a human. Only a fraction of his consciousness could enter the realm of dreams without flat out killing his human vessel.

While awake, he barely talked. I didn't know how to interpret his reaction. Zain clearly wanted my presence, and especially for me to touch him, but not in a sexual way. He craved for me to gently rub his back in a soothing motion, scratch his scalp, or caress his hair. It took me too long to realize my Nightmare wanted to be comforted, although I doubted that he was aware of it.

Until today, he had never truly experienced pain. It sucked that his initiation should have been at such an extreme degree. But, beyond the physical distress, I had begun to suspect that the battle had mentally scarred him as well. Over the following days, Zain displayed clear signs of a depression.

Although his bruises healed at an incredible speed, Zain continued to sleep an unusually high number of hours. He, whose appetite exceeded mine, dispassionately munched on his meals, leaving more than half in his plate. He was irritable and aggressive with everyone but me. However, he no longer playfully taunted me or pursued me with his sexual advances. And yet, every night, he insisted on cuddling with me despite his bruises.

The only thing that retained his full attention during his short waking hours were the combat and self-defense videos Tate had provided him to at least learn the theory until he was able to resume physical training. Every time I tried to get Zain to open up, he would change the subject or say all was well. As much as it pained me, I knew better than to pressure him. All I could do was let him know that I was here, and that he could talk to me about anything when he felt ready.

The few hours I had to leave the base to consult with my patients seemed to depress him even more. However, even without him, my current situation with the agency was untenable. I didn't want to live permanently inside a fortified base. I wanted to be back in my home, with my big backyard and in-ground pool. I wanted to be able to have friends over, or chill on my front porch with a tall glass of iced tea and a good book, while the neighborhood kids played in the street. Zain's presence was binding me here.

Obviously, the agency wouldn't be too keen on letting him leave the base. They only trusted him to behave in my presence, or during a specific mission in my absence. To my shame, I had to admit that I also wasn't certain to what extent I would trust Zain on his own not to cause harm. And yet, my gut said he would absolutely control his violent urges—not out of compassion, but because he understood the restraint he had to exercise in order to live in this realm.

On the sixth day, just as Anika was telling him that he was good to resume physical training, but not to overdo it, and to listen to his body for any sign of distress, a new victim was discovered. Darryl, who had been oddly quiet for the past week, had finally resurfaced. No cameras had captured his image, but the energy signature lingering around the desiccated remains matched his. That news seemed to crush Zain. Understanding finally dawned on me. That, too, I should have figured out sooner.

When we returned to my quarters, he immediately went to watch the news. I took the remote from him, turned the TV off, and forced him to look at me.

"I've been watching you eat yourself from within for the past week," I said in a soft, but firm voice. "You relentlessly pursued me, convinced me to be yours, and now you are shutting me out. You call me your mate, but you treat me as a stranger. I've been trying to figure out what was torturing you. I'd even started wondering if you had tired of me, but—"

"No!" Zain categorically said, interrupting me. "I can never tire of you. You are my life."

"Then if I am, why won't you talk to me?" I asked softly. "Why won't you let me help you? That is what mates do. I should be the one person you always feel safe to talk to about everything and anything, because I'll never judge you or turn my back on you. It hurts me to see you in pain and not be allowed to help you through it. I wish you would trust me. I am your woman, and you are my man."

An expression of deep pain crossed his features. Although he tried to hide it, a part of it lingered on his beautiful face, further breaking my heart.

"Am I?" he asked. "Am I still your man, Naima?"

I recoiled, my chest constricting with a painful feeling of rejection.

"Of course, you are!" I exclaimed, confused and hurt. "Or are you saying that *you* no longer consider yourself as such?"

Zain snorted and shook his head with a dejected expression. That he didn't answer right away to deny my question cut deep. Head bowed, gaze vague, my Nightmare appeared lost in painful thoughts. Silence stretched between us, filling the room, choking the air out.

"I do not know who or what I am anymore," Zain finally said in a low, angry voice. "I am a killer created to terrorize my creator who no longer wishes to be stalked. I am a predator who can no longer hunt without upsetting my mate. I am now supposed to be a protector, but I would have been defeated by an idiotic Nightmare if not for the aid of two frightened humans. I am a human who doesn't know how to be one. I am a Walker trapped in a vessel I don't comprehend, and in a world filled with nonsensical rules based on arbitrary and intangible notions."

He lifted his head to look at me. My throat tightened, and tears pricked my eyes at the sight of the despair on his face. Zain studied my features as if he was trying to memorize them. He lifted one hand and caressed my cheek with such care, you'd think I was a mirage that he feared would vanish any minute. I wanted to answer and appease his insecurities, but he had more to say. I couldn't risk stemming the flow now that the dam had broken.

"I cannot honor my commitment to you, Naima," Zain said in a broken voice. "I cannot make you happy. You no longer want what I was made to offer, and I am too weak to accomplish what you need from me. I cannot beat Darryl. He is ten times more powerful than Tobin was, and I barely survived that. Each passing day, he grows stronger while I stagnate. Unless I can freely hunt humans, I will never catch up to him. And you will never allow it. Even with all the training in the world, I will at best weaken him. In the end, he will still obliterate me. I have nothing to offer you, Naima. You are my life, my sole reason to exist. But what is my life worth if I am of no use to you?"

"You think I'm going to leave you!" I whispered, flabbergasted.

"Aren't you?" he said with a painful resignation.

"No, I'm not," I said with conviction before cupping his face in my hands. "That is *not* how relationships work. I didn't agree to be your woman in exchange for you saving my people. My affection is not for sale. I'm not a whore."

Zain recoiled in shock and horror, realizing what his fears involuntarily implied.

"Naima, I never meant—"

"I know," I interrupted, pressing my thumbs to his lips. "I know you didn't mean it that way. But that's exactly what it implies when you think that my feelings for you are merely linked to your ability to kill monsters. So, you need to stop thinking that. Yes, I am beyond grateful that you are able to help us, but that's not the reason I consented to be your woman. It was your arguments in the Mist that convinced me."

I scooted closer to him on the couch and slowly traced his noble features with my fingertips.

"The superficial part of me may be drooling over that drop dead gorgeous, godly body of yours, but it's the predator in you that turned me on. I love the sense of danger around you. As much as it unnerves me, it tickles me in all the right places to see that evil smile of yours. The malicious glimmer in your eyes when you are thinking of all the atrocious things you would do to those you consider prey turns me upside down. I've always wanted a wickedly bad boy. You make me feel weak and vulnerable every time you look at me with that hungry, feral expression. And when you hold my neck and squeeze, I feel faint and like my heart is going to beat out of my chest, because I know you could snap it like a twig without breaking a sweat. And yet, I fucking love every single one of those things because I know you will never harm me or perform those acts except in order to protect me."

Letting go of his face, I slipped my hands into his. Mine looked so small and fragile in comparison.

"I have searched my entire life for a man who would make me feel alive, who would give me the thrill and the adrenaline rush that I seek while also keeping me safe," I continued, my eyes flicking between his. "Someone who I can trust with my heart and soul, and who would never betray me. Like you said, you are not my Nightmare, Zain. You are my Darkest Desire. With you, I can be who I want to be without shame and without fear. *This* is why I belong to you, and why you belong to me. Darryl, the Fourth Division, and the rest of the world have *nothing* to do with *us*. The one thing that would make me leave you is you betraying my trust by hurting me for your own pleasure."

"That will never happen," Zain said with a slight trembling in his voice.

"I know. So, unless you find some other fucked up way to drive me away, then it looks like you're going to be stuck with me, forever," I said with a quivering in my own voice.

He stared at me with a look of such wonder, you'd think an angel had appeared before him.

"My mate," Zain whispered before drawing me into his embrace and capturing my lips in a kiss filled with such tenderness and devotion, I just melted against him.

My lips parted, surrendering to his tongue's imperious demand for access. I loved the dominant and possessive way in which Zain kissed and touched me. The greed and impatience of his hands undressing me reminded me of a starving man. He seemed on the verge of just tearing my clothes right off and devouring me whole. I could feel the feral beast, just below the surface, barely contained, and ready to pounce. That made my girly bits tingle.

Zain never stopped kissing me even as he stripped the clothes off my body. While pulling off my top, his lips teased the sensitive skin at the edge of my nape along the curve of my neck. When he was sliding my skirt down, his mouth paid homage to my breasts and my ticklish navel, forcing me to lie down on the leather couch.

We still needed to talk about the Darryl issue, but that

could wait. My brain all but stopped functioning when Zain lowered my thong, and his warm breath fanned over my sex. Fiery butterflies took flight in the pit of my stomach, which quivered with anticipation. I had previously felt his unusual tongue in the Mist, but this would be our first time together as humans.

His tongue was warmer, softer, but just as relentless and demanding. Zain's almost animalistic grunt of satisfaction as he dipped its tip in my opening set my skin on fire. Although he couldn't read my mind in this realm, he could still feel my emotions and leveraged this ability to the fullest. No one had ever been so attentive to each of my responses, as he licked and sucked on my little nub. His fingers, thick and long, zeroed in on my sensitive spot with an almost supernatural accuracy.

With one hand buried in his silky hair while he devoured me, I caressed and pinched the hardened nipple of one of my breasts with the other. My legs trembled as I began to crest. Zain growled again and accelerated the movement of his fingers inside me. While his mouth still massaged my clit, my lover looked up at my face. The savage, predatory glimmer in his eyes, and the shadowy aura swirling around him sent me over the edge.

As I rode my orgasm, my body shaking with spasms of pleasure, I watched Zain stand next to the couch through hooded eyes. He slowly removed his clothes, his gaze never straying from mine. He didn't make a show of it like a stripper would, but in a calculated—almost menacing—way that hinted that the warmup phase was over, and that I had better brace for what would follow. My stomach did a couple of backflips in a delicious mix of fear and anticipation.

Zain was magnificent. He looked like both a Samoan

warrior in his naked beauty, and a fallen god surrounded by the dancing flames of his shadowy aura. His thick cock, proudly erect, pointed at me in a menacing way; the threat further enhanced by the almost evil smile that stretched his sinfully plump lips. My inner walls constricted and throbbed with both eagerness and apprehension. I felt hollow, aching to be filled, yet dreading the burn at trying to accommodate someone of his girth.

We were not in the Mist anymore. Magical thinking wouldn't simply make me adjust.

Zain leaned towards me, and I opened my arms wide to welcome him. But instead of lying on top of me, he picked me up, facing him. My legs instinctively wrapped around his waist. I shivered with pleasure at the feel of his hard shaft pressed against my sex and of his burning skin against mine.

"Yes," Zain hissed, a lustful expression settling on his gorgeous face. He tightened his hold around me and rubbed his face against mine.

We had never been so close, with no barriers between us in this world. If the feel of him was messing me up so badly, I could only imagine how much more intense this was for him who was still adjusting to the sensitivity of human skin.

My man crushed my lips in a searing kiss while he carried me to the bed. His cock rubbed against my clit with each step, sending lightning bolts down my spine and the length of my legs. I wanted him inside me, yesterday. Zain lay me down on the bed before joining me. Despite his visible hunger—which I shared—he continued to kiss and caress me a short while longer while I reciprocated. With the way he responded to each caress on his feverish skin, I believed I could make him climax just by touching him.

When he began stroking my sex again, I realized the time

had come. A bolt of fire exploded in my nether region and expanded outwards. However, through the blazing red-hot haze of lust, a sliver of lucidity came to the fore.

"Wait," I whispered, pushing back on his shoulders to make him roll off me and onto his back.

He resisted for a half-second before complying, a frown marring his forehead as he stared at me with confusion. I climbed on top of him, kissing his lips before leaning towards the nightstand. I opened the drawer and retrieved a condom from the black box Anika had discreetly given me the day after we had moved Zain to my quarters. I had taken the time to get my contraceptive prescription renewed this week when I'd gone home to unlock my house. However, for the time being, I couldn't take Zain's seed inside me in any way, including orally, as it would bind him to me, to this world. His power would decrease, and with each passing day, he would become increasingly human while his ethereal essence faded.

His eyes widened in understanding at the sight of the small packet clasped between two of my fingers. Relief and anger battled each other on his face. I smiled and kissed him again. He was mad at himself for having been so lost in pleasure to have forgotten this critical point.

"We're a team, Zain," I whispered affectionately against his lips. "Everything doesn't always have to be on you."

Not waiting for his response, I kissed his lips again then began trailing a path down his neck and chest using my lips and my tongue. The way he moaned, whispered my name, and shivered beneath my touch was intoxicating. To think such perfection was entirely mine... That this predator, this blood-thirsty psychopath turned into a putty in my hands made me feel like a goddess among mortals.

A strangled cry rose from his throat when I clawed both

sides of his chest from below his clavicles, over the hard nubs of his nipples, and down the chiseled plains of his abs. I had put just enough pressure to give it a nice burn without causing pain. His legs jerked when I licked and sucked his navel before pursuing my journey further south.

Zain leaned on his elbow, his lips parted as he breathed heavily through his mouth. I could almost hear his heart pounding erratically with anticipation as my face hovered above his crotch. Eyes locked with his and a mischievous smile plastered on my face, I pulled my tongue out as far as I could to build up tension. Then, in a deliberately slow fashion, I licked his shaft from the base to the tip. Zain hissed with pleasure. Teeth clenched, he fisted the blanket with such force I expected it to rip any minute.

Taking my time opening the condom packet, I licked the head of his cock and teased the seam of his slit before taking him into my mouth. He cried out my name, his hips involuntarily jerking upwards. Thankfully, I had prepared for that eventuality and moved my head back in time to avoid getting my tonsils destroyed.

"Stop!" Zain ground between his teeth in a pleading tone that only spurred me into bobbing my head a couple more times over him.

Just as I was going to comply, Zain grabbed my hair at the nape with enough strength for it to give me a serious sting that resonated directly in my core. He yanked my head away from him while moisture pooled between my thighs. I looked at him with hooded eyes and licked my lips in the naughtiest fashion before smirking, unrepentant. Zain bared his teeth at me in a menacing way that only made me throb with impatience.

Still, I took my time unrolling the condom over his

massive shaft. It wasn't just the sadistic part of me that wanted to prolong the torture of the wait for both of us. Considering his girth, I was somewhat afraid to tear the condom if I rushed. I also wanted to show him how to unroll it on his cock as he had obviously never done this before.

As soon as I was done, I crawled back on top of Zain and sat on him, my sex aligned with his. I rubbed myself on him, covering his shaft with my essence while he leaned forward almost in a sitting position to kiss me. I felt him tense when I lifted myself onto my knees, and my hand blindly took his shaft to align it with my opening. He broke the kiss and locked eyes with me. Our faces inches from each other's, our breaths mingled as I lowered myself onto him. With careful and shallow movements, I gradually impaled myself on his cock.

Although it did burn a bit, I didn't care. I was lost in the eyes of my lover, surrounded by his love—obsessive though it was—by his godly body with his burning skin wrapped around me, and the vortex of his shadowy aura swirling around us. By the time he was fully sheathed, time and place had ceased to exist. My skin tingled from the ethereal energy emanating from him.

Zain hissed as I began riding him. His eyes all but rolled to the back of his head from the extreme pleasure the friction was giving him. His arms around me were almost crushing in the strength of their hold. It should have terrified me, but only turned me on further. I increased the pace while covering his neck and chest with kisses and caressing his back. When I raked my nails on each side of his spine, something snapped inside him.

I yelped as the room spun around me. Before I knew what was happening, I was on my back, helplessly pinned beneath

Zain. He slipped his arms behind my knees, forcing me to spread them wide while folding them towards my chest. He then held onto my forearms on each side of me. I was trapped, opened to him, with no other choice than to surrender to the unbridled assault he unleashed upon me.

Zain rammed himself in deep, a possessed look on his face while his shadowy aura spilled over the mattress like a black pool I would drown in if he let go of me. I gasped at the pleasure-pain of his brutal invasion. My inner walls contracted around him, having never been so stretched and so full, and yet eager for more. Zain slowly pulled out almost to the tip before slamming himself back in. I threw my head back with a strangled cry, electric sparks coursing through me. He repeated the motion a few more times, gradually accelerating into a savage pace that had me shouting his name, spurring him on while he pounded into me.

My orgasm was so violent, I thought my spine had snapped. Only then did Zain release me from the position he'd kept me trapped in. But he didn't stop thrusting into me.

"Again," he ordered in a voice so feral the word almost came out like a growl.

Capturing my lips in a conquering kiss, Zain slipped a hand between us and furiously rubbed my clit while still rocking in and out of me. I went off like a rocket in a blink. This time, Zain's body seized as my walls clamped down on him, and he roared his release. He thrust a few more times before collapsing on top of me and then rolling off to the side. His body trembled with the spasms of ecstasy. Breathing heavily, his muscular body glistening with a thin sheet of sweat, he stared at the ceiling with a dazed expression. Still, his hand blindly sought me. I curled up against him, and he wrapped a possessive arm around me.

It was too early to sleep, but I didn't think I could ever move from my current position. I'd never been so thoroughly fucked in my entire life. I probably wouldn't be able to walk for a week.

"I love you, my mate," Zain said in a throaty voice.

My heart leapt in my chest upon hearing those words. As much as I wanted to, I couldn't reciprocate. I was falling for him... hard. But I wasn't ready to say those words and genuinely mean them.

Propping myself on one elbow, I looked at his face staring back at me with an infinite tenderness laced with a fierce possessiveness.

"And you are sweeping me off my feet, my magnificent Zain," I whispered, caressing his cheek.

To my great relief, he smiled, satisfied with my answer. I caressed his muscular chest slick with sweat before resting my palm over his stomach.

"You're about to love me a lot less though," I said teasingly. He gave me an inquisitive look. I indicated his crotch with my chin. "You need to go get rid of that. Take it off carefully, make a knot, and toss it in the trash bin."

He stared in disbelief at the condom still hugging his deflating cock before gaping at me. I grinned with the most obnoxiously innocent look I could muster. Zain audibly closed his mouth, shock giving way to aggravation. He glared at me, then at his cock before rolling off the bed.

"Motherfucking human body..." he muttered under his breath while marching into the bathroom.

I burst out laughing while admiring the magnificent round and firm globes of his stellar behind as he disappeared from view.

My irreverent and spirited man was back.

CHAPTER 16

NAIMA

I kissed the top of Zain's head while massaging his shoulders. They'd grown so stiff from the anger bubbling within him that I might as well have been kneading cement.

"It's not your fault, sweetie," I repeated in a soft voice.

"If I had been there sooner, Peters wouldn't have gotten injured," Zain argued, his voice boiling with rage.

"You can't be everywhere at the same time," I countered in a slightly chastising tone. "We didn't even know that a new Nightmare had moved into our city. All that matters is that when you did get there, you beat his ass and saved many lives."

Zain grunted, somewhat mollified by my comment. In the three weeks since he had recovered from his brutal encounter with Tobin, he'd eliminated four more lesser Nightmares that had managed to avoid capture until now. Aside from Darryl who had gone suspiciously quiet, a sense of peace and an illusion of security had begun to set in. And then this Nightmare had jumped the two agents who had been investigating the site of the latest attack. Why he had remained in the vicinity of the crime scene was a mystery to everyone.

The Nightmare's tendrils had caught Agent Peters on his left side, fracturing two of his ribs. If not for his bulletproof vest, the damage might have been greater if not fatal. Along with his partner, Agent Taylor, and despite his injury, Peters had valiantly fired at his aggressor. Their joint efforts had forced the Nightmare to back away, giving them a chance to seek refuge in their reinforced van—the same vehicle the agents used when driving around in the Mist for emergencies. They'd holed up there, waiting for Zain and his team to arrive, stalked the whole time by the interloper.

"Peters still got hurt," Zain mumbled.

"Yes, he did. But his injuries are not grievous. He will make a full recovery in a few weeks," I said, in an appeasing tone. I then chuckled and ruffled his hair. "You know, you're starting to sound like you finally care about your colleagues."

Zain stiffened, and his head jerked left to look at me over his shoulder. "Do not speak nonsense, female."

"Deny it all you want," I said hopping off the mattress where I'd been kneeling behind him while he sat at the edge of the bed. "But I recognize the signs of caring when I see them."

He scrunched his face, and opened his mouth to argue, but I crushed his lips with a passionate kiss, silencing him.

"I've got some errands to run. I'll be back later. Be nice to your colleagues during my absence," I said, kissing him one last time before heading out.

I couldn't quite make out what he mumbled, but it still brought a smile to my face. Zain didn't technically care for his colleagues. He was incapable of that kind of feelings towards others that weren't me. And yet, over the past month, he had become protective of them in the same way a spoiled child would jealously watch over his toys. While he might personally abuse them should he be so inclined, woe unto anyone else who mishandled—or simply even touched—what was his. And the members of the agency were now all his... at least the way he saw it.

The day after that night when Zain had finally opened up about the cause of his distress, we had sat down with Director Thomson to discuss the hunt for Darryl. It had upset me that Thomson had not informed my man of the plan. I was also upset with myself that it hadn't crossed my own mind to prepare Zain for the greater role that the organization had for him.

In many ways, this past month had given him the opportunity to start seeing himself as part of a team instead of a solo predator. That first battle against Tobin had planted the seed. It had also made him realize the extent of his limitations. Although it stung him to admit that he needed help to defeat a rival, it all came down to the way we spun it. He didn't need help; they were merely more tools to help him achieve his goal. Knowing he would get to lead more Nightmares as his lieutenants with him as the general, and the agents as his soldiers, certainly held his attention in a positive way. Naturally, Thomson remained the man in charge, but Zain would be given the final word on which Nightmares were allowed to join our ranks.

Although he would never admit it, this greatly alleviated the fears that were gnawing at him and that had made him fall into that depression. Reading the literature Thomson had provided me about Nightmares and Wishes made many things so much clearer. The Mistwalkers defined themselves in large part by how relevant and desirable they were to their creator's needs and aspirations. Even though I had told Zain that our relationship was not contingent on his ability to fight the Nightmares on our behalf, that had continued to worry him.

Now, Zain had a role, something he could define himself by and strive for. He was the pack leader of the Mist Defense Squad, the protector of the humans, and my savior. He didn't need to be the most powerful as our rules prevented him from taking all the means to achieve that. However, he could assemble the most powerful team to ensure that no enemy who broke our rules could go unpunished. It was not the type of dominance he had hoped for and would always secretly desire, but it was still dominance with him as the apex Alpha.

It was good to see my old, insufferable, rude, antisocial, and arrogant Zain back.

As I made my way home, I started enumerating the adjustments I'd be making over the next few weeks for when Zain and I left the base to settle together in my house. Thomson had understandably been reluctant to let my Nightmare roam free in the city. But as the weeks went by, I no longer had to escort him whenever he left our room, and the security measures surrounding him became increasingly lax. Thomson knew he couldn't keep me forever trapped in the base either. Furthermore, displaying trust towards Zain was an important step in the relationship between him and the Fourth Division.

Although he acted nonchalant about it, Zain was impatient to meet his first two potential recruits tonight when the Mist would rise again. The holding cells to receive Riley's and Julia's Nightmares were already prepared, including the bed where they would take their human form, assuming they received my mate's blessing to cross over.

I pulled up into the driveway of my house, a two-story stone cottage with a black iron fence closing off my large backyard. The street was unusually quiet. Then again, the children were in school and their parents at work. Under different circumstances, I would also have been at the office.

I first went around watering my plants before running upstairs to throw a few more clothes into a bag. I then proceeded to shut down the house in preparation for the Mist. I didn't have a fully automated system as those were on the very pricey side. However, with the new crazy salary I was earning at the Fourth division, and considering all meals were provided for free at the cafeteria, I'd be saving enough money to be able to get a major upgrade in the next couple of months.

I was still flabbergasted by the abundance of meat served at work. It was only recently that Thomson had confessed that there was no shortage of meat. The government had simply seized the tragedy of the first Mist to do the major overhaul that had been needed on so many levels. The environmental cost of meat production farms had been addressed by reducing the general population's consumption and upgrading production farms with better systems to convert methane into energy to fuel the farms' equipment. It also helped to address the issue of people's excessive meat consumption, bringing it down to healthier levels.

However, the rich naturally still wanted to have their meat. And the producers didn't complain as the new prices allowed them to bring in a healthy profit with a much lower and far more efficient production.

After securing all the windows on the second floor, I was heading back downstairs when the doorbell rang, startling me. I frowned, wondering who that could be. I hurried to the front door and opened it, stunned to find a rather handsome, dark-haired man staring at me through the screen door.

"Yes?" I asked as greeting.

"Sorry to bother you," the man said in a rather pleasant and polite voice. "I've just moved into the neighborhood. My son was flying his kite with the other children a couple of days ago, and I'm afraid it ended up getting stuck in your backyard. He came ringing, but there had been no answer. I saw a car parked outside, so I figured I'd come check if anyone was home," he said with a sheepish grin.

"Oh, right," I said with an apologetic smile of my own. "I've been away for business."

"No worries," he said, with a look of understanding. "I know what it's like to be on the go all the time. Would it be okay for me to come in and retrieve it?"

"Wait right here. I'll get it for you," I replied.

"I wouldn't want to trouble you—"

"Don't worry, I've got it," I interrupted. "I'll be right back."

Not waiting for him to respond, I turned on my heels and went out to the backyard through the patio door. For a moment, I had feared the kite might have fallen in my inground pool, but then realized it was much too far from the street to have reached it unless the rope had broken off. I circled around to the side of the house, wondering where it had fallen. I mentally kicked myself for not asking more questions before I left, but I was a little distracted. I wanted to be in and out of the house to run a few errands before I returned to the base. I had some naughty plans for Zain and me tonight in the real world before he snagged me into the Mist.

My heart nearly jumped out of my chest when I turned the corner to see the tall silhouette of the man standing right in front of the gate of the fence. I'd often considered changing it into a large board wooden fence that would give complete privacy. However, the current black iron fence was vintage with some impressive detailing, and the part of the backyard where I normally hung out was hidden from view.

The man smiled and pointed at the side of the house. Only then did I finally notice the kite. It had somehow gotten tangled on the satellite dish of my TV network service. I cringed, realizing how high the damn thing was. Heights and I didn't get along, and I doubted my ladder would be tall enough to allow me to reach the kite. I lifted a finger towards him to indicate one minute then headed back around to the shed to retrieve the ladder. When I came back and put it down, one glance sufficed to confirm it wouldn't be enough.

The intense stare of the man unnerved me. I always felt uncomfortable with people watching me work. But this was all the more irritating in that I didn't know the man and that he was exuding very strong 'Why don't you just let a man do it?' vibes. I didn't even bother trying to climb the ladder and headed back inside to pick up a broom. When the man saw me return with it, he gave me a condescending smirk that made me want to punch him in the throat.

"If you let me in, I could handle this for you," he offered. "I have a greater reach."

"I've got this," I said in a voice that brooked no argument.

This was now a personal challenge. I would prove his sorry ass that no, a woman didn't need a man to do everything for her. Sucking it up, I climbed the ladder with the broom clutched in my hand. I silently addressed a prayer that I wouldn't make a spectacle of myself or become paralyzed with fear at the top. Leaning against the wall, I reached with the broom to try and knock the kite out of there. After a couple attempts, I nearly succeeded, but the damn thing just tilted back into the nook that kept it stuck.

I growled with frustration but refused to let myself be defeated.

"Please, welcome me in," the man insisted. "And this will all be over in a blink."

His persistence pissed me off. However, something in his wording rubbed me the wrong way. A sense of unease settled in the pit of my stomach. I turned to look at him. He held my gaze unflinchingly for a few seconds before casting a meaningful glance at the gate.

I didn't answer, and turned my attention back to the wretched kite. I gave it a couple of solid knocks with the tip of the broom. This time, it almost fell, but the broom slipped out of my hand, and I barely caught myself before I would have fallen off the ladder.

"For fuck sake!" the man exclaimed this time with obvious exasperation. "Just welcome me in your damn house."

My blood turned to ice in my veins as understanding finally dawned on me. My head jerked towards him. Eyes wide, mouth gaping, I stared at the stranger's face looking for some feature I would recognize from all the videos I had watched, but there were none. The branding on my chest began throbbing, and the tingle of ethereal energy made my small hairs stand on ends.

I carefully climb down the ladder, my stare never straying from him. A malicious smile stretched his lips, confirming he knew I had realized what he was. For some reason I couldn't explain, I turned to the kite and pulled on the rope that was now dangling. The kite came falling down, and I caught it before it would hit the ground.

Turning back to the Nightmare, my gaze locked with his. "You are not welcomed inside my house. You're not welcomed in my backyard. In fact, you are not welcomed anywhere on my property," I said in an icy cold voice.

His face immediately constricted, but he swallowed back the pain of trespassing to continue staring at me. This time, so much hate burned in his eyes that a cold shiver ran down my spine. That he hadn't collapsed to the ground, screaming in agony, or attempted to run the minute I had revoked his access to the public part of my residence proved that he was a very powerful Walker. Aside from Darryl, there had been no other Nightmares of this caliber reported in the neighboring cities. So, who the heck was he?

"As for this, you're not getting it back," I said, waving the kite in front of him. "As we say, finders keepers. Now, get the fuck off my property."

"Oh, little Naima, how I'm going to make you pay for your insolence," the man said.

My stomach churned upon hearing him use my first name. The male chuckled maliciously in response to the shocked expression on my face.

"I know everything about you and about that feeble Dark Desire called Zain," he said in a voice filled with evil glee. "Enjoy him all you can tonight. By the time the Mist is over, Zain will be no more. And as for you, I will not kill you. I will keep you, feed off you, and teach you not to fuck with Darryl."

"Darryl?!" I whispered in a horrified voice. "You can't be him."

"I am a man of many faces, little Naima," Darryl said. "I will enjoy feeding on your terror and your pain, and wrecking that tight little cunt of yours. Dream of me, my beauty. Whether you want it or not, I will haunt every single one of them."

On a reflex, I picked up my phone in my pocket and snapped a picture of the Nightmare who made no effort to hide his face. The cocky son of a bitch even struck a pose. Turning on his heels, he finally walked away towards an inconspicuous silver-grey vehicle parked in front of my house. I ran to the gate and took as many pictures as possible of the vehicle and of the license plate as he drove off.

Feeling faint, I leaned on the wall for support while calling Thomson. He ordered me to lock myself inside the house and not go anywhere until they arrived. I forwarded the images I had captured and took refuge in the living room.

I sat on the couch, staring out the window for any sign of their car. By the time Zain, Thomson, and Agent Richmond parked in front of the house, I had finally stopped shaking. I had never been one to easily let strangers inside my home, but I finally understood how easily most people would have welcomed in their death.

Zain stormed out of the vehicle and raced to my door. I opened the first door at the same time he was climbing the handful of stairs. Just as I was reaching to unlock the screen door, he stopped dead in his tracks. He wrinkled his nose as if he'd been struck by a nasty smell. A horrified expression suddenly descended on his face, and his head jerked towards the two agents also running up to the house. They gave him an inquisitive look, seeming as baffled as I felt by his strange reaction.

Without a word, Zain turned back towards me, his face having reverted to one of concern for me. He yanked the screen door open with such brutality he nearly tore it off its hinges before drawing me into a bone crushing embrace. To my shame, tears of both fear and relief burst out of my eyes, and I began to sob pathetically on his shoulder. Zain carried me inside the house. He sat on the couch, settled me on his lap, and gently cradled me in his arms. He caressed my hair without speaking a word, allowing me to expend the overwhelming emotions that had been choking me since that encounter.

By the time I regained my composure, Richmond was sitting at the other end of the couch, and Thomson was extending me a glass of water, which I gratefully accepted. Feeling a little embarrassed, I wiped my face with the back of my hand and gulped down nearly half the contents of the glass.

The men gave me a thorough interrogation about everything that had just happened.

"His power is insane," Zain said grimly. "That he was able to stand there and converse with you that long after you had banished him says a lot. But how can he have a different face? When was your last video of him recorded?"

"The last one where we actually see his face was before the last Mist," Thomson said pensively. "Even though he has been quiet for the past few weeks, I doubt he underwent some kind of aesthetic surgery. So, we can only assume that during the last Mist, he chose to be reborn in a new body. But why?"

"It would have made sense if you wanted to hunt incognito," Richmond reflected out loud. "But then why show his face to Naima? Why reveal his identity?"

"Because he wants to send us on a wild goose chase," Zain said in an angry tone. "And because he also wants to flaunt just how powerful he is. No one recreates a body just for the heck of it considering the energy cost involved. He's making a statement about his endless resources. He's telling me to run because I will never be able to defeat him."

Silence settled over the room with every eye locked on

him. He had stated the last sentence in a factual, almost nonchalant, manner. I hated that I couldn't read his mind to know his mental state. Over the past few weeks, Zain had learned the art of the poker face.

"I will enjoy watching the light fade from his eyes when I drain the last of his lifeforce," Zain finally said with such hatred in his voice that goosebumps erupted all over my skin.

I didn't know how he intended to defeat Darryl, but something had changed in my man. My money was on the fact that the Nightmare had made it personal by attacking his mate.

"What I want to know is how the fuck does he know my name and yours? How does he know where I live?" I asked, still shaken by the events.

"For your address, he might have followed you from the base," Thomson said, frowning. "Many of the sentient Nightmares have realized the Observatory is a governmental agency. Even though your name isn't indicated on your mailbox, he could still have gotten it off your mail. But that doesn't explain how he knows of Zain."

"Could he have witnessed us killing the other Nightmares that roamed the city?" Richmond suggested. "After all, we would have mentioned Zain's name. And when he stood outside your screen door, he could have felt your energy, recognized it as matching Zain's and put two and two together."

I nodded slowly. Technically speaking, it actually worked. But I wasn't fully sold. Zain, staring at the floor with an unreadable expression on his face didn't help.

"Let's take my mate back to the base. Time is ticking. The Mist approaches. I can feel it in my bones," Zain said in a stern voice.

The others agreed and stood as one. They patiently waited

as I went around to lock the rest of the entry points of the house and activated the shutters. Zain sat in the passenger seat of my car as I drove back to the base. Thomson and Richmond followed in our wake. Zain didn't say a word during the entire ride back. He wasn't depressed or beating himself up as I had expected he would. Something was troubling him, and I could see his wheels turning. I had to bite my tongue multiple times not to ask him what was going on in his head. But at a visceral level, I knew he needed this time to sort out his thoughts and therefore left him alone.

When we arrived at the base, Zain didn't go back to our quarters with me. He waited for Thomson to come out of his vehicle and immediately requested a talk in private. No sooner had Thomson said yes than my Nightmare was already heading towards the elevators. Richmond and I stared at the two men with confusion.

So much for our kinky pre-Mist evening.

CHAPTER 17

ZAIN

I was fuming, angry with myself for not having seen it sooner. But I was just as furious with the Director that he, too, should have been so blind to what was so obvious. This entire time, I had wondered how Darryl had been so effective in avoiding capture. Reading through their files, it had been uncanny how he systematically found the most powerful newborns in the midst of crossing over, so that he could feed on them in their most vulnerable state. It had been far too convenient that every time he siphoned the victim, it always happened to be at a time where no agent was in close enough proximity to intervene in a timely fashion. And the time they would have been close enough, out of sheer luck there happened to be no cameras in the area that could have given them an early heads up.

There were too many coincidences to continue to deny the truth.

When the lift stopped on the second floor where the offices were located, I made a beeline for his. I didn't wait for Thomson to open the door, letting myself in before taking a seat in one of the two leather chairs in front of his desk. The Director eyed me warily, a frown marring his forehead.

"You wished to speak to me?" Thomson said while circling around his desk to take a seat.

"Darryl knows what is going on in this base," I said matter-of-factly but in a slightly harsh tone. "You've been suspecting as much for a while now. And yet, you allowed my mate to leave this place without an escort and put her in harm's way."

Thomson cringed and lowered his gaze, guilt washing over his features. However, I didn't give a shit about his guilt or any remorse he may feel.

"You are right. I had begun to suspect information was somehow being leaked to him," Thomson said in a grim tone. "I trust every one of my agents and cannot believe for one minute they would do such a thing. Why? What could they possibly gain from it? Every single person in this project has been thoroughly vetted. And yet, despite my doubts, I actually launched an internal investigation to root out the traitor," he added, running his fingers through his hair with a dejected expression. "We have found absolutely nothing."

"And you won't," I said in a calm voice. Thomson recoiled, his blue eyes widening in confusion. "Tell me Director Thomson, what is your greatest fear?"

His frown deepened, and he looked at me in a way that said he didn't see what that had to do with anything.

"I bet that the thing that keeps you up at night is the fear that something will come out of the Mist, so powerful, so evil, so relentless, that it will decimate the population of the city you have sworn to protect, and that you'll be helpless to eliminate it," I said in a conversational tone. "I bet you have nightmares about the men and women you've grown to consider as family getting obliterated by a vile and unstoppable monster. And as the months and years go by, one by one, your greatest fears are coming to pass. Why do you think that is, Director Thomson?"

The blood drained from Thomson's face, a horrified expression descending on his features.

"No," he whispered, shaking his head in denial.

"Yes, Thomson. Yes. Darryl is *your* Nightmare," I replied in a tone that brooked no argument. "Every night, you feed him vital information about this operation and the people within it."

"THAT'S A LIE!!" Thomson shouted. He jumped to his feet, fury etched on his face. "I would never—"

"SIT DOWN!" I shouted back, interrupting him.

"You don't—"

"Sit your ass down *now*, or I will make you," I hissed in a threatening voice.

Thomson swallowed hard, his anger giving way to fear as my tendrils came out. More waves of fear and confusion wafted to me from behind. I didn't need to look over my shoulder to know that the handful of agents who hadn't gone home for the Mist, were panicking at the sight of what they could only interpret as me having turned on their boss... on them.

"You tell them to stay outside," I warned in a dangerously low voice. "Anyone comes in, I *will* hurt them."

A slew of emotions crossed the Director's features before he gestured at the people outside to stand down. He then resumed his seat, no longer knowing what I would or wouldn't do. Over the past month, he had become compla-cent, overly confident that I was 'tamed' by my mate.

Foolish man.

I crossed my legs and leaned against the backrest of my chair before brushing a non-existent piece of lint off my pants.

"Every time a human goes to sleep, his Wish, Nightmare, or Dark Desire gets an open window into that person's thoughts, hopes, dreams and, naturally, fears," I explained in a conversational tone. "Humans also use that time of rest to sort out the things that plague them, the problems they couldn't solve, or to confirm if the steps they have taken to address an issue were right. Just like you have your daily physical hygiene routine, humans do their nightly mental hygiene."

Thomson let out a shuddering breath, and his shoulders drooped with understanding.

"If I thought you had deliberately betrayed the men and women of this organization, you would be drawing your last breath as we speak," I said in a harsh tone. "I do not fault you for creating that monster or for involuntarily giving him the ammunition to fire back. It is the natural way the human mind works in conjunction with the Mist. But I do blame you for not seeing it sooner. My mate has already mentioned that her preliminary evaluation of your agents has led her to believe they are spawning half of the Nightmares haunting your streets. And that if they haven't yet, they will soon, without steady stress and PTSD therapy."

Thomson nodded, a pained expression on his face. Although I couldn't read his mind in my human form, with the Mist increasingly approaching, I could feel his emotions with a greater acuity and a hint of the thoughts that had fueled them. In this instance, I could clearly sense the guilt gnawing him at the thought of the agents and the civilians that had died because he hadn't been able to manage his fears.

This whole remorse business was such a waste of time. Humans devoted too much energy crying over spilled milk. It was absurd. People had died... oh well. Rather than wallowing in a pointless sense of guilt, he should channel that energy into focusing on preventing this from happening again.

"I need to remove myself from this situation," Thomson said.

"Yes," I said, surprised he didn't seem intent on arguing.

"But if he's been reading me, he knows the plans about the Squad," he reflected out loud with a frown. "He knows that Letho and Merax are coming back tonight."

"To be interviewed by me," I countered. "He doesn't know the outcome. He also doesn't know their power level. If they were diligent and committed to their promise to build their energy level until the next Mist, those two will have gorged for the entire month and should be of a respectable level. The three of us combined will be a force to be reckoned with."

Thomson cast a glance at the clock on his desk. "If I leave now, I can make it home before the sirens go off. To think I told Tate to take some time off this Mist, and Belinda is home with her family," the Director said with annoyance.

"Tell Tate to return," I ordered in an imperative tone.

"He's out of town. He wouldn't be back until tomorrow morning," Thomson argued.

"Bring. Him. Back," I snapped. "Do you really want *me* running the show?"

Thomson blinked, taken aback by my comment. I could literally read the thoughts fleeting through his mind as he assessed the current situation. He knew damn well Tate was the only one of his agents whose authority I would defer to. All others would be my bitches.

"I will call him," Thomson said with a heavy sigh.

"Good man," I replied in a taunting tone.

He leveled me with a hard stare, and I couldn't help but admire how ballsy it was for him to act in a threatening fashion towards me.

"Do not patronize me, Mistwalker," the Director said in a clipped tone. "This is still my organization, and you still report to me. You do not order me around, shadow tentacles or not."

"They're tendrils," I corrected.

"I don't give a flying fuck what they are," he snapped back. I raised an eyebrow, impressed to see the tougher side of our division's leader. "I'm *temporarily* stepping aside to avoid further jeopardizing the safety of the people of this organization, and the residents of this city. Don't get too cocky. You will assess the two Nightmares as soon as they come in, and report back to Tate right after you're done, understood?"

I should have snapped his neck for his insolence, but the old man was growing on me. I smirked and rose to my feet.

"Safe journey home, Director Thomson," I said in a taunting tone while walking out of his office.

"Arrogant son of a bitch," Thomson muttered while picking up a few items from his desk.

I chuckled and left his door wide open. I strolled past the dozen agents gathered outside his office, putting as much swagger as possible in my steps. The poor humans didn't know what to think or how to react. I entered the elevator and turned to face them. As the door closed, I winked at them, which earned me a barrage of swear words quickly cut off by the doors shutting.

I made a beeline for my quarters to find my female on a video call with one of her psychologist colleagues. She quickly ended it, which pleased me immensely. I liked being her main priority.

"Sweetie, is everything okay?" Naima asked as she came to stand in front of me.

I drew her into my embrace and kissed her deeply. She melted against me, yielding the control I craved, and responding to my passion in equal measure. My female was a drug I could never get enough of.

"I'm sorry I wasn't there when he stalked you," I whispered against her lips.

Naima frowned and pulled back to look at me. "What did I tell you about it being impossible for you to be everywhere at once?"

"I know, but that doesn't change how I feel," I said before nipping at that plump bottom lip of hers that always drove me crazy.

She yelped in surprise when I picked her up and carried her to the couch before sitting her on my lap. I gave her a summary of the discussion I just had with Thomson. Although she was floored that Darryl was his Nightmare, she wasn't surprised he had been spawned by someone within the agency. She had suspected two other agents instead.

"I would like you to list all the agents you believe to be at risk, and for us to compare their energy signatures to those of both victims and Nightmares that have been eliminated over the past year," I said. "We need to know who else might be leaking, and to nip in the bud any new Nightmare in the making. I need to hunt tonight anyway. Might as well kill two birds with one stone."

"Okay, I can definitely do that," Naima said, her eyes flicking from side to side as she mentally reviewed the agents she had already started having sessions with. "I'll get on it right away. Who knows if one of their Walkers will show up tonight during the recruitment."

I bit back a growl of annoyance. I understood the urgency of finding more potential Nightmares to join our ranks, but the timing couldn't be more rotten. I didn't want to spend the next few hours evaluating the Wishes, Nightmares and Dark Desires that might come stalk the candidates. I wanted to hunt and then to lose myself in my woman.

"When the Mist is over, I want you to promise me not to go out again without some sort of escort," I said, abruptly changing the subject.

I had expected her to balk at this invasion of her privacy—a thing humans seemed pretty big on—but to my pleasant surprise, she merely nodded.

"Yeah, I was just thinking that," she said pensively. "That bastard has it in for us. I do *not* want to give him the opportunity to corner me alone anywhere."

I kissed her one last time then let her get to work.

I watched the new groups of candidates enter the Observatory. Eyes wide with excitement and curiosity, their emotions buzzed with confusion, hope, and a sliver of fear of the unknown. Without context, appearances were so incredibly misleading. A month ago, when Naima's light had beckoned me to this place, I had presumed this to be some sort of a rich folks gathering to enjoy the view of the freaky creatures of the Mist. Never in a million years would have I guessed they were here as bait to lure monsters like me.

At a glance, I could already tell who wouldn't have spawned the type of Walker we needed. A dozen of them had taken seats at one of the tables grouped in the center of the room to free the area around the windows so that others could walk around it in the hopes of getting spotted by their Mist-walker. Two more groups would be brought here within the next hour once they completed their screening back at the HQ.

I felt the portals opening a split second before the city's sirens resounded in the distance. A wave of energy surged deep within, and a sense of peace, of being home washed over me. The humans around me gasped in awe and fear at the sight of the white fog that appeared to rise from the ground to quickly swallow the world. But in my case, a terrible longing was urging me to run outside and give myself over to the loving embrace of the Mist. And then the first Beasts and Sparks appeared in the distance before slowly making their way towards us, drawn by the bright lights illuminating the large Observatory.

While the first group of candidates began walking around the perimeter of the room with a great deal of trepidation, a second group arrived. Among them, Riley and Julia who were immediately taken down to the secured area of the base by Agent Peters. Naima would be happy to see them, especially Riley with whom she had formed an almost instant friendship.

Although Naima's affection for anyone other than me displeased me, I didn't feel any particular urge to bash Riley's head in since he clearly didn't feel any sexual attraction towards my mate—or any other woman for that matter. However, I had to admit that the appreciative glances he'd cast my way had both flattered and offended me. I was well aware of my tremendous ego. For one such as myself, instilling awe and admiration in others felt like my due. At the same time, I was insulted on behalf of my mate that he would covet what belonged to no one else but her. I'd only spared him because he hadn't acted on it.

Minutes later, two Mistwalkers arrived together and

circled around straight to the side door that had first taken me inside one of the holding cells of the base. It was an incredibly odd sight. Nightmares usually didn't play well together. Maybe, there was hope after all.

I headed down to their holding cells. Initially, each cell had been in an individual room with the 'safe' front half for the human, and the glassed-in area filled with Mist. For the sake of expediency, the wall separating two such rooms had been taken down, making it one large room with two holding cells occupying the back wall. I walked in before the Walkers arrived and found Naima in an animated conversation with Riley and Julia. Agent Peters was holding the remote which controlled the access doors from the tunnel into the cells.

With his fractured ribs, Peters should have gone home and taken some time off to recover. But the foolish man had insisted on staying. Like many of his colleagues, he was too eager to meet the two potential new recruits.

As soon as he noticed my presence, the agent beamed at me while approaching to hand over the controller to me. Young, with short black hair, and a face that would probably eternally look like he'd never quite ended puberty, Peters was my hardcore fan. He'd already been in awe of me previously, but saving his life when that foreign Nightmare had infiltrated our city had sealed the deal. If he had a tail, he'd no doubt be wagging it something fierce right now. He was my cute little pet.

"I'm staying in the Observatory to handle the candidates," Peters said. "Agent Tate has returned and said he would supervise the men luring Beasts into the holding areas instead."

My brows shot up. "Already? I thought he wouldn't be back until morning."

Peters nodded. "That's what we all expected, but he had changed his mind about that vacation. You know how much he loves training new recruits. He didn't want someone else working with the new guys."

Just as he spoke those words, the first Nightmare entered one of the cells, followed shortly thereafter by the second one in the other cell.

I grunted in acknowledgement to the agent's statement then turned my attention towards the Walker to the left: Merax. The predatory way with which he stared at Riley had given him away. His creator slowly approached the double reinforced glass locking in the Nightmare. Riley buzzed with a mix of excitement and apprehension that reminded me of Naima's reaction during our first encounter in a similar setting.

A sideways glance at my mate revealed that she, too, was reminiscing about that day. She'd been terrified when I'd busted through the glass to nab her. How far we'd come since that day.

Despite the double glass wall separating us, I could easily read Merax's thoughts as if we were both back in our realm. The great amount of power I had acquired over the past month from syphoning those condemned and the Transient Nightmares—enhanced by the nearby Mist—made it child's play.

Just like with Naima and me, Merax was Riley's Darkest Desire. But unlike me who had loved to hunt and terrorize my creator, he wanted to hurt his. I was a stalker and a killer; he was a bully and a sadist. The one thing we had in common: we were both madly in love with our creators. However, Merax had some rude awakenings in his future.

From what I could read from Riley, he would enjoy a certain level of pain. He was a masochist who had been mishandled by the partners to whom he had given power over him. My gut said Riley only dabbled on the lighter side of the kink and wasn't a true submissive. Like my Naima, he wanted a partner with whom to explore the darker sides of his fantasies that he could also trust to keep him safe.

Merax placed his palm on the glass, like I had previously done. Riley responded in kind. By the ethereal energy swirling around the human male, I could deduce Merax was mind-speaking to him. The redness creeping on his creator's face made obvious the nature of his words.

"You will acknowledge me as your alpha," I mind-spoke to Merax.

His head jerked towards me, and he glided through the Mist filling his room to come face me.

"On the field and during missions, I will defer to your command," Merax said in his disembodied voice. *"But when it comes to my mate, you will not interfere."*

"As long as your actions do not jeopardize his physical and mental health, you are free to handle him as you see fit," I replied with a dismissive gesture of my hand.

His mostly featureless face tensed with blossoming anger, and he advanced menacingly towards me, as close as the glass wall allowed.

"What is it to you? Why do you care for MY mate's welfare?" Merax hissed.

I snorted with disdain at the petty jealousy. *"I don't give two shits about his welfare, except to the extent that he is my mate's friend. Any harm to him will upset her. Upset my mate in any way, and I will personally deal with you."*

That seemed to pacify him.

"Then we are in agreement," Merax said after a beat, his stance relaxing.

"You will initiate your cross over immediately," I ordered.

Not waiting for his answer, I used the remote to close the tunnel door that led to his holding cell. I turned to look at the other Nightmare, only to be met by three humans staring at me with bated breath. I gave them a stiff nod. Riley fisted his hands in a victory gesture and silently mouthed 'yes' while looking at his spawn. Merax mentally said something to his creator who nodded. He then glided to the large bed at the back of the room to initiate his human birth.

Julia nervously shifted on her feet as I approached her Nightmare's cell. Letho was no Dark Desire. Even in his ethereal form, he twitched and restlessly paced like a junky in bad need of another hit. In his mind, complete and utter chaos lurked beneath an infinite thirst for blood and murder. He wasn't just a Nightmare, he was insane. There were no bonds of love between him and his creator. Yet, a powerful connection linked them: pity and guilt from her, complete and utter dependence from him.

"Not you," I said out loud while gesturing for Letho to exit through the tunnel. "He's insane," I added as sole explanation to the others.

Turning on my heels, I made to leave, but the Nightmare frantically tapped on the glass wall, calling me back.

"HUNTER! Wait! Take me! Take me, too!" Letho telepathically shouted to me. *"I fight and kill with you... FOR you!"*

I paused and turned back to face him.

"Your mind is too chaotic," I mind-spoke to him. *"You would jeopardize the missions and put the humans at risk."*

"I don't. I won't. Letho listens. Letho obeys," he begged, his palms and face pressed against the glass. *"Purpose quiets the noise. Give Letho purpose, Alpha. I listen. I follow. I hunt for you."*

I glanced at Julia, who uncomfortably shifted on her feet. A thick cloud of guilt swirled around her.

"I… I think he could help," the army veteran said in an apologetic tone.

It was my first time seeing her display so little confidence. She didn't know for sure what her Nightmare was but had a strong suspicion as to why his mind was fractured. Through the chaos of Letho's memories, I could see glimpses of what had made him this way. The poor bastard was the embodiment of Julia's ordeal as a POW. In him, she had poured all the agony, terror, helplessness, and hatred that had festered inside of her. He was the reason she hadn't gone mad. Through him in her nightmares, she had vicariously become the hunter, slaughtering all who crossed their path.

"The human Director gave Letho focus: hunt, grow power. Letho obeyed," the Nightmare pleaded again. *"Apex Alpha Zain, give Letho focus. I obey."*

It then dawned on me with crystal clarity. Letho's purpose had been to take away Julia's pain and channel it towards destroying her enemies. Since her retirement, and following therapy that had helped her cope with most of the trauma, her Nightmare no longer had a purpose. That left him day in and day out drowning in the chaos of his mind. Thomson's directive for him and Merax to spend the past month hunting to build their reserves before they crossed over had given him focus. Focus had silenced the madness. I could give him focus with training and missions. But was he worth the hassle?

"He's a strong and gifted hunter," Julia said, as if she'd read the thoughts crossing my mind. "Yeah, he's a little broken, but he can fight for our cause. And, in between that, I'll look after him… like he looked after me."

Her voice slightly broke on those last words, erasing any doubt I held about her knowing why he was like this.

"He was indeed swift and quite capable during the last Mist," Riley added warily.

Naima walked up to me and placed her hand on my upper arm. She lifted her beautiful face to look at me. Even before our gazes connected, she'd already won.

"Is he a threat to the agents or to the general population?" my mate asked in a soft voice.

"Under my control, no," I admitted, reluctantly.

"So, he could help then. Yes?" Naima insisted.

"He could, or he could become a nuisance," I grumbled. The wretched female gave me a shy smile and shamelessly batted her eyelashes at me. I growled in annoyance before glaring at Letho. "If you become a pain in my ass or jeopardize a mission, I'll permanently kill you myself."

"I won't! Letho listens to Alpha," the Nightmare said enthusiastically. *"I cross over now."*

I made a disgusted gesture with my hand and closed the tunnel access to Letho's holding cell while he rushed to his bed to initiate his transition. In the cell next door, a white cloud crisscrossed by lightning already surrounded Merax's ethereal body.

Come what may, those two misfits were now my pack.

CHAPTER 18

NAIMA

My eyelids were growing heavy, but my two companions had no interest whatsoever in calling it a night and going to bed. I couldn't blame them. I, too, had wanted to stay right next to my Nightmare the minute I'd found out he was crossing over. We'd brought in a table and three chairs for Julia, Riley, and me to sit in front of the two holding cells where the Walkers were forming at an impressive pace.

It stroked my ego that they weren't forming as quickly as my Zain had. My man had completed his transition in the record time of five hours and twenty-six minutes. We had passed that mark a little over ten minutes ago with these two. Nevertheless, Merax and Letho were definitely ahead of the curve according to the average total birth time of ten to twelve hours that Thomson had reported for Transients born in the wild. By my estimate, they should awaken in the next hour or so. A part of me wondered if being in a completely safe environment drove them to expend more energy to form faster. Normal Transients might have gambled with taking a longer time to save as much energy as possible to sustain them while looking for their creator.

Although sleeping quarters had been prepared for both Riley and Julia, the silly man had begged and pleaded to have a camp bed brought into the room so that he could sleep next to Merax's cell. Riley was determined to be right there when his Nightmare first woke up. To my dismay, Agent Peters had managed to get two beds in here, one for each of my companions.

But where Riley awaited the birth of Merax with the eagerness of a lover impatient to be reunited with his partner after a long separation, Julia waited with the gentle patience of the devoted mother of a child with special needs. I had never even imagined the possibility of such a scenario. It was my hope that with time, a genuine affection would develop between them instead of this relationship based on guilt, duty, and dependence.

After Zain had left us to go back to assessing the candidates' Walkers, I'd spent the first hour or so catching my companions up on what had happened during my first month here. In between anecdotes, I'd walked them through the training program they would have to follow with their respective Mistwalker. In retrospect, it blew my mind to realize what a long way Zain had come since that first night he'd been hellbent on terrifying me.

While I didn't go into too many intimate details about my relationship with Zain, I gave them some insights about defining the terms of our interactions, my hard and soft limits, and making him understand that the confused child that had spawned him had evolved into a woman with different needs.

"All right, you two," I said, fighting back a yawn. "This

chick needs to get her butt to bed. You should do the same as well. Tomorrow will be a busy day."

"You just want Mr. Gorgeous and Grumpy to yank you into dreamland to play naughty," Riley said teasingly.

"Mr. Sexy As Fuck is busy hunting in the Mist," I retorted, despite the heat creeping on my cheeks. "I'm going to pass out in bed and dream of rainbows and unicorns."

"And he'll ditch all of those Beasts to chase your fluffy tail the minute he feels you falling asleep," Julia said in the same mocking tone.

I chuckled and shook my head. "You're both perverts," I said with a false air of despair. "Now, you two get some Zs. Otherwise, you'll regret it in the morning. It's already midnight!"

"Yes, Mother," Riley said with a long-suffering sigh.

I barely resisted the urge to ruffle his hair. Getting up, I cast one last look at the two Nightmares in the final stages of their human birth then left the room. I had just started walking down the long hallway when a shrill, but muffled cry of a Beast nearly made me jump out of my skin. Startled, I turned around to look at the opposite side of the hallway from whence it had emanated. Granted, the cells were located at the end of the L-shaped corridor, but the holding area was perfectly soundproof, even when their outer, reinforced doors were opened.

This time, a vicious roar resonated from the same area, but much louder.

The door to the Nightmares' birth cell jerked open, startling me again. A very worried Riley poked his head into the corridor. He cast an inquisitive look towards me. I shook my head to indicate I didn't know what was going on. Raising one finger to tell him to hang on, I ran down to the end of the

hallway towards the secured area. At the L-shaped intersection, I glanced at the large, reinforced doors with the
'restricted access' label on them. My blood ran cold at finding
the doors ajar, and at the sight of red lights blinking all around
the frame.

Just as I was going to turn around and hightail it, the doors
fully opened with a clanking sound and a hiss. I nearly fainted
at the thought a Beast would come charging out of there, but it
was Agent Tate's tall silhouette that came walking out.

"Tate!" I said with a sigh of relief. "What the fuck is
going on?"

But even as the words left my lips, a wave of unease
washed over me. It took a second for my conscious mind to
rationalize the red flags that my brain had picked up. Why
was Tate still in the holding area at such a late hour? Why
were the wires from the doors control panel all hanging out
like the security system had been gutted? Why was he
nonchalantly strolling out of there, tools still in hand, like he
didn't have a care in the world? Why was he smiling like that?

Zain's brand on my chest began throbbing at the same
instant I noticed the white smoke of the Mist slithering on the
floor behind him before pouring into the hallway.

The base had been breached.

"Miss me?" Tate asked. A malicious grin stretched his
lips, and dark, shadowy tendrils began swirling around him.

"Darryl," I whispered with dread.

The sadistic expression that descended on his face
confirmed I'd rightly guessed.

"We have a score to settle, you little cunt," Darryl said,
continuing his slow advance.

"I banish you!" I shouted. "You are not welcome in this
base. I banish you!"

For a split second, I feared I didn't have the authority, like it had been the case with Zain during our first encounter here. But Darryl hissed and flinched, taking a couple of steps back. Thankfully, this place had all but been my home for the past month. However, Darryl didn't flee. With the Mist catching up, then passing him, it overrode my banishment. Wherever the Mist could enter, so could its dwellers. Darryl's grin returned, and he resumed advancing towards me in that terrifying, casual pace of the stalkers in slasher movies.

He burst out laughing when I turned on my heels and started running. If not for the Mist's slow advance, constraining him, there was no doubt in my mind Darryl would have given me chase.

I need to alert the agents!

But even as that thought crossed my mind, I realized it would be suicidal for them to confront Darryl without Zain. But Zain was in the Mist, and Merax and Letho were both still being born. If Darryl got to them...

The loud screech of a Beast resonated behind me, turning my blood to acid.

"What's going on?" Riley called out as he saw me running towards him.

"Get back in!" I shouted while barreling down towards him.

At the same time, Agent Peters and Agent Richmond came running from the other end of the hallway which led to the cafeteria and the private quarters. Disheveled and still adjusting their clothes, they'd clearly been dragged out of bed.

"Darryl is inside!" I shouted to them, stopping right in front of the holding cell where the Nightmares were being born. "He let the Mist in! We need to lockdown the base!"

I looked over my shoulder just in time to see the first

plumes of the Mist slithering on the floor, turning the corner to flow into the main corridor I stood in. Peters cursed and gestured with his head for Richmond to get going. Without a word, Richmond turned around and headed back from whence they'd come. Peters rushed to me, his hand cradling his injured ribs.

His eyes widened when Agent Tate finally emerged in the corridor we were in. His steps faltered at the sight of the sadistic expression on the face of his long-time colleague and friend.

"It's not Tate! It's Darryl," I said, my heart pounding into my throat.

Peters ran inside the room, and we shut the door behind us. Julia and Riley approached us with the same panicked expression on their faces. The agent tapped a few instructions on his phone, and the alarm went off. He then used his device to connect to the base's intercom system.

"To all members of personnel, this is not a drill," Peters said in an urgent but controlled voice. "The base has been breached. Darryl is inside, and the Mist is flooding the facility. Immediately initiate all lockdown measures. Do not, I repeat, *do not* let the Mist enter your secure sector. Remain confined until further notice. Be warned that Darryl has returned with the appearance of Agent Tate. I repeat: Darryl has taken the appearance of Agent Tate. Do not let him approach you. Do not open the door for him. He is to be handled with extreme prejudice."

A frightening thought crossed my mind as Peters spoke those words. Whipping out my own phone, I called Agent Tate.

"Hello," Tate answered at the second ring.

To my utter relief, there was no sound of sirens in the

background of where he was answering from, confirming he wasn't the Nightmare lurking in the base.

"It's Naima. Where are you?" I asked.

"I'm driving back. I'm still thirty to forty minutes away," Tate said, worry creeping into his voice. "What's that noise? Is that the breach siren?"

"Yes," I replied with a tensed voice. "Darryl is inside, and he has taken on your appearance."

"WHAT?!" Tate shouted.

"He's let the Mist in and released the Beasts from the holding areas," I continued while trying to rein in the fear that threatened to choke me. "I banished him, so he can only stay within the areas that the Mist can access. Peters is locking down the base to try and contain him."

"Good thinking. Where is Zain?" Tate asked.

"He's hunting in the Mist. I need to go get him," I said, glancing at the beds Peters had brought in for my companions.

"The Nightmares?" he asked.

"Still about an hour to go before they wake," I said heading towards one of the beds. "When you get here, make sure to contact Peters first to avoid friendly fire."

"Will do. Be there soon," the agent said before hanging up.

As I sat down at the edge of the bed, another terrible thought crossed my mind, and I stared suspiciously at Agent Peters.

"Darryl disabled the alarm," I said to him. "How did you know something was going on?"

Peters didn't flinch or recoil and held my gaze unwaveringly.

"Before he left, Thomson said there might be a breach. He didn't want to know what measures we would take but only said to account for that possibility," Peters replied. "I activated the backup security system and only informed Richmond. That system is silent and is triggered the minute anyone tampers with the base's lockdown system."

That alleviated some of my worries. Then again, he had weapons, and we didn't. If he'd meant to harm us, he'd have already done so. The thumping sound of a Beast's heavy steps in the hallway and its growl reminded me that time was of the essence.

"I'm going to get Zain," I told my three companions. "Whatever you do, don't let Darryl in, I added before lying on Julia's bed.

I closed my eyes and prayed that Zain would pull me in.

CHAPTER 19

ZAIN

I'd never thought the day would come when hunting would feel so lackluster. With too few high-level Beasts in the vicinity, I easily mowed through the Sparks and other creatures roaming around. To think that, just a month ago, some of the ones I'd defeated today would have required some effort and strategy.

I was buzzing with an insane amount of power. A single blow with my tendrils could all but split one of my prey in two. Between the convicts, the Transient Nightmares, and feeding daily from my woman's emotions, especially during our lovemaking, my power had grown by leaps and bounds.

Naima had been right to fear I'd grow addicted to hunting humans—or at least highly sentient beings. These helpless Mist Creatures presented no challenge. That didn't stop me from gulping down everything I could get my claws on. Despite the boredom of the chore, I felt happy: an emotion I'd never thought would ever be associated with me.

Throughout the years spent preparing myself to cross over, I'd imagined a million ways my physical reunion with my creator would go down. After their unexpected offer of joining the Fourth Division, I'd been uncertain if I'd managed to adapt to their world, their rules, and their expectations. In truth, after the battle with Tobin, I'd fallen into a terribly dark place unlike anything I'd ever experienced before. The certainty that I'd soon lose my mate had been eating me from the inside out. I'd even started thinking of ways to convince Naima to leave the Mortal Plane and just come live with me in the Mist. But she never would have agreed.

And yet, here I was today, part of a team and the leader of my own Squad. I had high hopes for Merax. As long as he didn't develop unrealistic ambitions, he could make a solid right hand. Letho was a train wreck. However, if he could be trained as an attack dog, in my hands, he could become a formidable weapon. I had seen two more Nightmares stalking their creators in the Observatory tonight that might make a good addition to my team.

Only a few weeks ago, the agents of the Fourth Division had been terrified of me. While they still feared my power and my ability to annihilate them without breaking a sweat—as they should—they now admired and respected me. I had never expected to derive greater pleasure from their idolizing awe than from their fear. My pet, Agent Peters, certainly knew how to stroke my ego without even trying. It was the sincerity of his admiration and appreciation of me that affected me so deeply. It disturbed me to want to provoke more such reactions from others. Being liked didn't mesh with the persona of an apex predator.

In the end, however confusing this concept of teamwork felt at times for a solo hunter like me, it made me feel stronger. It gave me confidence that we could overcome any challenge, even Darryl. And *that* made me *very* happy.

Although nothing would ever make me as happy as my mate. In many ways, Naima had changed me. Yet, for all that, they were small and superficial changes that, combined, had a powerful impact, allowing me to function in her world. But at the core, she had accepted me and learned to love me the way I was.

I couldn't wait for her to finally go to sleep. Although she had tried to keep it a secret, Naima had planned a special evening for us tonight. That fucking bastard Darryl had ruined it. However, I, too, had planned a special evening here in the Mist for just the two of us. I intended to push her boundaries, test her limits, and make her shed the last of the inhibitions she still held on to in the name of those silly human principles.

Why the fuck was she taking so long, anyway?

Just as that thought crossed my mind, I finally felt my female's consciousness poking at the portal of the realm of dreams. Excitement surged within me, and I almost drew her to me before remembering that this no man's land wasn't an ideal location. Granted, I'd pretty much cleaned the place out of anything that could even remotely present a threat, but still... I cursed under my breath when I realized how far I'd wandered from my domain.

As I began to race back towards my territory, a sense of unease took root deep within me. Something felt off. Naima was attempting to fall asleep with such frantic impatience—almost desperation—that it instead caused her consciousness to bash against the portal, making it resist the assault. She needed to ease herself in for the Veil to yield.

This was unlike her. I reached for my mate through my brand on her chest. The wave of fear, panic, and urgency that smashed into me left me reeling. Something terrible had happened. Stopping dead in my tracks, I erected a protective wall over a small radius around me. It burned some of my energy but finding out the source of my mate's distress was more important. As soon as it formed, I pulled Naima's consciousness to me. For the first time, I hated the slow transfer of her soul into my world, manifested by the fall of her ethereal body towards me. Her shape and features became more defined as she neared the ground.

Her eyes snapped open right before she landed. They immediately searched for me.

"Zain!" Naima exclaimed, throwing herself into my arms the instant her feet touched the ground. "You must come back! Darryl is inside the base. He has let the Mist and the Beasts inside."

"WHAT?!" I shouted, my hands tightening on her upper arms. "Tell me everything."

She gave me a quick rundown of what had transpired. Her quick thinking and Peters' foresight had helped avert a tragedy. But knowing he was there, with a simple wall between him and my mate had me on the verge of panic. Even though he couldn't breach the walls without sustaining extreme pain and energy loss now that he had been banished, there were workarounds. I only hoped he wouldn't think of it.

"Stay put," I ordered, my mind racing. "I'm coming,"

"Okay," Naima said in a shaky voice. "Please, hurry. I'm scared."

"I will *not* let anything happen to you, Naima. You are my life. I love you," I said before crushing her lips in a desperate but brief kiss. "I'm sending you back now. I'll be there soon."

"Okay. I love you, Zain," my mate said, her eyes blinking furiously to stem the tears that threatened to rise.

I sent her consciousness back to her body then allowed my

own to flow back into my vessel. Naima's words should have elated me. She had never actually said those three words before. Despite the fear crippling her, my mate had meant them just now. However, she had spoken them thinking that this could be her last chance to do so. Naima didn't think she would survive the night.

I felt my consciousness heavily fall back into my naked corporeal vessel, which I had put in stasis while hunting in the Mist. I jerked up into a sitting position, but a wave of dizziness forced me to lie back down. It always took a few seconds for my soul to mesh again with my human body.

I grabbed some clothes, not bothering with underwear, and threw them on while accessing the camera feed of the base through Naima's computer. The agents had done a good job locking down the living quarters section, the Observatory, the offices, the cafeteria, and the gym. The Mist flooded the hallways along the cells where Naima and the others were trapped, the armory, the garage, and the four holding areas where the Beasts and Sparks had been detained for me to feed.

Darryl, wearing Tate's appearance, was near the holding areas, luring Beasts towards the cells. My blood turned to acid in my veins as I knew exactly what he intended to do.

I called Peters' phone.

"Peters," he answered.

"Darryl is going to try and break into the room," I said without preamble. "I will try to slow him down, but you can't stay there. Take my woman and the others into the tunnels leading to the exit. You know the maze, right?"

"Yes," Peters responded.

"Good. Take them to one of the other holding cells, as far as possible from this one. Repeat as needed if he chases you.

He won't be able to take the pain of breaking through multiple doors."

"The Nightmares?" the agent asked.

"Leave them. Moving them during the crossover might kill them," I said, cursing inwardly that they hadn't completed their birth.

Maybe if I could delay Darryl long enough, they might awaken in time.

But they will be too clumsy to control their new human vessels and deal with gravity.

My heart sank further at that depressing thought. I couldn't say how effective Darryl was combatting in his ethereal form. But he had certainly mastered combat in a human vessel. Whereas it was the opposite for me.

I froze, struck by a sudden realization.

"Can you see the camera feeds?" I asked Peters.

"Yes, we have a laptop here," he replied, thankfully keeping to the strict information of importance.

"I am in my room. I will come out in my ethereal form. As soon as I'm in front of the confinement wall, open it just long enough for me to get to the other side, then shut it down," I ordered. "Open the path to the training room. That's where I intend to fight Darryl. Once I get him there, send backup."

"Understood."

"Peters... Do not let any harm come to her," I said with a barely veiled threat.

"I'll protect her with my life."

I didn't answer and hung up before returning to lie down on my bed. I allowed my ethereal form to come out, leaving my human vessel behind. As a Transient that had not yet been bound to the Mortal Plane, it was an easy task. Remaining contained was normally the challenge. I glided to the door, opened it, and slipped into the hallway. Without the Mist to facilitate my movements, it felt a little like walking with heavy weights attached to my ankle—if I'd had any in this form.

As I closed the distance with the reinforced walls that blocked off access to the rest of the base, Peters activated it. It no sooner started rising up than the Mist greedily rushed in to invade this section of the hallway. I swiftly slid under the partially opened confinement wall, my speed aided by the fog. The moment I cleared it, the agent lowered it. The handful of Sparks and the Beast that I had spotted on the camera feed, greeted me on the other side. While the Beast had a sliver of awareness, it wouldn't attack unless it felt threatened. Right now, I had no intention of stirring that pot.

Gliding at maximum speed, I raced down the hallway towards the holding cells. The pained and enraged roar of a Beast spurred me on. The powerful aura of energy that struck me when I turned the corner into the main hallway nearly made my innards liquefy.

Darryl was beyond powerful.

How the fuck could he still have so much power after two rebirths in the past thirty days? He had just performed one last night after stalking Naima at her house. I would never be able to defeat him on my own. Even with the agents shooting him, I wouldn't survive the encounter long enough for them to finish him. He would slaughter us all. Our only chance was to delay enough until Merax and Letho awakened and joined the battle in their ethereal forms.

Darryl had made one huge miscalculation. He hadn't realized that I'd figured out the identity of his creator, and that the domino effect of this revelation would result in Peters detecting his intrusion and shutting down the base. My mate banishing him before Peters arrived only ensured the agent could enact the security protocols in a timely fashion. Without that, Darryl would have been able to open every door and every room, letting the Mist and its Beasts in while we all slept, unaware.

He would have slaughtered us the coward's way.

But now, unlike me, Darryl would have to remain in his human form to battle, with all its gravitational restrictions and the huge energy cost required to shield it from damage. Should he be so foolish as to exit it in order to leverage the benefits of his ethereal form, a single bullet through the head of his discarded human form would end him.

With a dozen tendrils swirling around him, Darryl was battling a creature that resembled a giant gorilla covered in scales instead of fur. It possessed a rhinoceros' head and sharp spikes along its spine. A blind fury descended over me as I watched the Nightmare swipe his tendrils at the Beast, three grouped together at a time, to send the creature crashing against the wall. The Beast roared again in pain, both from the tendrils' blow and from the trespass backlash of damaging the wall. Its spikes were beginning to pierce through the thick walls, while its mass had already severely dented it.

Despite its massive size and long arms, the creature couldn't move fast enough to strike at the Nightmare. Darryl was quick, far more than a regular human, and chain-swiped his tendrils at his prey before it could recover enough to counterattack.

I shifted into stealth mode, rendering myself invisible as I had done that first night I'd brought Naima into the Mist. It cost next to nothing if I remained motionless but consumed a great deal of energy to maintain the faster we moved while cloaked.

I darted towards Darryl while he was pummeling the Beast. He sensed my presence moments before I was upon him. His head jerked right. Eyes wide, he raised two tentacles in my general direction to block the attack he knew was incoming. Without slowing down, I whipped two of my tendrils with all my strength right below his. They both met their mark, colliding with his right side and thigh. The impact made me flash into existence for half a second before I vanished again.

The force of the blows sent Darryl flying sideways. He crashed onto the floor, half-stunned, then roared in agony. The arrogant fool hadn't surrounded his vessel with a thick enough shield, thinking himself invulnerable. I hadn't inflicted any fractures, but that pain would torment him. He'd had such an easy ride for so long, his tolerance to pain would be low. I just needed to get in as many licks as possible while avoiding his blows.

I flipped around to strike at him before he could get back up. Anticipating that move, Darryl swiped his tendrils forward in the area I'd be coming from. I veered hard left, barely avoiding getting clipped. The Nightmare jumped back to his feet, holding his injured side only to get back-handed by the gorilla. It knocked him a couple of meters away. Darryl landed hard on his ass before banging the back of his head on the hard floor. To my chagrin, although the blows had certainly caused him some level of discomfort, the bastard had cranked up his shield after I'd first gotten him.

Nevertheless, I swooped in and whipped him twice more in a fly by. Even as he shouted in pain, Darryl retaliated with a swipe of his own. Knowing I'd never get out of its path, I dissolved into a vaporous form, letting his tendril pass right through me, leaving me unscathed. Once again, that made me visible for a split second before I vanished from view.

Enraged, my nemesis got up and flapped his tendrils in every direction, waving them like a madman in the hope of landing a lucky blow.

"Show yourself, and fight me as a human, you coward!" he shouted, hitting the gorilla a few times instead.

I grinned, pleased to see him exert so much energy in vain —not that it made a significant dent in his insane reserves. But every bit he lost was a step closer to a potential victory for us. More importantly, it bought me time.

Drawn by the ruckus, a couple more Beasts came looking for prey. I glided away, at a safe enough distance not to get caught by a blow intended for another. One of the two creatures could have been the offspring of a peacock and a pterodactyl. When the freaky bird started spitting on him something that looked like acid, it almost gave me a hard on.

Such poetic justice.

The acid was doing a number on the Nightmare's shield, forcing him to burn more and more energy to reinforce it. The other creature looked like a carnivorous plant hydra mounted on the body of a giant porcupine. It nipped at Darryl with its nine heads, forcing him to juggle parrying it and the gorilla, leaving the acid bird to safely fuck with him.

For a moment, I considered luring more creatures his way so that they could keep him tied up, then thought better of it. I needed to preserve my energy, and this hallway was too narrow for the Beasts to give him a real run for his money.

That decision was reinforced by the fact that the Nightmare expressed no fear, only anger to have his plan turned against him. Fury also emanated from him that I should have gotten a few hits in while he still had yet to score a single one against me. It was inconceivable to Darryl that a being so inferior to him could have the upper hand.

Unfortunately, the battle didn't last long. The wretched Nightmare was too powerful and the creatures too weak in comparison. In his rage, Darryl also killed the gorilla, regretting it immediately.

He stood there for a moment, fuming. His gaze flicked back and forth between the pile of ashes from his victims, and the damaged wall. I couldn't believe the fool was actually considering finishing breaking the wall himself. He had the energy reserves to do it and survive the cost. The agony he would endure though would overwhelm him.

I was hoping he would do it.

While he'd been battling the gorilla near the cells, I'd felt my mate leave, the strength of our connection dimming as Peters led her and the others through the tunnel. Merax and Letho were protected by the double, reinforced glass walls. Breaking through those would require even more power and inflict significantly more damage than this first wall. It would wreck him.

Seeming to come to the same conclusion, Darryl snarled with rage, his gaze blindly looking for me in the corridor, empty but for the Mist and the ashes of his victims.

However, as much as Darryl wanted to kill me and harm Naima, his creator had not spawned a mindless idiot. Smart leaders like Thomson never did. Their monsters were usually the cold and calculated types, which made them even more dangerous. And this specific Nightmare was coming to the conclusion that his perfect plan had encountered too many hiccups to justify pushing through.

He had thought that by the time the agents would have realized what was happening, half of them would have already been dead, and that the remaining ones would have rushed him in a desperate effort to retake the base. Instead, we had trapped him in a limited set of narrow corridors with me in stealth form preventing him from breaking into the locked rooms by cheating. But I couldn't let him leave. While I had not expected our confrontation to go down this way, our current situation was actually stacking the cards in my favor. I needed to lure him inside the gym before he decided to bail.

I carefully glided past him towards the high security area before turning around. I dashed forward swiping at him with three of my tendrils, hoping to catch him in the face with at least one. It was always the least protected part. However, just as I initiated the blow, Darryl sensed my approach. He didn't try to parry the hit he knew was coming but swung six of his twelve tendrils at me. Two of mine connected solidly with his left arm and shoulder, and the third landed like I had hoped on the side of his face.

Repeating my earlier tactics, I switched to an intangible form, but not fast enough to avoid getting struck by his first tendril. It caught the tail end of my ethereal form, sending an excruciating wave of agony through me. It felt as if someone had swung a spiked mace at my ankle with all his strength. I clenched my teeth through the pain and continued gliding at high speed towards the training room. Turning this setback to my advantage, I flickered in and out of stealth as I flew away. Hopefully, my nemesis would assume he'd inflicted a grievous enough injury that the debilitating pain was keeping me from properly going back into stealth mode.

Darryl's triumphant laughter as he gave chase confirmed he had taken the bait.

"Running away, you little coward?" Darryl taunted, the sound of his footsteps pounding the floor as he ran after me filling the hallway. "Not so ballsy when you can't hide to strike from the shadows. And *you* are the Fourth Division's champion? You pathetic little worm, I'm going to enjoy syphoning your lifeforce. And when I'm done, I'm going to destroy your human pets, one by one, but not your bitch. Her, I will keep as my sex toy and my energy battery. Every month, maybe even every week, I will fuck her cunt, her ass, and her face with a new body. By the time I'm done with *my* Naima, she will have had more cocks than the Mortal Plane's greatest whore."

A red haze descended before my eyes. While Darryl's primary intention was to taunt me into losing my head to anger, I also knew his words to be truthful. He would use her this way, feeding on her pain and terror, and leeching her life-force. He would leave her with just enough so that she couldn't fight his abuse while remaining fully conscious and aware of the torture he subjected her to. In due time, I would make him pay for having even entertained that thought.

I reached the door of the training room, stopping just long enough to turn the handle and yank it open. To my shock, Darryl was already upon me. Before I could try to fly inside the room or dissolve into my intangible state, one of his tendrils hit me square in the chest, sending me flying down the corridor leading to the personal quarters. I collapsed to the floor, the wind knocked out of me. For a split second, I feared losing consciousness. If I did, all would be lost. Beyond the agony radiating around the point of impact, I couldn't feel the bottom half of my ethereal body. Although I could see the rest of me, it felt as if I'd been split in two.

Darryl rushed me. Fighting through the pain, I flew towards the creatures I had passed on my way out of the personal quarters area. Once behind them, I turned back into stealth mode. This time, I was genuinely struggling to maintain it. The Nightmare charged right through the creatures, tendrils flaying. The Sparks collapsed into ashes at the first blow. The Beast reared and attempted to fight back but it, too, was defeated in a handful of powerful strikes from Darryl.

I curled into a small ball at the bottom left corner of the corridor, my back pressed against the confinement wall. Shifting into my intangible form while remaining in stealth mode through this level of agony took all of my willpower. I would not be able to fly past him and through the door without at least one of my two abilities collapsing. And at the rate keeping them up was eating through my energy reserves, I could only last so long. I only needed for him to keep flailing at the ceiling long enough for me to recover and make a dash for it.

"DARRYL, YOU PIECE OF SHIT, GET THE FUCK OUT OF OUR BASE!"

Hearing my woman's voice shouting from the connecting hallway felt like a bucket of acid had been poured over me.

No, my love! No!

Why the fuck did Peters let her out? With a malicious grin on his face, Darryl turned on his heels and ran to the training room door directly in front of the T intersection that led on the right to the cafeteria and on the left to the holding cells. Abandoning my intangible form, I rushed in stealth mode towards him. As soon as Darryl reached the intersection, shock replaced the evil glee on his features. A barrage of bullets greeted him, stopping me dead in my tracks.

The Nightmare roared with rage and started racing towards the shooters. I glided toward the intersection, peering from the top corner of the wall by the ceiling to avoid eating a stray bullet. My jaw dropped at the sight of Tate—the real one

—Peters, and Director Thomson standing in front. Naima, Riley, and Julia, standing behind them, had also been shooting. But they were now rushing back inside the room, quickly followed by the agents. They slammed the door shut with time to spare before Darryl could reach them.

Seething with fury, my nemesis struck violently at the wall next to the door with both his fists and one of his tendrils, making an impressive dent in it. He immediately hissed, his knees nearly buckling from the backlash of trespass. Thankfully, the wall held as it had been undamaged prior to this assault. This was a different room than the one the Nightmares were forming in and that Darryl had attempted to breach earlier.

I wanted to strangle the agents who had put my mate in even a sliver of danger—although I didn't doubt for a minute that she had insisted on helping. After all, we had both begun weapon's training over the past month. At the same time, I could have kissed them for creating the distraction I needed to get out of that tough spot.

"Apex," Merax' voice suddenly said in my mind, startling the living daylights out of me. *"I have awakened. What is this sound? Why is my outer wall damaged?"*

"Leave your vessel behind," I ordered, my heart soaring. *"Darryl is in the hallway, about twenty meters from your room. Letho?"*

"Waking. He should be conscious any minute now."

"Hang on," I replied.

I glided to the training room and opened the door.

"You'll have to learn to move faster, you piece of shit, like my woman so eloquently labeled you," I telepathically taunted Darryl, while holding the door open.

In our ethereal form, we didn't have a physical voice in

the Mortal Plane. And our speech range with humans was fairly limited, although much greater with our anchor or another Walker.

Darryl hesitated. His situation had become even more precarious. This time, his survival instincts were starting to take over his bloodlust. If he returned to the Beasts holding area, he could escape. I needed him to walk into my trap. Then again, the Mist had thinned. I repressed the grin, realizing Thomson and Tate would have closed the external access and activated the venting system to purge the Mist inside the base.

"Naima, ask Thomson to get a group of agents to the armory to block off Darryl's path if he attempts to flee," I mind-spoke to my mate. *"Merax has awakened, he will provide support."*

I couldn't hear her answer. She would have needed to verbally speak it back to me. But the connection had been clear enough for me to know she'd at least received it.

"Is the high and mighty Darryl too terrified of a handful of humans to finish what he started?" I telepathically mocked my enemy.

"You can't goad me with your taunting, Zain," Darryl replied out loud with contempt. "You're the one that hid and fled rather than stand and face me."

"All right, then. Run off like a little bitch, you pussy. We'll finish spanking you another time," I said with disdain. *"We'll see just how smart you truly are now that you won't be able to leech insider information from your creator. Thomson doesn't like spies."*

Darryl blanched with both fury and shock that I knew his creator's identity, and what that would mean for him moving forward.

"Apex, Letho is awake and in his ethereal form," Merax mentally said to me.

"Excellent. I grant you permission to freely roam within the base but wait for my order to move. You do not harm the humans. Only the Transient Nightmare Darryl," I ordered him, before repeating the same to Letho.

"Understood, Apex," Merax said.

"I obey," Letho replied with the feral glee of the hunter.

Darryl glanced once more at the door keeping him from the humans inside, before looking back at me. An air of determination descending upon his features. He stomped towards me, his pace accelerating with each step until he broke into a full run. It was clear that the Nightmare had no intention of entering the training room. He was too smart to fall for that. But that didn't mean he couldn't be coerced into it.

"Come out now!" I ordered my Nightmare Squad.

I waited until the very last second before rushing inside the room, giving Darryl the illusion that he had stood a chance of yanking me out. He shouted in pain when his tendril missed me and struck the door instead. As soon as I was out of the way, a volley of bullets showered him. Darryl turned towards his attackers. His eyes widened in shock, and the first glimmer of fear crossed his features. My Nightmares had come into play.

He had known they would likely form this weekend. I believed this had prompted his attack on the base to nip the potential Squad in the bud. But he hadn't expected them to finish forming so quickly, let alone to face them in their ethereal forms instead of their weakened, new human bodies.

Darryl couldn't run to the right side of the T intersection which was a dead-end leading to the closed off cafeteria. Not knowing the full power of the two Nightmares supported by the agents shooting, attempting to bowl through them to flee could prove too risky. But when the confinement wall leading to the personal quarters opened in front of us, revealing a dozen agents also firing at him, Darryl had no choice but to seek refuge inside the training room. He knew he would never manage to cross the fifty meters between him and this new team of shooters before the wall closed again.

I flew further back inside the room. Understanding that this was do or die, Darryl threw all caution to the wind and raced after me. Knowing it would hurt like a motherfucker, I transferred a maximum of energy to my ethereal shield and allowed him to catch up. To my shock, instead of simply whipping at me with his tendrils while I lured him farther to the back, Darryl wrapped his tentacles around my body and yanked me to him. While every single one of his tentacles were attempting to crush me, Darryl's hands were clawing at the back of my head. If he managed to break through my shield and inflict a bleeding wound, he'd be able to suck my lifeforce right out of me.

Teeth clenched, I forced myself to keep advancing forward to the back of the room where the Mist trickling in from the corridor hadn't reached yet. When he finally realized what I was doing, Darryl attempted to reverse course, which slightly loosened his hold. Merax and Letho flew inside the room, tendrils swirling, ready to strike. The delicious scent of Darryl's blossoming fear tickled my nose. He released four of his tendrils surrounding me—further reducing the pressure on me—to parry the oncoming attacks from my Squad, while attacking my neck in a frenzy.

"Whip him towards the back," I ordered my minions.

With all my might, I dragged him forward, clearing the thinning plumes of Mist. Darryl shouted in agony. Before I could make myself intangible to break free of his hold, my nemesis released me to attempt a mad dash towards the exit. Carried by my momentum, I flew up and did an aerial back-flip to bring down all four of my tendrils on his back. He would have face planted but, just as he was falling forward, Merax' and Letho's tentacles whipped him back with enough force to send him crashing against the back wall.

Darryl shrieked in agony and scrambled to his feet only to be showered by bullets from the agents who had invaded the room. Having understood my plan, Thomson closed the door of the training room to prevent any more Mist from entering. He tapped a few instructions on his phone, the blaring of the breach alarm stopped, revealing the rushing sound of the ventilation system sucking the Mist out. Sure, it made it harder for us to fly and glide in our ethereal forms, but Darryl was as good as dead.

With my minions following my lead, we swooped down on the Nightmare like birds of prey, whipping him back before flying back out of range. Where Merax struck powerful and well calculated blows, Letho moved like a snake, striking and retreating at lightning-speed, leaving his target reeling. Shifting my vision to seek the weaknesses in his armor, I made my tendrils razor thin and their tips sharp. Fighting the urge to target the big fracture on his chest that would guarantee instant death, I stabbed at the ones in his legs, crippling him.

Darryl fell to his knees, throwing his hands in front of him to avoid smacking his face on the floor. Raising a palm towards the agents, I gestured for them to hold their fire.

"Feed," I told my minions.

"Gladly, Apex," Merax said with greed.

"Thank you, Apex," Letho replied with a childish excitement that was almost cute.

They swooped down, hovering long enough over an open wound to leech some of Darryl's lifeforce, moving away before he could swat them. But the fight was bleeding out of our prey, drowning in a world of agony. The Mist had receded from the room. I couldn't begin to imagine the extent of the excruciating pain of trespassing he was currently experiencing. Not that I particularly cared. I gorged on his terror as he vainly tried to crawl towards an exit he would never reach. I stabbed him some more, this time in his arms to put an end to his efforts to flee.

Gliding down in front of him, I fisted his hair and yanked his head back to make him look at me.

"Nightmares controlled by their bloodlust and their ego never last long," I mind-spoke to him tauntingly. *"You were too greedy in your feeding, too arrogant in your killing and, ultimately, too stupid in your overconfidence. Never hunt on enemy territory without at least two exit plans. But thank you for contributing to making me the most powerful hunter in this realm."*

Darryl opened his mouth to say something, likely to plead for mercy, but I didn't give him a chance. I sucked the lifeforce from him with feral avidity. A glowing electric light flowed into me like a tsunami. For all the damage he had sustained, Darryl still possessed three times the amount of the combined power between Merax, Letho, and me.

The Nightmare's groans faded into a gurgling sound and then silence only disturbed by the electric sizzle of his lifeforce leaving him from three places, and the thumping sound of his limbs' dying spasms.

My gaze never strayed from his to make sure he didn't die

or lose consciousness before he was too weak to flee. But even then, I continued deriving great pleasure from watching the light fade from them. With his last breath, his hair turned to ashes in my hand, making me lose my grip. But his face never struck the floor, also crumbling into a fine grey dust before it landed.

Only then did I feel a presence behind me. Turning around, I found Thomson staring at the remains of his Nightmare with a savage, almost cruel smile.

I liked that.

He turned to look at me with the strangest expression. The emotions emanating from him towards me held a depth of affection that unnerved me.

He placed his hand on my shoulder, my shadowy aura swallowing it while he gave it a gentle squeeze.

"Thank you, son... for everything." He turned to my minions and slightly bowed his head. "Thank you as well, and welcome to the Fourth Division."

Without another word, he turned around and slowly walked out of the room. Following in his wake, the Walkers of the Fourth Division exited the room under the cheers and applause of the agents... our new people.

CHAPTER 20

NAIMA

That night, after Zain reintegrated his body, I could literally see electric coils slithering over his skin like those inside a plasma ball. Although grateful that his human vessel had remained sheltered in our room, I had seen the savage blows Darryl had given him, and the way he had tried to crush him.

"I am fine, my mate," Zain said while discarding the clothes he'd previously donned before deciding to battle in his shadowy form. "Whatever damage I sustained, Darryl's life-force has mended, and then some."

Zain slipped out of his pants and dismissively tossed them to the ground. Since he hadn't taken the time to put on any underwear after I'd called him for help in the Mist, he was now stark naked. The sight of his massive cock proudly erect as he prowled towards me with a predatory look had my core throbbing with anticipation. And yet, it wasn't a shiver of excitement that coursed through me as I watched him approach.

"What is it, my love?" Zain asked as he closed in on me.

I instinctively backed away, but he continued his advance until my back met the wall, ending any further possibility of retreat. Zain invaded my personal space and leaned against the wall with his forearms on each side of my head, caging me. My pulse picked up, and my breathing became shallow from the growing fear and unease he was provoking in me. The excessive energy flowing through him had my skin erupting in goosebumps and my hair standing from all the static.

"Why do you fear me?" he demanded in a dangerously low voice, almost menacing.

I shuddered, my palms finding their way to his chest as if to keep him at a distance, even though his face was already inches from mine.

"My... My brand hurts, and y-you don't f-feel the same," I stuttered.

How was I supposed to tell him that his ethereal aura that normally felt delightfully dangerous now had a slimy edge to it that reeked of Darryl? That it was both turning me off and freaking me out?

"It is normal," Zain said in the same low voice that was definitely not giving me warm fuzzies. "I have absorbed a large amount of his lifeforce. His evil, malicious energy you feel will fade by morning. Undress, my love."

The matter-of-fact way he said that, as if talking about the rain but in that creepy voice, was really making me want to get the fuck out of the room. I did *not* want to play naughty with him feeling that way.

I licked my lips nervously and forced myself to hold his gaze. "I don't want to get naked with you right now. Not like this. Not when you... feel like him."

There used to be a time when I would have simply given

in for fear of upsetting my boyfriend, for fear he might get violent. But I'd buried that girl the day I'd buried Jared. I wasn't going back to that. And I certainly didn't want my intimate moments with the man I love soiled by the lingering presence of a monster.

I braced for how he would respond. To my shock, a satisfied smile stretched his lips. It still had that extremely dangerous edge he'd been sporting since leaving the training room, and yet it somehow soothed me.

"I'm not asking you to fuck, Naima," he said with a predatory grin, deliberately needling me. "Although I'm always ready and willing... But I recall my woman saying she didn't like going to bed with the filth of the day. Come shower with me. You can help me wash the stench of Darryl off me."

Taken aback by the unexpected answer, I gaped at him for a second before smiling, relief washing over me.

"Yes," I nodded. "I need that."

Zain's face softened ever so slightly, but not to the extent he normally used to. Something had changed in him. I wanted to believe this harder edge would fade with the slime of Darryl.

He ended up doing most of the work undressing me. Despite a raging hard on that never abated, Zain was very clinical and gentle while doing so. He then led me to the shower where we mutually washed each other. Once again, it was tender and affectionate but in no way sexual.

When we finished, Zain dried me then carried me to bed, both of us still naked—but then we always slept in our birthday suits. He turned off the light then, drawing me into his embrace, he kissed my forehead before closing his eyes.

Now that the fresh scent of soap had washed away some of Darryl's presence, a part of me regretted that Zain hadn't insisted. Yet, the minute I rested my head on his muscular chest, the exhaustion and high stress of the day crashed into me. I couldn't even recall closing my eyes before sleep swept me away.

Zain didn't lure me into the Mist that night. I believed he, too, had needed a good night sleep to recover from his own ordeal and for his body to adjust to the insane amount of power that now bubbled within him.

I didn't remember dreaming, only that my sleep had been extremely pleasant and rejuvenating. I emerged from my slumber to Zain's plush lips covering my face with soft kisses and his fingertips drawing fleeting patterns on my naked skin. My eyelids fluttered open, and my gaze rested on his gorgeous face. His green eyes bore into mine with an intensity that left me breathless. Zain still buzzed with an incredible amount of power, but the stench of the Nightmare was gone.

His hand's gentle caress along my arm and the curve of my shoulder became far less innocent. It slid down to my chest, fondling my right breast in a slow and sensual motion before flicking my nipple with his thumb. It then continued its journey south, the touch of his fingertips so light on my skin it almost tickled. They paused at my outie navel, teasing it before giving it a gentle pinch. I inhaled sharply, my lips parting and my breathing shortening as my mate's hand slipped further down.

Zain's green eyes darkened, and his pupils dilated in that way they always did whenever he was aroused. But there was something different this time that I couldn't put into words. His gaze still locked with mine had me hypnotized. I shivered as two of his fingers gently traced the seam of my sex. The familiar heat of desire blossomed in the pit of my stomach.

"Do you love me, Naima?" Zain asked in an almost whispered voice.

"Yes," I said with sincerity.

"Do you wish to spend the rest of your mortal life here with me, and afterwards eternity in the Mist by my side?" he asked.

My heart skipped a beat at the realization of where this was headed. I licked my lips nervously. The delicious torment of his full hand now rubbing my sex in a possessive fashion made it hard to concentrate.

"Yes, Zain, I do."

He examined my features as if he was seeking confirmation that I truly meant it. I held his gaze unflinchingly. That night in the Mist when we had first made love, I had already known this would be for the long haul. The past few weeks had only confirmed it.

"Bind me to this world," Zain whispered. Although he said it as a statement, it was a request. Despite its extreme subtlety, the underlying pleading tone was undeniable.

"Are you sure?" I asked, my eyes flicking between his.

It would slightly lessen some of his power, and with each passing day, he would increasingly become human, unless he continued to refresh his ethereal essence by spending a maximum amount of time in his realm during the three days of the Mist. It would also allow us to have children should we so choose at some point in the future.

"I am certain," Zain said with a conviction that erased any hesitation I still felt.

I didn't speak and merely lifted my head to kiss his lips. Zain's response was immediate, commanding and possessive. My mate's ability to go from zero to one thousand in a split second always turned me on. I gladly yielded to his dominance, my lips parting to welcome his invading tongue, and my legs as well to accommodate his venturing hand.

Zain slipped two fingers inside of me while his thumb rubbed my clit. I moaned against his mouth, and my own fingers found their way through the silky strands of his dark-brown hair. He broke the kiss then his mouth roamed over my face and along my jawline. It stopped for a brief moment by my right ear to suck on my earlobe. Zain nibbled at that sensitive spot just at the side of my neck near my nape, before pursuing his exploration. He made love to my body with his hands and his mouth, before his expert tongue took over the exquisite torment to which his fingers had subjected my clit.

This time, however, Zain stopped just as I was about to topple over. I stared at him in disbelief as he straightened to climb on top of me. My words died in my throat at the feral look of lust on his face.

"You will come on my cock," Zain commanded in a voice so filled with desire it sounded like a growl.

My lover pushed himself inside of me, visibly struggling to keep himself under control. Even with us going at it like rabbits, he was still a tight fit and required some care when first penetrating me. Legs spread wide, I placed my hands on his ass, my nails digging into the round and firm globes, spurring him on. I would welcome a bit of extra pain just to have him deep within me, filling the void that ached for him.

The look of pure bliss on my man's face when he finally was fully sheathed nearly undid me. Zain was an extremely sensual male. After all this time, his human body and nerve endings still remained very sensitive to the slightest touch or sensation. This was our first time without any barriers between us, and it was wrecking him.

The intensity of his pleasure seeping through our connection, radiated from the brand on my chest and throughout my body. Compounded by the feel of his thick cock filling me to the brim and stretching me to the fullest, each stroke fanned the flame raging inside me.

In no time, my Darkest Desire had me on the edge. Sensing my impending climax, Zain slightly shifted his thrusts and struck my sweet spot with deadly precision. I threw my head back and cried out as my orgasm slammed into me. I clawed at his back, overwhelmed by the intensity of our combined pleasure. But that only seemed to trigger him.

Zain lifted one of my legs over his shoulder and pounded into me, the blunted tip of his cock zeroing in on my sweet spot with each movement. I thought my spine would split open from the violence of the third orgasm that ripped through me. This time, Zain roared my name in unison with my own cry of ecstasy. He slammed himself home. Buried deep within me, my lover held my hips in a bruising hold while his human seed and ethereal essence shot out inside of me. It felt like a river of liquid lava had been poured into my womb, setting me ablaze from within.

Zain's ethereal essence seeped into every tissue, every organ, sending electric sparks throughout my body as he bound himself to me. A maelstrom of pleasure-pain engulfed me, my fourth climax building up even as I still glided on the wings of the third one.

My body writhed beneath his sensual assault, my skin slick with sweat, and my nerves ending on fire. I lost count of how many times he made me climb the highest peaks of ecstasy and filled me with his essence.

By the time he took mercy on me, I was a trembling puddle of bliss.

"We are bound for eternity, my mate," Zain said, gathering me in his arms.

With my throat too sore from screaming so much, I didn't verbally respond but tightened my hold around him with a possessiveness that spoke volumes.

And on my chest, the burning tingle of my brand, expanding to its final form, marked us as bound for life.

EPILOGUE

NAIMA

The public announcement of the death of the Thornhill Killer at the hand of the special unit of the Fourth Division was received with extreme euphoria by the distressed population of Cordell. We used the picture I had snapped of Darryl with my phone for the press. However, not before doing some Photoshop retouches to tweak his appearance in case he had created this body based on an existing innocent individual like he had done with Tate.

The agents' morale within the agency had never been so high. For months, they had felt helpless, fighting a losing battle while watching the men and women they had sworn to protect get slaughtered in the streets. Worse still, they would go on missions and watch their colleagues, some of whom they had grown to consider as brothers and sisters, get split in half by beings far too powerful for them to ever defeat.

No wonder so many of them had terrible nightmares. Judging by the database I had put together, a little over a third of the Nightmares that had crossed over had indeed been spawned by members of the agency, mainly the men and women on the frontline. The now compulsory psychotherapy sessions I had with each member on a regular basis helped them cope with the stress and trauma of their profession.

Even with the Squad by their side, some victims still died in terrible ways, but thankfully, rarely during missions. After that battle with Darryl inside the base, a strong bond had formed between the agents and the Squad. I wouldn't call it friendship, but there was an undeniable protective ownership from the Walkers towards their human colleagues.

In the past six months, Zain had recruited four more Nightmares for our team. To our general surprise, he had deemed that he wouldn't recruit more than ten in total for the time being. I would have expected him to want to dominate a large group of devoted minions. However, he was quite serious about running his Squad in an efficient and appropriate way. He proved not only extremely picky, but also thorough in the training his minions received.

In many ways, where Tate was Thomson's right hand, Zain was his left. The level of trust and autonomy that he had been afforded went a long way into feeding the loyalty he displayed towards the agency.

Nevertheless, I was beyond relieved when, a week after Darryl's death, Zain was finally able to move into my house. It also opened the opportunity for us to teach him what a normal life in the real world felt like. From movie nights, to dining in the city, to theme park rides, and a swim in the ocean, I rediscovered so many things through his virgin eyes. Many such moments gave rise to hilarious situations, but all contributed to me falling in love all over again with him, time after time.

Zain was fundamentally antisocial. We would never have a huge circle of friends or frequent double dates, but that was fine with me. I'd always been a bit of an introvert myself, so activities alone with him suited me just fine. However, to my surprise, Zain showed a particular taste and natural talent for dancing, especially Latin dance. To this day, I still cracked up remembering the first time we had gone to a Latin club.

My man had been so ridiculously sexy in his skintight black T-shirt and those fancy black dress pants that hugged his perfect ass in the most amazing way. We'd taken the dance floor by storm, showing off the sleek moves we'd learned during the salsa dance lessons we had been taking. The number of patrons drooling over us, and more specifically over my magnificent beast, had pissed him off to no end.

A woman in particular who had shown, without any subtlety whatsoever, that she tremendously appreciated his appearance and sexy moves, earned his ire. To have him flat out tell her to keep her damn eyes to herself had required all my willpower not to burst out laughing in her face. I had always hated those shameless bitches in clubs who thought it was okay to hit on a man they clearly saw was accompanied. I didn't need to be jealous, *ever*. Zain took care of telling skanks to keep walking—he was already spoken for.

Nevertheless, we did occasionally hang out with Riley and Julia, although Zain considered it as us hanging out with Merax and Letho. For Zain, Riley's Nightmare had become his right hand. Whereas Letho had become a strange mix of a little brother and an attack dog.

Both of my human colleagues had also taken their respective Nightmares home.

Riley and Merax were officially a couple. I still didn't fully understand the dynamic between them. Merax was a bully and a dominant. However, Riley was no pushover. I suspected some interesting exchange of power occurred between them in private. As curious as I felt about them, I respected their right to indulge in their kinks. After all, I had my own, including getting spanked, gently choked, bitten, and some bondage.

Julia's relationship with her Nightmare was quite moving. He was too broken mentally to be left to his own devices. Officially, Julia and her husband—who had no children of their own—had adopted Letho as their son. A genuine affection had developed between the three of them. Letho required a well-established routine to thrive. He needed specific goals for every hour of the day for him to function. Focusing on clear and simple tasks—be they training or relaxation time— kept him from becoming overwhelmed by the chaos that otherwise reigned in his head. His greatest reward was seeing Julia smile.

Although he didn't suffer from autism, his behavior matched many of the symptoms attributed to that condition. As he responded well to the type of treatment used in such cases, we pursued that method. Initially, Julia had believed making Letho play video games would help him vent some of the excessive aggressivity that constantly boiled deep within him. But he had no interest in first person shooters or combat games. Then again, it was a myth that playing video games promoted violence in the real world, just like watching slasher movies didn't turn people into serial killers. Instead, Letho developed a passion for puzzle and match-3 games, especially those that required the ability to recognize patterns to perform well.

I loved how much the welfare of his Squad mattered to Zain. He had naturally shown it during that battle against Darryl by allowing his team to feed first instead of hogging all that power for himself. That, in turn, earned him their undivided loyalty. Zain merely perceived it as him taking good care of his guns so that they didn't break in the middle of a shootout. Although he believed it and that, in some ways it was certainly true, I also knew that a loving, caring side of him lurked beneath his cynical exterior.

In the years that followed, the services of the Squad were requested to assist with neighboring cities and states. Zain even ended up supervising the recruiting process for some of their local Squads. But most of his time was devoted patrolling the streets of Cordell during the Mist to help prevent domestic tragedies such as the one that had almost cost me my life, stop foolish teenagers or gullible cultists from committing mass suicide in Mist Pacts, and protecting vulnerable Wishes from getting devoured during their cross over. The rest of the month, they assisted local police forces or federal agents in the manhunts against the most vicious criminals or illegal Mist battle arenas pitting humans versus Beasts.

As for me, I was happy. I had a job I loved, which allowed me to make a positive difference in the lives of men and women who selflessly put themselves on the line to protect others. I had an insanely sexy man who was entirely devoted to me. Even after all this time, mind-blowing sex with him still had me speaking in tongues.

The semi dark cloud in my perfect blue sky stemmed from Zain claiming he didn't want to have children. I was still on the fence myself as to whether or not I wanted any. If I insisted, he would cave in. And judging by the way he looked after his Squad, I didn't doubt for a minute he would be a great father to our children. My man didn't mess around when it came to what was his. But we still had plenty of years left to make a decision on that front. For now, I was more than happy to settle on practicing baby-making.

We watched the Mist rise through our living room window. In a couple of hours, Zain would have to go to work. Until then, every single inch of his drool-worthy body was mine. Clad in his Squad uniform so that he'd be ready to head out at the drop of a dime, he closed the shutters, and picked me up in his arms.

I wrapped my arms around his neck while he carried me like a bride to our bedroom.

"Are you prepared to be sacrificed to the vampire?" Zain asked in a delightfully menacing voice.

"I will not go down so easily. Tell that fiend I have learned quite a few tricks to escape monsters," I replied with defiance, my excitement rising as he climbed the stairs to the second floor.

"That's okay. He loves to hunt. Nothing excites him more than feasting on prey after a good chase."

Zain entered the bedroom and carefully laid me down on the bed before stretching his tall frame next to me.

I no sooner closed my eyes than the falling sensation swept me away. Moments later, I gently landed in the middle of a dark forest with leafless, tortured trees, bending this way and that as far as the eye could see. The moon provided the only source of light in the darkness of night. The shiver that ran through me wasn't due to me wearing nothing but a diaphanous, white negligee.

A howling sound in the distance startled me. I spun around, my bare feet slightly sinking in the strange, padded surface of the forest's ground. Three hundred meters away, the dark silhouette of a giant bat flew down from the midnight sky and landed on its feet. It shifted into a human form, with red eyes glowing. His mouth stretched in an evil grin, baring a frightening pair of fangs that glistened in the moonlight.

My stomach fluttered, my nipples hardened, and moisture pooled between my thighs at the sight of my most beloved predator.

"Run away, little girl," the vampire mind-spoke to me in a voice promising a world of pleasure and pain.

Without a word, I turned around and ran.

THE END

:

ALSO BY REGINE ABEL

THE VEREDIAN CHRONICLES
Escaping Fate
Blind Fate
Raising Amalia
Twist of Fate
Hands of Fate
Defying Fate

BRAXIANS
Anton's Grace
Ravik's Mercy
Krygor's Hope

XIAN WARRIORS
Doom
Legion
Raven
Bane
Chaos
Varnog
Reaper
Wrath

THE MIST
The Mistwalker
The Nightmare

BLOOD MAIDENS OF KARTHIA
Claiming Thalia

VALOS OF SONHADRA
Unfrozen
Iced

PRIME MATING AGENCY
I Married A Lizardman

EMPATHS OF LYRIA
An Alien For Christmas

THE SHADOW REALMS
Dark Swan

OTHER
Bluebeard's Curse
Alien Awakening
Heart of Stone
The Hunchback

ABOUT REGINE

USA Today bestselling author Regine Abel is a fantasy, paranormal and sci-fi junky. Anything with a bit of magic, a touch of the unusual, and a lot of romance will have her jumping for joy. She loves creating hot alien warriors and no-nonsense, kick-ass heroines that evolve in fantastic new worlds while embarking on action-packed adventures filled with mystery and the twists you never saw coming.

Before devoting herself as a full-time writer, Regine had surrendered to her other passions: music and video games! After a decade working as a Sound Engineer in movie dubbing and live concerts, Regine became a professional Game Designer and Creative Director, a career that has led her from her home in Canada to the US and various countries in Europe and Asia.

Facebook

https://www.facebook.com/regine.abel.author/

Website

https://regineabel.com

Regine's Rebels Reader Group

https://www.facebook.com/groups/ReginesRebels/

Newsletter

http://smarturl.it/RA_Newsletter

Goodreads

http://smarturl.it/RA_Goodreads

Bookbub

https://www.bookbub.com/profile/regine-abel

Amazon

http://smarturl.it/AuthorAMS

Made in the USA
Coppell, TX
11 September 2021